A Magica...

EUGENIA RILEY
LISA CACH
VICTORIA ALEXANDER

A Magical Christmas Present

LOVE SPELL   NEW YORK CITY

LOVE SPELL®

October 2008

Published by

Dorchester Publishing Co., Inc.
200 Madison Avenue
New York, NY 10016

A Magical Christmas Present copyright © 2008 by Dorchester Publishing Co., Inc.
"The Ghost of Christmas Past" copyright © 1993 by Eugenia Riley Essenmacher
"A Midnight Clear" copyright © 2000 by Lisa Cach
"Promises to Keep" copyright © 1996 by Victoria Alexander

ISBN 10: 0-505-52789-8
ISBN 13: 978-0-505-52789-9

The name "Love Spell" and its logo are trademarks of Dorchester Publishing Co., Inc.

Printed in the United States of America.

10 9 8 7 6 5 4 3 2 1

Visit us on the web at www.dorchesterpub.com.

✳

A Magical
Christmas Present

TABLE OF CONTENTS

EUGENIA RILEY

The Ghost of Christmas Past

This story is dedicated, with love, to our newest Riley,
our own Christmas angel, my precious niece—
Sarah Carter Riley
born December 22, 1992
—and with special congratulations to Mom and Dad, Philip
and Cay.

CHAPTER ONE

*You are invited to meet
The ghost of Christmas past. . . .
"Through this portal, take your leave,
You'll come back on Christmas Eve. . . ."*

Sitting in a quaint café across from Piccadilly Circus, Jason Burke sipped his cappuccino and stared at the two cryptic messages inscribed on the strange invitation that was included among a stack of invitations given to him by his employer. Of the half-dozen or so announcements for the Christmas Candlelight Tours he was covering here in London, this one was by far the oddest. The peculiar notice was printed in old-fashioned gold script, on ancient-looking yellow parchment banded by red. Beneath the two messages was written, "The Simmons Hotel," followed by an address Jason had never heard of.

Not that he was that familiar with addresses here in London. An American, Jason was a reporter in England on assignment for a New York newspaper. Ever since Finias Fogg, an Englishman, had established the *Manhattan Chronicle* over 150 years ago, the paper had published an annual spread on Christmas traditions in England. As an added touch of whimsy, the series had always been run under Fogg's byline. This year, Jason had been awarded the dubious honor of becoming the sainted Mr. Fogg, and thus he was reluctantly writing the Yule spread.

Reluctantly. Now that was an understatement. Only a few months ago, Jason would have scoffed at taking on one of those softer, fluffier assignments for the women's pages or the Sunday supplements. Until recently, he had been a hard-edged news reporter who had covered trouble spots all over the globe.

But that was before he had lost his edge.

He sighed, wondering when he had lost his incisiveness, his vision. Had it been in Africa, when he had held in his arms that frail, pitiful child too weak to take the food he had offered? Or perhaps in the Middle East, when he had watched one of his best friends, a world-class photographer, lose his life when he had accidentally stepped on a land mine? Or maybe it had been the day a few months ago when he had returned to his Manhattan apartment, only to discover a note from Shelley breaking their engagement, telling him that he was too self-absorbed to make a good husband, and that she had gone off to "find herself" in L.A.

Whenever it had happened, at 29, Jason had become burned out. He had arrived at a point where he had ceased to care what he wrote—until his editor had yanked him off the fast track and had given him less-challenging assignments as a sort of enforced sabbatical. When Jason had revolted, refusing to cover whooping crane lectures or museum openings, his editor had given him an ultimatum: Prove yourself, or leave.

He hadn't left. He wasn't a quitter. He would prove himself and get his edge back, if only to escape the boredom of these frothy assignments.

Covering the West End Candlelight Tours here in London had to be the most frivolous so far, he mused. Over the next three nights, decked out in black tie and a forced smile, Jason would trudge through the formal, high-society affairs, going from one upscale London home or bed-and-breakfast establishment to another. The theme of the tours was "A Christmas Carol," and Jason presumed that there would be feasts, carolers, stuffed boars' heads and plum pudding ad nauseam. In fact, he understood that the homeowners or innkeepers were to dress in period costumes and to pose as citizens of Dickens's London.

He glanced again at the invitation from the Simmons Hotel and had to smile ironically. Now, it appeared that one of the tours was even to be led by an actual "ghost."

Hearing laughter at the table next to him, Jason turned to watch a large family group jovially toast a couple who were obviously celebrating an anniversary. He felt a sense of melancholy drift back over him. In truth, he rather disliked himself for greeting his current assignment here in England with such cynicism. After all, he had gotten to travel on expense account to London, and ordinarily he loved England. No doubt, too, the readers of the *Manhattan Chronicle* deserved far better than his world-weary approach to Yuletide.

Only, his life felt so empty at the moment. And thus he feared he would perform his current duties with all the enthusiasm of a true Ebenezer Scrooge.

"Will there be anything else, sir?"

Jason glanced up at the waiter, who stood in his apron and gartered shirt, with pad in hand.

"Do you know where this address is?" Jason asked, handing the man the invitation.

The waiter took it, turned it over, and frowned. "A very odd invitation, sir. Why, the paper looks almost as old as the address itself. Why the strange wording, do you suppose?"

"I'm covering the West End Candlelight Tours for the *Manhattan Chronicle*," Jason explained. "And it seems that the tour of the Simmons Hotel is to be led by a ghost."

The waiter broke into a grin. "Oh, yes, sir. You're referring to the annual wingding when all of London's high society dress up like they're straight out of Queen Victoria's time?"

"That's it."

The waiter handed the invitation back to Jason. "The address is off Belgrave Square, sir. I'm not really sure just where, but perhaps if you navigate over in that direction, you'll find it in good time."

"A comforting prospect," Jason quipped. "Now, if I can just remember to keep my rental car on the right side of the road—or rather, the left."

The waiter laughed and handed Jason the check. He paid the bill and left the cozy restaurant. Outside, the cold December air hit him, and he lifted the collar of his coat against the chill. Regent Street, with its three- and four-story classical facades, was jammed with cars and ablaze with lights. Mammoth glittering chandeliers hung suspended above the streets, and sprays of electric lights cascaded from one doorway to another. Late shoppers, diners, and theatergoers thronged the sidewalks, and the mood was one of holiday ebullience. Jason caught his reflection in the window of a china shop and saw a tall, black-haired man with cleanly cut features and shuttered dark eyes. He hurried on, feeling somehow uncomfortable to be looking at himself too closely. He arrived at his small rental car, unlocked it and ducked inside, groaning as he folded his tall form into the cramped driver's seat. He debated whether he should consult the map in the glove box, then decided that the waiter's advice would probably work just as well. He may as well begin his evening with a ghost or two, he mused ruefully as he started the car and ground the gearshift into first.

Jason followed the flow of traffic, eventually wending his way down through Trafalgar Square with its spectacular soaring Christmas tree next to the fountain and Nelson's Column. He maneuvered his way past the stately offices and clubs on Pall Mall, and finally out onto Knightsbridge near the park. He turned south into Belgravia and circled past the stuccoed embassies on Belgrave Square. He then began methodically following the side streets that fanned outward from each corner of the square. More than once, he got lost amid the endless rows of fashionable shops and elegant houses. At one point, he found himself out of Belgravia entirely, and inching his way through heavy traffic past the glittering spectacle of Harrod's on Brompton Road. At last, he wended his way back into the residential area, where the thickening fog and dimly lit streets further impeded his progress. He was to the point of giving up when, to his exasperation, he became even more hopelessly ensnared in the maze of streets, and couldn't even find his way back to the square!

At last, in disgust, Jason pulled up before a three-story Greek revival town house, hoping to ask for directions. He got out of his car and approached the steps to the pillared portico and suddenly, he was there! To his amazement, he looked up at the lettering over the door and read #10 Belgrave Lane—the very number on his invitation. And, on the frosted glass panel of the door was emblazoned, "The Simmons Hotel."

Looking up and down the stately three-story white brick structure, Jason frowned. He was at the right address, all right, but it looked as if no one was at home. The house had an eerie, near-deserted quality about it. Only the wannest light could be discerned glowing behind the yellowed window shades. And there were no trappings of Christmas to be seen at all—no wreath on the door, only a small sconce spilling out a dim puddle of light. Perhaps the owners had deliberately created this chilling ambiance for their "ghost tour"?

Hugging himself to ward off the cold, Jason sprinted up the steps and knocked on the door. He was half-expecting no response at all. But to his surprise, a moment later the door creaked open and a young woman stood before him, with a lit candle in her hand.

Unaccountably, a chill shook Jason, and for a moment he could only stare at her. Never had the sight of any woman so compelled or mesmerized him! She stood in a pool of light so dim that Jason could barely make out her features. A spooky feeling racked him as he realized that this lovely creature very much resembled a ghost.

She was quite beautiful, but also quite pale. There was something haunting, almost ethereal, about her countenance. She had a delicate face, eyes as light as honey, and lips as pale as faded rose petals. Her golden-brown hair was piled on top of her head. She wore an old-fashioned, brown velvet gown, with a skirt that swept wide and dragged the floor.

Jason smiled at her. "Hello," he murmured, in a voice that trembled oddly. "You must be the ghost of

Christmas past—and I must say, a lovelier ghost I've never seen."

"Good evening, sir," the woman replied in a sweet, lyrical voice. She lowered her gaze self-consciously. "I am Annie Simmons, daughter of the hotel's owner, and your guide for this evening." She stepped back. "Won't you come in?"

"Thank you."

The disquieting feeling continued to grip Jason as he moved through the portal. Meanwhile, his ghostly tour guide moved farther away from him. Only when he was several feet beyond her did she turn to shut the door. He regarded her bemusedly.

"Follow me, sir," she murmured.

Jason glanced about in perplexity as they filed down the barren hallway with its high ceilings and carved frieze. The walls were darkly wainscoted, the faded wallpaper above hinting of a grander time.

"I take it I am the first to arrive on the tour tonight?" He laughed almost nervously. "If the others have the difficult time I did in finding you, Miss Annie Simmons, I'll wager they are all lost, just like I was."

She turned to stare at him. "You are not lost, sir."

Inexplicably, her statement—and the odd light in her eyes—unnerved Jason. She seemed to be talking about so much more than geography, and it suddenly struck him that he had felt lost, so lost, for such a long time.

He followed her into a large, barren room that obviously had once been a parlor. A crystal chandelier, unlit but still glorious, hung from a carved plaster medallion at the center of the room. The walls were papered in shades of faded, flocked rose damask.

At the fireplace, she turned. In a low, almost haunting voice, she said, "My father bought this hotel in

1832. I was born here the following year. My mother died that day, and my father raised me."

Jason regarded the woman with skepticism and uncertainty. While logic argued that she must be a member of a local historical society who was now merely reciting rehearsed lines, something about her visage almost had him believing this "ghost" was for real.

Trying to stave off the disquieting feelings she stirred in him, Jason took out his notebook and tried a stab at humor. "So, you really are up on your history, aren't you, miss?" He grinned. "Did it take you long to practice your role for tonight's tour?"

Again her pale, lovely gaze met his. "I am not playing a role, sir."

Jason forced a laugh that sounded oddly hollow. His guide turned to brush a bit of dust from the mantel of the fireplace.

"This room used to be our drawing room," she went on poignantly. "By the 1850s, our hotel was quite prosperous, the rooms always full. We would gather here with our guests each Christmas and sing carols and drink wassail."

"And did all the young men try their best to catch you beneath the mistletoe?" Jason teased.

For the first time, she smiled at him. "We called it the kissing bunch, sir."

"Ah, the kissing bunch," he replied approvingly, jotting down the term. "So you have done your homework. I'm impressed."

She did not comment, and the dimness of her visage, as well as the enigma of her shuttered expression, compelled him to study her at closer range. He edged toward her, but even as he moved, she was already sweeping away from him—as if she had read his thoughts! Feeling frustrated, he followed her out of the room.

In the hallway, she pointed toward another large, barren room where a bay window jutted out at the front. "This is where we all gathered for our meals. On Christmas Day our cook, Mrs. Chandler, would bring in the plum pudding aflame with brandy."

"Ah, the glories of Christmas Day," Jason murmured, unable to contain a hint of cynicism. "I do hope dear Mrs. Chandler didn't ignite the curtains when she set ablaze her culinary delights."

She stared at him sadly. "You don't much like Christmas, do you, sir?"

Again, the woman's uncanny insight knocked Jason off-balance. Before he could ponder a reply, the lovely "ghost" turned and started up the stairway. He followed her, wondering at the strange, spooky aura that radiated about her. Reason again argued that she was merely an actress playing a role—and yet his emotions were in turmoil, and he felt strangely drawn to her. Whatever he had expected on the Candlelight Tours tonight, it was definitely not this barren house and this sad, solitary "ghost."

Upstairs, his guide led him down a hallway, pausing at each doorway to tell him the history of each room: "This is where my Uncle Jed stayed, until he married a widow lady in 1848. . . ." "This is the room where Miss Media used to sit by the window and do her knitting. . . ." "In here, over against that wall, was the bed where I was born, and my mother died. . . ." "In this room, we had newlyweds—until the fever took them both. . . ."

With each step they took down the hallway, with each detail his tour guide uttered, Jason's feeling of unreality heightened. Annie Simmons—or whoever she was—made each statement with such conviction that it was becoming more and more difficult not to believe her!

Again, he wondered why he was the only person taking this bizarre "ghost tour." And why were there no furnishings, no Christmas decorations, no refreshments in sight? Somewhere along the way, Jason had even put away his notebook, and was now simply watching Annie, listening intently, fascinated, half-hypnotized.

She was now nodding toward the stairway that led to the third story. "Up there is where our servants used to sleep." Wistfully, she added, "But it's only storage now, with everyone gone."

Again, Jason tried to move closer to her, and again she glided away, elusive as a mist. He longed to touch her, but some instinct warned him not to. She led him back toward the stairs.

"If everyone is gone," he teased gently, "then who are you?"

She glanced at him over her shoulder. "I thought you knew, sir," she replied with a strange, almost chilling smile. "I am the ghost who haunts this hotel."

And, leaving him to reel in the wake of her eerie statement, she swept on.

Jason followed her downstairs. When she reached the first floor, she turned to stare at him, just a few steps above her. A haunting light played over her features as she murmured in a monotone, "I died on these steps on Christmas Eve in 1852, when I learned that my true love had deserted me."

Her words, her expression, sent a shudder through Jason. Intrigued and electrified, he hurried down to join her. It was uncanny as hell, he thought, but when she had just spoken, she actually had him believing she was a ghost!

"But why did you die?" he implored. "You must tell me more."

But again, she was already evading him, heading off toward the front door. "I'm sorry, sir. Your tour has ended now."

Jason felt strangely bereft. "Please," he murmured, "I'd really like to see you again. And I'd like to learn more about this hotel."

She smiled that same, eerie smile again. "Oh, but you will, sir."

She stood back so he could pass through the portal.

Taking one last, near-anguished look at the lovely, ethereal creature, Jason left. He headed back down the steps, feeling bemused and shaken by his "ghost tour."

When he turned back to look at the town house, all the lights were extinguished, and he could see only darkness.

CHAPTER TWO

The next morning as he ate breakfast in his hotel room, Jason found himself endlessly reliving the moments he had spent on the "ghost tour" last night. It had undoubtedly been the strangest ten minutes of his entire life—and yet, on another level, the most compelling. His tour guide had in every way personified an actual ghost; indeed, when she had whispered, "I died on this staircase . . .", Jason had felt hard-pressed not to believe her.

And why had she been so careful never to let him venture too close to her, or to touch her? Her ethereal, elusive qualities fascinated him. Even though logic still argued that she had only been playing a role, he knew that he wanted to see Annie Simmons again, to get to know her better. He couldn't deny that something had sprung to life inside him during the brief moments they had shared. On some uncanny level, she seemed both to know and to understand him, to reach out to the emptiness in his heart and soul. Already he felt a deep bond with her.

Jason picked up the phone and called his editor in the States. He reached Bill Turner at home.

"Jason. How is it going?" Bill muttered, stifling a yawn.

"Okay. I'm working on the feature on the West End Candlelight Tours right now."

"Will you get the piece in by the deadline?"

"Don't I always?"

Bill chuckled. "What about the photos? Is Steve McCurdy on top of them?"

Jason groaned. "I'm afraid Steve has a touch of the flu."

"Oh, Lord."

"Don't despair. The tours are running for two more nights, and Steve has promised me he will play catch-up either tonight or tomorrow night."

"I love a photo finish," Bill quipped. "Listen, the spread is going to run in just over two weeks—"

"We'll get it in," Jason reiterated. He cleared his throat. "I do have a question for you, Bill."

"Shoot."

"Can you tell me anything about the Simmons Hotel? An invitation from them was included with the ones you gave me."

"Let me grab my briefcase and see if I can put my hands on the list of people and establishments we've been in contact with."

Jason waited, then heard Bill pick up the phone again and rustle through some papers.

After a moment, Bill said, "You know, this is odd. I don't see the Simmons Hotel on the list of homes and inns you are to cover."

Jason was mystified. "But I've got the invitation right here in my hand."

"Are you sure you didn't pick it up somewhere else?"

"Definitely not. It was in the envelope with the other info you gave me."

"I'll be damned," Bill muttered. "Maybe an invitation was sent, but the hotel wasn't included on the master list I was given. Tell you what—why don't you contact this Mrs. Jessica Fitzhugh? She's the chairman of the tours, and is serving as our London liaison."

Jason flipped through some of the papers Bill had given him. "Oh, yeah. Her number is right here with the other materials. Why didn't I think of that?"

"And you say you're on top of things?" Bill asked skeptically.

"You'll get your article on time," Jason said, and the two men hung up.

"Mrs. Fitzhugh?" Jason asked.

"Speaking," replied the elderly sounding, feminine voice at the other end of the line. "May I help you?"

"I'm Jason Burke, the reporter who is covering the West End Candlelight Tours for the *Manhattan Chronicle*."

"Ah, yes, Mr. Burke," the woman said eagerly. "I've been expecting to hear from you. Indeed, we were hoping that you would stop by our home last night."

"Oh, that's right," Jason muttered. "The Fitzhugh home in Mayfair is featured on the tour."

"You should have been here," Mrs. Fitzhugh related excitedly. "We had a crowd of hundreds, and carolers came by from our parish church. We couldn't have planned it any better."

"Sounds wonderful," Jason commented without enthusiasm. "I'll be sure to get by your home tonight. In the meantime, I have a question for you."

"Yes?"

"Can you tell me anything about the Simmons Hotel? An invitation for a tour of the inn was included in the package you sent my editor."

"Why, forevermore!" gasped Mrs. Fitzhugh. "I never

mailed your editor any such invitation! And if that isn't the oddest thing I've ever heard of!"

"What do you mean, odd?" Jason asked.

Mrs. Fitzhugh laughed. "Why, the Simmons Hotel is not included in the West End tours. Indeed, during the forty years I've been chairman, the hotel has never been included in the tours."

A chill swept over Jason. "Then how can you explain my having the invitation?"

"I have no idea. A joke, perhaps?"

"If so, not a very funny one," Jason replied. Frowning to himself, he added, "But you do seem familiar with the hotel."

"Oh, yes," she replied. "However, you must be aware that there no longer is a Simmons Hotel as such—indeed, there hasn't been one for over fifty years."

Now Jason had to protest. "There, you are wrong. You see, I toured the hotel last night. The tour was led—"

"Yes?"

Reluctantly, Jason admitted, "By a young woman posing as a ghost."

He heard Mrs. Fitzhugh laugh. "Oh, Mr. Burke! Now you are pulling *my* leg!"

"Not at all," Jason argued. Feeling frustrated, he added, "What can you tell me about the hotel?"

"Well, as I recall, the Simmons was established in the nineteenth century. If memory serves, it closed down in the early 1940s, and thereafter was split up into flats or something. I believe it is now vacant and boarded up—if it hasn't been razed."

"But that makes no sense," Jason put in vehemently. "I tell you, I was there last night."

"Perhaps you were at a different address, and only thought you were there."

Jason frowned. "Do you know of any way I can find out additional information on this hotel?"

"Ah, yes. I believe the Simmons is included in a book on historic inns of the West End. You might ask for it at the library."

"Thanks."

"Oh, Mr. Burke?"

"Yes?"

Mrs. Fitzhugh paused for a moment, then related awkwardly, "I don't know quite how to tell you this, but the Simmons Hotel has always been rumored to be haunted."

The Simmons Hotel has always been rumored to be haunted.

That very statement was still haunting Jason Burke an hour later as he maneuvered his small car through the maze of streets in Belgravia. Navigating was somewhat easier by the light of day, and in due course, Jason managed to find his way back to Belgrave Lane—and to the town house he had toured last night.

What he saw astounded him. The candlelit inn was gone. In its place stood a crumbling edifice with soot-blackened brick, sagging roof, and boarded-up windows!

Jason left his car and strode onto the walkway, staring in disbelief at the derelict structure. The building standing before him had obviously been closed down for some time now—there was even graffiti decorating the graying boards.

Nothing made sense! Nothing made sense at all! There were no signs of life around the old edifice; in front of it, a sign proclaimed that the structure would shortly be renovated into an office building.

Feeling more bemused than ever, Jason got into his car and drove off. What on earth had happened to him last night? Had he gotten lost? Had someone truly played a joke on him? Had he been hallucinating? Or had his tour been led by an actual ghost?

Jason visited the renowned Guildhall Library not far from the London financial center. The librarian was very helpful, showing Jason to a table and bringing him the requested book on historic inns of the West End.

For a moment, he felt too unnerved to open the volume.

Five minutes later, Jason was staring at a faded daguerreotype of Annie Simmons and her father, both of whom were standing before the staircase at the Simmons Hotel in the year 1850.

Jason could not stop trembling. For he was staring at the very ghost who had guided his tour last night!

To his deepening sense of amazement and mystification, the other details of the article confirmed just what Annie Simmons and Mrs. Fitzhugh had already told Jason—that the inn had known its heyday in the 1850s, that Annie Simmons had died there due to a tragic accident late in 1852, and that, for generations afterward, Annie's spirit had been rumored to haunt the hotel.

Jason buried his face in his hands and groaned. What was happening to him? Had he lost his mind? Was the woman he had met last night a descendant of Annie Simmons? But how could that be if Annie Simmons had died young and unmarried?

He was falling in love with a ghost!

*　*　*

That night as Jason drove his car through the zigzagging streets of Belgravia, he was still questioning his own sanity. Since the Candlelight Tours were to continue for two more nights, he had again donned his formal attire and had gone searching for the Simmons Hotel and Annie Simmons. He seemed compelled by forces too powerful and complex to understand.

Again, he got lost in the fog, in the maze of streets. He was growing intensely frustrated when some inner voice told him that perhaps he should give up his search for now and go visit the other homes on the tour. He suddenly felt a compelling need to conclude his business here in London.

Thus, Jason drove out of Belgravia and made the rounds of half a dozen homes on the tours, visiting a charming 18th century house in Queen Anne's Gate, a stunning Adamesque town house on Portland Square, a magnificent estate overlooking Regent's Park. Jason was warmly received at each home and, despite his impatience to locate the Simmons Hotel again, he enjoyed the lavish decorations and costumes, the wassail and hymn singing, much more than he would have thought. He visited the Fitzhugh home in Mayfair and at last met the charming Jessica Fitzhugh. When the elderly woman asked Jason if he had ever found the Simmons Hotel, he merely smiled enigmatically and said that perhaps he *had* gotten lost.

He did not finish with the tours until well past midnight, and when he returned to his hotel, he felt impelled to write the articles. He pulled out his laptop computer and worked feverishly throughout the night, completing all four features and then typing in his byline, "Finias Fogg." At dawn, he tumbled into bed and caught a few hours of sleep. At noon, he called Steve McCurdy and checked on how the photo shoot was coming along. Afterward, he went out and mailed the floppy disk with the articles to his editor in the States. He also mailed his parents a Christmas card, sending them his love.

That night, again in black tie, Jason drove back to Belgravia and circled through the darkened streets. A feeling of heightened tension gripped him as he realized that tonight would likely be his last opportunity to find the Simmons Hotel and Annie Simmons.

But this time, he found #10 Belgrave Lane much more easily than he would have thought—indeed, the structure appeared lit up like a beacon. "My God!" he cried as he braked his car to a halt.

Jason shut off the ignition and all but bolted out of his car. He stared in amazement at a far different Simmons Hotel that loomed before him tonight. Gone were the boards, the sagging structure he had seen yesterday. The Greek Revival facade now seemed perfect in every detail, and the windows sparkled like a Christmas tree! Indeed, the spirit of Yule was evident tonight in the garlands gracing the front steps and the freshly cut wreath on the door.

Jason bounded up the steps. He didn't know where he was headed, but he did know that he wanted with all his heart to be right here on this stoop!

He knocked, and this time—to his astonishment and delight—his knock was answered by a far different Annie Simmons, who swung open the door and regarded him with a friendly smile.

This woman, who so strikingly resembled his ghostly guide from two nights ago, was very much alive! Jason sensed that at once. She was dressed in a bright-red velvet gown, her cheeks were bright, and her eyes gleamed with merriment. Beyond her, the hallway was lavishly carpeted and furnished, as well as decorated in the spirit of Yule. He could hear the sounds of happy voices and soft music coming from the parlor. He could even smell the intoxicating aromas of Christmas—the spice of wassail, the crisp scents of cedar and pine. Indeed, he could see the "kissing bunch" she had mentioned two nights ago—a masterpiece of holly and mistletoe, pinecones and lit candles, hanging directly above her head.

Jason was tempted to pull this lovely vision into his arms and kiss her!

But she made the first move, reaching out to take his hand. Her flesh was warm and electric on his, and he felt suddenly as if he were hovering on the brink of some magical discovery.

"Hello, miss," he murmured.

"Good evening, sir," she murmured back. "You must be our expected guest from America. Won't you come in out of the cold and join us?"

Before Jason could think of a response, she tugged on his hand and pulled him through the portal. A sense of unreality swamped him, and he suddenly remembered the verse, "Through this portal, take your leave . . ."

For a moment, Jason felt genuinely disoriented, almost frightened. "Where am I?" he asked his hostess as she tugged him toward the parlor. "What is going on here?"

Her lyrical voice somehow soothed his fears. "Don't worry, sir. You are where you belong now."

CHAPTER THREE

"Father, we have a guest," said Annie Simmons.

After taking Jason's overcoat, Annie led him into the drawing room. Jason could only glance about him in awe, and had to struggle not to gape at the astounding tableau unfolding before him.

Immediately, he sensed that this was hardly a scene enacted from the past, such as he had witnessed at several London homes last night. Instead, he was gripped by the intense, eerie feeling that he had stepped right into an actual Victorian parlor!

The same crystal chandelier he had spotted two nights ago gleamed overhead, casting about warm sprays of light. A vivid royal-blue-and-rose oriental rug covered the floor, and mauve-colored flocked wallpaper graced the walls. The furniture was fashioned of elegant carved rosewood, with silk damask coverings. Behind handsome brass andirons, a fire blazed in the grate. Everywhere were Christmas decorations, from the holly festooning the mantel to the Nativity scene on the tea table, to the Christmas tree in the front window, which gleamed with small lit candles, and was gaily decorated with everything from candied fruits, toys, and clocks, to sugarplums, doll furniture, and pieces of jewelry.

And the people! There seemed to be at least a dozen

guests present, gaily visiting in the parlor—gentlemen in black tailcoats, matching trousers, ruffled shirts, and elaborate silk neckwear, ladies in sweeping floor-length gowns similar to Annie's. At the beautifully carved cabinet grand piano, an elderly woman was playing the sweet strains of "The Holly and the Ivy."

What on earth had happened to him? Jason wondered. He had the uncanny feeling that he had somehow arrived at the Simmons Hotel during its heyday—and that explanation could only make sense if he had somehow traveled through time! Such a possibility seemed preposterous.

Yet how else could he explain the resurrection of the hotel from the ramshackle structure he'd seen yesterday to the magnificent edifice in which he now stood? And how could he account for the transformation of Annie Simmons from the ghost who had mesmerized him two nights ago to the enchanting, beautiful, very much alive creature who now stood next to him?

A balding man with muttonchop whiskers now strode up to join them, glancing rather perplexedly at Jason. "Annie, who have we here?" he asked the woman.

"Father, our visitor from America has arrived," she explained.

"Ah, yes. We hadn't expected you for a few more days, sir." The man extended his hand toward Jason. "I am Oscar Simmons, proprietor of this inn. I see that you've already met my daughter."

Jason smiled at Annie. "Yes, I have."

As the two men shook hands, Oscar Simmons regarded Jason quizzically. "Then you are Finias Fogg, sir?"

"Finias Fogg?" Jason was amazed. "You mean the founder of the *Manhattan Chronicle?*"

"Why, yes. Mr. Fogg recently wrote us reserving a room for his stay in London." Scratching his jaw, Oscar Simmons appeared perplexed. "Are saying you saying you are not Mr. Fogg?"

"I'm afraid we have a misunderstanding here," Jason explained awkwardly. "I am definitely not Finias Fogg—except perhaps in a whimsical sense." As, father and daughter exchanged bemused glances, he quickly added, "However, I suppose I am a representative of Mr. Fogg, since I do write for the *Manhattan Chronicle*. My name is Jason Burke."

"Ah, Mr. Burke," Simmons murmured.

"Then you have come to London in Mr. Fogg's stead?" Annie suggested with a puzzled smile.

Jason had to restrain a chuckle. "Perhaps in a manner of speaking, I have."

"And what is the purpose of your stay in our city, Mr. Burke?" Oscar Simmons asked.

Jason decided the truth might best suffice. "Actually, I am here gathering information to write a series of articles on Christmas traditions in Great Britain."

"Oh, how fascinating!" Annie cried with an expression of delight.

"Indeed," her father concurred. "As it happens, we are hosting a bit of a Yule gathering here tonight for our guests and a few friends. Won't you join us, Mr. Burke?"

"I wouldn't want to impose," he replied hesitantly.

"Nonsense," Annie said. "This gathering is for folks just like you. And you must stay here the night, as well."

"But if you were not expecting me—that is, Mr. Fogg—as yet—"

"Don't be silly," Annie cut in brightly. "At Christmastime, you will never see a sign at the Simmons Hotel reading No Room at the Inn."

"You must really like Christmas then, Miss Simmons," Jason felt compelled to murmur.

"It is my favorite time," she replied.

While Jason still felt highly confused and unsettled regarding his new surroundings, he managed to hold his own as Annie and her father took him about and introduced him to several of their guests. He met a farmer and his wife from Chiswick, as well as the owner of a nearby jewelry shop, and two elderly spinsters, sisters who shared a room at the hotel. When Jason learned that one of the spinsters was named "Media," he felt a chill grip him as he recalled Annie Simmons's "ghost" mentioning the same name two nights ago.

Although from their bemused expressions, it seemed the guests found both Jason's sudden appearance and his attire to be peculiar, all graciously made no comment to indicate that they found the newly arrived guest the least bit out of place here. Within minutes, Jason had a cup of warm wassail in one hand, a plate heaped with fruitcake and gingerbread cookies in the other. Annie had drifted off to visit with a couple of the women, and Jason hung about a small circle of men, which included Annie's father, and listened intently to their conversation.

"I hear Disraeli presented his new budget to the House of Commons today," the shop owner was saying.

"And an inspired proposition 'tis," said the farmer, "reducing the taxes that have so long burdened those of us who work the land."

"Ah, but with the increasing taxes on houses,

innkeepers such as myself are bound to suffer," put in Oscar Simmons.

The shop owner turned to Jason. "What is your tax situation like in America, Mr. Burke?" He laughed. "Or are all of you too rich from mining gold out in your California to care?"

Jason smiled thinly. "Taxes do seem to be an eternal blight for us all."

"Aye," added another. "And I do wonder if the earl of Derby's regime will even survive the four weeks needed to see the year of our Lord 1853."

1853. This announcement of the coming New Year set Jason reeling. Feeling desperate to regain his equilibrium, he moved away from the group and headed toward the front window. What he saw as he moved aside the velvet drapery and glanced down at the street hardly comforted him.

Unfamiliar, ancient-looking three- and four-story houses lined the street, while on the corners, elegant gaslights spilled out their radiance. He noted that his car—indeed all the cars!—had disappeared. Gone was the asphalt street, replaced by time-worn cobblestones. As Jason watched, fascinated, a horse-drawn carriage rattled past, driven by a coachman who wore a heavy cloak and a top hat. Then, on the sidewalk, he observed a bedraggled woman in a long dress lumber by, pushing a flower cart.

So he had been thrust back in time to early December of 1852! His sense of amazement was overwhelming. And, if this were true, then—good heavens!—he had arrived at a juncture only a few weeks before Annie Simmons would die!

Jason was still reeling with this knowledge as he

heard a lyrical voice murmur, "Mr. Burke, are you all right?"

He turned to see Annie Simmons standing beside him. He studied her delicately drawn face—the youthful skin, large, bright eyes, wide mouth, and charming dimples. A sudden anguish rent him. Oh, God, he thought, staring at her, she was so real, so lovely—

And in so much peril!

Jason managed a tremulous smile. "I suppose I'm feeling just a bit disoriented."

"When did you arrive here in London?"

"Only tonight."

She snapped her fingers. "And we didn't even ask about your luggage."

Jason coughed awkwardly. "It's a long story, but I'm afraid that I don't have any."

Annie was gazing at Jason in perplexity when a man stepped up to join them. He was blond, blue-eyed, tall, slender, and quite handsome.

"Annie, dear, you are ignoring me," he murmured. He glanced sharply at Jason. "Do I sense competition here?"

"Oh, Stephen, don't be silly," Annie scolded the gentleman. "This is our new guest, Mr. Jason Burke, a newspaperman from America. I'm only trying to help him gather his bearings a bit." To Jason, she added, "Mr. Burke, this is a very special friend of mine, Stephen Prescott."

"How do you do?" Jason asked, shaking hands with Stephen.

"So you're a newspaperman—and an American." Stephen studied Jason's attire cynically. "Perhaps that is the reason for your rather eccentric garb?"

Before Jason could reply, Annie's father called out from near the piano, "You young people, come over here and join us! Miss Mary is going to play some carols, and let's all gather round the piano and sing."

Jason, Annie, and Stephen dutifully gathered with the others, singing several Yule hymns—"Deck the Halls," "God Rest Ye Merry Gentlemen," and "I Saw Three Ships." Watching Annie stand so close to Stephen, and observing the smug, self-satisfied grin on Prescott's face as he stood with his arm possessively at Annie's waist, Jason felt a strange sense of foreboding and powerlessness wash over him.

After the songs were completed, Oscar Simmons held up a hand. "Ladies and gentlemen," he began proudly, "I have an announcement to make." He smiled at Annie and Stephen. "It is my honor to inform you that my beautiful daughter Annie will shortly marry Mr. Stephen Prescott."

As a cheer went up from the guests, Annie and Stephen smiled happily. Jason felt a chill grip his very soul. He knew now that he had been thrust back in time to a period when Annie Simmons was still alive, albeit she might have only a few weeks left to live! Was he too late?

For Jason had the strong feeling that he had just met the very man who would be responsible for Annie Simmons's death! And yet there she stood, holding Stephen's hand, the very image of the blissful bride—totally oblivious to the disaster hurtling toward her!

Now, the guests swarmed around Annie and Stephen, offering congratulations and hugs. Jason walked over and dutifully extended to both Annie and Stephen his best wishes. Annie responded with a shy smile, Stephen with an indifferent handshake.

In the meantime, Oscar Simmons was making his rounds, handing out glasses of Madeira for a toast. Jason retreated toward a corner, where he could hear the farmer and the shop owner conversing quietly nearby.

"Looks like our dear Miss Annie has found herself a good match," he heard the farmer say.

"Oh, I'm not so sure," replied the shop owner. "When young Prescott came into my shop recently to buy Annie a brooch, he brought along a chap from his club who was giving him the very mischief over his plan to keep on his mistress after the wedding."

"Well, I'll be hanged!" said the farmer. "Prescott plans to philander following the nuptials? Do you suppose we should warn Annie or Oscar?"

"Nay, leave it be," advised the shop owner. "As our Mr. Bulwer-Lytton says, 'Boys will be boys.' Besides, it is not as if young Prescott's attitude toward wedded bliss is that unusual, now is it?"

As the two men chuckled behind him, Jason felt staggered by their disclosures. He again stared helplessly at Annie, who now kissed her father's cheek as he handed her a glass of wine, while Stephen looked on approvingly. Again, he remembered her chilling words from the present, "I died on these steps on Christmas Eve in 1852, when I learned that my true love had deserted me."

Jason had been back in time for less than an hour, yet he already knew not only who would betray Annie Simmons—but also how and why.

CHAPTER FOUR

"If you'll just follow me, sir, the room is down here."

Two hours later, while Annie Simmons's father was downstairs bidding the remaining guests goodnight, Jason Burke was following Annie down the third-story corridor of the hotel. She strolled a few feet ahead of him, holding high a taper to light their way. With the long shadows spilling about them, their sojourn down the darkened hallway bore a spooky resemblance to Jason's "ghost tour" with Annie's spirit two nights ago—and almost a century and a half away! The very thought staggered him.

Not that he wasn't already reeling from his evident journey through time. He felt half-afraid that if he pinched himself, the entire fantastical world to which he had been whisked might simply disappear.

He wondered if Annie remembered taking him on the "ghost tour" two nights ago—and so far away! But, of course, she wouldn't, because he had returned to a period in time before she'd even become a ghost. That realization seemed mind-boggling. Was it then his mission to save her from the catastrophe that would all-too-soon spur her tormented spirit to haunt the Simmons Hotel for so many decades to come? If, indeed, he were even allowed to stay here that long?

Annie creaked open a door. "Ah, here we are."

Jason followed her inside a small, plain room that was furnished with little more than a narrow bed and a nondescript dresser. A couple of oil paintings of English pastoral scenes, as well as airy curtains at the window, lent a feeling of warmth.

Annie gestured toward the grate, where kindling had been laid out. "You can light a fire if you wish. I'm sorry we haven't a finer room available tonight."

"Don't apologize. This will do just fine."

Annie laughed, revealing her charming dimples. "You are very easy to please."

Jason couldn't resist winking at her. "But then, you please me so easily, Miss Simmons."

Jason could have sworn he watched her struggle to hide a guilty smile as she turned away to the dresser, using her taper to light the oil lamp. "We use this room for the occasional overflow of guests, when all our second-floor rooms are occupied." She turned to him. "You say you have no luggage?"

Jason suddenly felt very awkward, and shifted from foot to foot. "Actually, I have arrived not only without luggage, but also without appropriate funds to pay you for this room."

Although she appeared taken aback, she quickly protested, "Oh, please, you must not concern yourself about paying for the room just yet. But it does distress me that your employer, Mr. Fogg, did not adequately provide for you."

Jason grinned sheepishly as he improvised an explanation. "I must confess that I was not entirely truthful downstairs. Indeed, Mr. Finias Fogg may yet show up here."

"What do you mean?"

In a low, conspiratorial tone, he confided, "You see, I

am not an actual employee of the newspaper in America. I'm what you might call a stringer. I've done assignments for the *Manhattan Chronicle* before, and I was simply hoping to sell them some articles on Christmas here in Great Britain."

"Oh, I see." Annie grew thoughtful, frowning as she placed a finger alongside her jaw. "Then perhaps—"

"Yes?"

"I do not mean to be presumptuous, but—"

"Please, feel free to speak."

"Would it be helpful if you could find employment here?"

"Indeed," Jason concurred with a dry laugh.

"You see, my father is good friends with a Mr. Spencer, who owns a local newspaper," she continued with some excitement. "Perhaps we could speak with him on your behalf—"

Jason held up a hand. "You are very kind, but I do feel that you've already done enough for me. Besides, even my staying here must be an imposition."

"Not at all. We want you to feel at home." She paused to study his formal black suit, then grinned almost impishly. "As for your clothing . . . I must say that styles seem to differ greatly in America these days."

"So they do," Jason concurred dryly.

"Across the hallway is a storage room where we keep items left behind by various guests. You're welcome to take anything you need, Mr. Burke." Again, she looked him over, her expression pensive. "As a matter of fact, a few months back, one of our boarders, a Mr. Haggarty, passed away of the fever, and he was about your size. I was going to include his things in the Christmas baskets my church is making up for the poor—but please feel free to claim anything you want first."

"You are far too generous."

"I'm just glad you can put the things to good use." She smiled rather shyly. "Well, is there anything else?"

A *kiss*, Jason thought suddenly, noting how adorable she looked, standing there and gazing at him so expectantly. *Yes, a kiss would do just fine.*

To her, he said reluctantly, "No, I have everything I need."

Appearing satisfied, she swept away toward the doorway, smiling at him over her shoulder. "Well, then, good night, Mr. Burke."

Watching her leave, Jason was rent by sudden anguish. He felt compelled to touch her again. He quickly closed the distance between them, took her free hand, and kissed it. "Good night, Miss Simmons. And thank you for all your kindnesses."

She blushed then, a look of delight spreading across her angelic face that almost had Jason pulling her into his arms—especially as he felt her fingers trembling in his.

Then, gently, she extricated her hand from his. "Good night, Mr. Burke."

Annie Simmons flashed Jason a happy smile as she left.

Jason lit the fire and, as the room warmed up, strode over to the window and gazed out. He studied a skyline that was curiously the same, yet vastly different from the world he had left behind. All modern structures were conspicuously absent. In the distance, he could spot the Belfry Tower of Westminster Abbey, the gothic spires of Parliament, the trees of St. James Park, and the solid outline of Buckingham Palace. Close by on the gaslit street, he watched smoke curl from tall chimneys, and observed another carriage clattering down the cobblestones. A fine powder of snow was beginning to flutter over the rooftops, and the glass of the windowpane felt cold against his fingertips.

Annie's hand had felt warm in his—so warm, he thought. Her flesh had felt so soft against his lips. The memory brought a stab of longing to his heart. Again he hungered to kiss that wide, sweet mouth that had smiled at him tonight with such joy, with such innocence. Annie—his enchanting, untouched 19th century lady. Though he had been with her only briefly, he already knew that she was like no one he had ever met before—a total departure from the worldly-wise girls he had dated back in the present. She was so young, so fresh, so beautiful.

So fragile. Remembering her with Stephen, he frowned darkly. Again, he wondered what he could do to stop the insidious catastrophe that might soon smash Annie's tender young heart to pieces—and end her very life! Protecting that precious life was much more important than his own budding feelings for her.

A weary sigh escaped him. Somehow, he must help Annie—but now, especially after last night's writing marathon, he knew he needed rest. He had definitely brought every bit of his exhaustion with him here to the 19th century.

Moving away from the window, he unbuttoned his jacket and automatically pulled out his wallet. In amazement, he stared at the leather billfold. Flipping it open, he examined his ID, credit cards, and traveler's checks. Everything was still there, intact. The contradiction of this reality astounded him. He was obviously now living in the year 1852—and yet he held in his hand proof that he had actually come from over 140 years in the future!

He laughed ironically. A lot of good these items would do him here now! He chuckled at the prospect of trying to cash one of his pound sterling traveler's checks, or of going to a restaurant and pulling out one of his credit cards. If he told anyone here where he had actually come from, he would likely be labeled a lunatic and carted off to Bedlam. He took his wallet, along with his wristwatch and keys, and placed the items at the back of the top bureau drawer.

Wondering what he might wear to bed, he took the oil lamp and crossed the hallway to the storage room Annie had mentioned. He sniffed at the unpleasant, dank air. Broken or worn furniture, as well as thread-bare or patched linens, were stacked about.

Near the window, he examined two dusty, musty-smelling chests—one held women's clothing, the other held men's. Jason smiled at the sense of Victorian propriety that extended even to segregating old clothing in the storage room.

Turning to the collection of men's attire, Jason pulled out the items one by one. He could only shake his head at the curious contents—felt bowler hats, quaint men's coats with shawl collars, silk brocade vests with braided lapels, finely pleated linen shirts, white silk cravats, walking sticks, and boots. Concentrating on the least worn of the items, Jason selected a brown suit and hat, a white shirt, black cravat, a pair of boots, and a nightshirt. He took the items back to his room.

In bed, with the lamp extinguished, Jason found sleep elusive. His woolen nightshirt felt scratchy and the softness of the feather tick made him feel strangely adrift compared with the firm mattress he was accustomed to in the present.

He turned, punched down his pillow, stared at the dying fire, and wondered what tomorrow would bring. All his instincts told him that he had come here to 19th century London for a reason. Again, he remembered the rhyme on his invitation—"Through this portal take your leave; You'll come back on Christmas Eve."

He knew he had arrived here in early December 1852. Could it be that his time here would be limited, that he would be thrust back to the present on Christmas Eve—hopefully, after he had accomplished his purpose? Had he indeed been sent here as some sort of guardian angel or troubleshooter meant to save Annie Simmons from disaster?

He considered his flight through time from another perspective. Could it be that he had been sent here to learn something, just as Scrooge had experienced a spiritual awakening when he had taken his mystical journey with "the ghost of Christmas past"?

Then he groaned as he again remembered the feel of Annie's baby-soft flesh against his mouth. One thing he knew for a certainty—his first objective while he was here would be to remove Miss Annie Simmons from the clutches of Mr. Steven Prescott.

Downstairs, as she tiptoed about tidying up and snuffing out lamps, Annie Simmons found herself feeling consumed with thoughts of Jason Burke. She felt strangely drawn to the handsome, mysterious American who had appeared on their stoop tonight.

What an enigma he was—showing up here, so

strangely yet elegantly attired, and yet arriving without appropriate funds or even luggage! Even his explanation about being sent by the newspaper had seemed odd as well as dubious.

Yet Annie couldn't deny that she found the American both interesting and intriguing. She considered his arresting face—the deep-set brown eyes, beautifully chiseled nose and firm mouth, the cleft in his strong chin. His physique was tall and trim, his hair thick and black as midnight.

There was a haunted, passionate quality about him that drew her most of all. Heretofore, the only man who had been important to her romantically was Stephen—and Jason Burke was all darkness, all intensity, to Stephen's lightness and charm.

She knew she had agreed to marry Stephen mostly to please her father. Oscar Simmons was getting along in years, and his heart was not as strong as it once had been. Annie knew her father wanted most of all to see his daughter happily settled with the successful haberdasher. She and Stephen had been friends for years, and she had found the prospect of marrying him to be pleasant enough.

Yet honesty compelled her to admit that, ever since she had set eyes on their dark, mysterious stranger who had arrived from America tonight, ever since he had pressed his warm, masterful lips to her flesh, she was having second thoughts about becoming Stephen Prescott's wife.

CHAPTER FIVE

"Did you sleep well, Mr. Burke?" Oscar Simmons asked.

Early the next morning, Jason, dressed in the quaint brown suit he had selected last night, sat in the dining room, eating breakfast with Annie Simmons and her father. Also present were the two spinsters, Miss Media and Miss Mary Craddock. The repast laid out on the lace-covered mahogany table was sumptuous—hot chocolate and coffee, scones and rolls, cranberry bread and cheese. A fire in the grate warmed the room, and the enticing aromas of the freshly baked goods filled the air. More than once during the meal, Jason had looked up in amazement as the pink-cheeked cook, Mrs. Chandler—the very servant Annie's ghost had told him about in the present!—lumbered in wearing her uniform, apron, and mobcap, and bearing a tray laden with more coffee, marmalade, or toast. With every moment that passed, it sank in upon Jason more that he was actually living in 19th century London—for whatever reason.

Now Jason glanced, smiling, from Annie, who sat across from him, to her father, who sat flanking him at the head of the table. "I slept splendidly, thank you, sir," he replied. "It was kind of you and your daughter to take me in on such short notice."

"And what are your plans now that you are settled?" Oscar asked. "Will you be pursuing your duties for your employer?"

When Jason, feeling at a loss, did not immediately reply, Annie filled the gap. "Father, I thought I might take Mr. Burke round to meet your friend Mr. Spencer, the newspaperman. You see, it seems that Mr. Burke is in need of a post during his stay in London."

Oscar Simmons scowled sharply at Jason. "I thought you said you were already employed by the American newspaper."

Jason coughed. "Our arrangement is an informal one."

"So it appears," Simmons murmured, an undercurrent of disapproval in his tone. He nodded toward his daughter. "Perhaps it would be best if I take Mr. Burke by to meet my friend Harley."

"But, Father," Annie protested, "you know the surgeon has cautioned you not to over-do in this weather. Besides, I must be out today, anyway. I had planned to go by Covent Garden to select the nuts and fruits for my Christmas baking." She smiled shyly at Jason. "I thought I might show Mr. Burke a bit of the town."

While Jason returned Annie's smile, Simmons slanted an admonishing glance toward his daughter. "My dear, may I have a word with you?"

"Of course, Father."

Simmons nodded to the others. "If you'll excuse us?"

Jason stood as Annie got to her feet. He watched the father and daughter leave the room together, then sat back down, nodding to the two spinsters—both of whom had been observing the exchange with expressions of fascination.

"Will you be staying in London long, Mr. Burke?" Media asked.

Jason mused that the old lady doubtless could not begin to understand the irony of her question. "I really have no idea."

Across the hallway in the drawing room, Annie and her father were talking in low, intent voices.

"Have you taken leave of your senses?" Oscar demanded of Annie.

She lifted her chin. "I really have no idea what you mean, Father."

He sighed in exasperation. "My dear, you are a promised woman. It is highly improper for you to be gadding about town with this stranger—a bachelor about whom we know nothing."

"But Mr. Burke is a newcomer to our country," Annie argued. "It is only common courtesy that we should help him get acclimated."

"You are letting your own benevolent nature rob you of all good sense!" Oscar declared. "It would be one thing if Stephen were accompanying you—"

"Stephen is quite busy at his shop, especially as it is the Christmas season," Annie pointed out. "Furthermore, are you saying that I am not trustworthy, Father?"

"Certainly not!" he said, flinging his hands wide. "I am simply trying to point out your error in judgment. You have always been far too generous for your own good, my dear. To become a mentor to this . . . newcomer—"

"Father, Mr. Burke is destitute," Annie cut in. "He arrived here without a farthing. He needs a post and a place to stay."

"But there are charitable institutions to see to his kind."

"Now you are sounding as dreadful as Mr. Dickens's Scrooge," Annie scolded. "And I must say that it is quite unlike you to be so stingy. Charity begins at home, Father. It is Christmastime—and I am going to help this man get on his feet."

"Very well," Oscar grumbled, realizing that he was defeated. "You may go out with this man. Just don't make a habit of it." He smiled gently at his only child. "You, I trust. But as for this American upstart—that's another matter altogether."

"Your father doesn't like me much, does he?" Jason asked.

Thirty minutes later, Jason and Annie were seated across from each other inside the family coach. They were headed out of Belgravia and toward Piccadilly. The day was quite chill, and Jason wore his wool overcoat over his suit. He noted that Annie looked simply adorable in her fur-trimmed pelisse over a carriage dress, and a feathered silk bonnet tied with a satin bow.

She smiled at him. "I'm all Father has. You see, Mother died when I was born—"

"I'm so sorry. Then you are an only child?"

"Yes. I suppose that is why Father is so protective of me. He won't be completely happy until I'm wed to Stephen."

"And what of you, Annie?" Jason asked, gazing into her eyes. "Will you be happy when you are wed to Stephen?"

She was pensively quiet for a long moment, avoiding his eye. At last, she said carefully, "Mr. Burke, I am glad to help you. But you must realize, as my father has just reminded me, that I am a promised woman."

Jason could not help himself. He reached out to touch her gloved hand—and again, her honey-gold gaze flicked up to his. "Should you need reminding, Annie?"

She did not reply, but Jason noted to his satisfaction a guilty blush staining her cheeks as she pulled away and turned to stare out the window. Jason also took in the passing sights. They were moving through Hyde Park Corner, with its view of the verdant park and the Corinthian columns of Apsley House. Jason stared at the Wellington Arch, complete with a statue of Wellington that had been absent in his own time. He was amazed. He watched a regiment of Royal Horse Guards trot past, on their way to exercises in the park. That particular London tradition had not changed, he mused.

As the coachman turned the conveyance onto Piccadilly, Jason marveled at the throng of coaches and omnibuses that had supplanted the usual cars and double-decker buses. In place of the usual shops and tourist bureaus, a polyglot of Italianate, Georgian, and Regency structures delighted his eyes. He recognized the familiar lines of Burlington House and the Adamesque façade of St. James Hall.

After a moment, Jason turned to see Annie regarding him with an expression of amusement. "What is so funny, Miss Simmons?"

"Your expression," she admitted. "I've never seen anyone so enthralled with the sights and sounds of London. Clearly, this is your first visit."

"In a manner of speaking, it certainly is," Jason concurred.

While she appeared bemused by his cryptic reply, she did not comment directly. "Tell me of your background, Mr. Burke," she suggested.

"Such as?"

"Your family."

He sighed, deciding the truth might best suffice. "They live in the American Midwest, on a farm in Missouri."

"Have you sisters and brothers?"

"Two sisters."

"And do you see your family often?"

"No," he replied almost curtly.

She at once picked up on the tension. "I'm sorry. I did not mean to broach a painful subject."

He flashed her a contrite smile. "I am the one who must apologize for almost biting your head off. It's just that my family and I, we've never thought much alike. My father wanted me to remain in Missouri and help him run the farm."

"While you wanted to seek your fortunes in the big city as a newspaperman?"

He grinned. "You are very perceptive."

"I think that it is often difficult simply to place oneself in a mold created by a parent. I do admire your courage in pursuing your own destiny, Mr. Burke."

"Perhaps you could use a little of that courage yourself, Miss Simmons?" Jason could not help but suggest wryly.

Again, she appeared reluctant to comment, and a new, awkward silence ensued. Glancing out the window, Jason noted that they had headed south, in the general direction of the Thames. They were now passing through Trafalgar Square with its dramatic statue of Nelson, the magnificence of the National Gallery serving as a backdrop, and the breathtaking spire of St. Martin-in-the-Fields just beyond.

Soon, they clattered along the stately Strand, with its three- and four-story Palladian and Tudor buildings, its lovely view of St. Mary-le-Strand to the east, and the panorama of the gleaming, vessel-jammed Thames running parallel to them to the south. The coachman pulled the conveyance to a halt in front of a storefront whose window was emblazoned with "The Bloomsbury Times."

Annie turned to Jason. "This is Mr. Spencer's newspaper."

As the coachman opened the door, Jason hopped out and escorted Annie out of the coach and into the office. They were greeted by a busy cacophony. Jason glanced in amazement at the old Hoe rotary press, which was whirring away, attended by a harried pressman. Various clerks were scribbling at their desks or scurrying about with papers.

Annie led Jason directly to the back office. "Mr. Spencer," she called out from the doorway.

An elderly, bespectacled gentleman with a balding head and a pleasant, round face looked up at them from his desk. "Why, Annie Simmons! Come right in here!"

Tugging Jason along by his sleeve, Annie stepped inside. Smiling brightly, she said, "Mr. Spencer, I'd like you to meet a guest from our hotel. Mr. Jason Burke is a journalist visiting here from America."

Mr. Spencer grinned in obvious approval and stepped forward, extending his hand. "How do you do, young man?"

"Fine, thank you. And I'm most pleased to meet you, sir," Jason replied, shaking Spencer's hand.

"What newspaper do you write for?" Spencer asked.

"I'm a stringer for the *Manhattan Chronicle*."

Spencer scratched his jaw. "The *Manhattan Chronicle?* Strange, I've never heard of it."

"It's one of the newer—and smaller—newspapers in New York City."

Spencer nodded, then glanced from Jason to Annie. "So what may I do for you two today?"

Annie smiled. "Mr. Spencer, Jason needs a post while he is here in England, and I was wondering—"

"If I can use an extra newsman?" Spencer finished, winking at Annie.

"Yes."

Spencer chuckled, then turned to Jason. "How long are you planning to be in our country, young man?"

"I'm not sure—but probably at least through Christmas."

He scowled. "So you are really only looking for a temporary post here?"

Jason glanced at Annie. "It could work into something permanent."

"What kind of writing are you accustomed to doing?"

"All kinds," Jason replied. "Both current events, and lifestyle pieces."

"Lifestyle pieces?" Spencer repeated in confusion.

Realizing his foible in tossing out a decidedly 20th century buzzword, Jason quickly explained, "You know, articles on the way people live in various locales."

"Ah, yes," Spencer murmured.

"Jason is hoping to sell a series on English Christmas traditions to the New York newspaper."

"Hmmmmm." Spencer stroked his jaw thoughtfully. "You know, Charles Dickens has had such success with his *Household Words* magazine. I might also be interested in the type of pieces you are planning to do, Mr. Burke—that is, unless you are already committed on the series to the *Manhattan Chronicle?*"

"No, we have no formal commitment."

"But I think I would want a more personal slant," Spencer went on. "Say, what it feels like for an American to celebrate Christmas in England for the first time."

"I'd be delighted to give it a try, sir," Jason said sincerely.

"Then you are hiring Jason?" Annie cried with delight.

Spencer again winked at Annie, then turned back to Jason. "Who could resist this Christmas angel? Tell you what, young man. Come back by tomorrow, and we shall discuss this matter further."

"Thank you for helping me," Jason said.

"You are most welcome," Annie replied.

A few moments later, Annie and Jason stood in the vast main arcade of Covent Garden, amid stately pillars and high archways lit by gaslights. They had paused at a fruit stand, where Annie was selecting bright red apples from a cart piled high with the gleaming fruit.

Jason was amazed by the sights and sounds of the market. The huge building teemed with noisy humanity, from the best-dressed gentleman shopping to the most raggedy urchin begging for coins. Shoppers haggled with fruit peddlers and flower girls, while merchants waved their wares and shouted to gain the attention of passersby. Around them swarmed organ grinders with their monkeys, vendors displaying the newest toys, hawkers with squawking parrots on their shoulders, pea-shuckers busily at work, and porters dashing about with baskets on their heads. Nearby, a group of children were gathered about a puppet show. The myriad booths displayed everything from fresh and candied fruits, nuts and spices, to flowers, cut holly, and even the freshly cut Christmas trees that Annie told Jason had been made popular by Queen Victoria's husband, the German Prince Albert. Despite the chill, a riot of smells laced the air—everything from cedar and spice to smoke and garbage.

Annie paid the vendor for her purchases. After the man wrapped the apples in brown paper and twine and handed them to Jason, they strolled on.

"You know, I've been thinking," Annie murmured.

"Yes?"

She flashed him a quick smile. "Well, if you are going to successfully write a series on Yule here in London, you will need to make the rounds and see how we celebrate. My father, Stephen, and I are invited to a number of Christmas gatherings and events—and we would be happy to have you accompany us."

Jason had to laugh. "You are too kind, Miss Annie Simmons," he chided gently. "You might be willing to have me tag along for the revelry—but don't speak for your father or Stephen."

That comment brought a frown to her lovely mouth. "But I cannot imagine either of them being anything but gentlemen about it, under the circumstances. After all, you are a guest who needs our assistance."

Before Jason could comment, Annie paused, smiling down at three ragtag street urchins who were crouched on their haunches, selling flowers. She handed each child tuppence, and the oldest boy popped up, bowing and presenting Annie with a nosegay of violets.

"Thank you dearly, miss," the lad cried in a heavy Cockney accent, a broad smile splitting his thin, smudged face.

Annie touched the boy's filthy hand. "Please, you must keep the flowers."

"Oh, no, miss," he protested. "They is already paid for, good and proper. You must take them."

"Very well, then. God bless you."

"And you, miss."

As Annie and Jason started on, she glanced over her shoulder at the tattered orphans. "It breaks my heart to see the young ones so," she murmured to Jason. "Of course, those stuck at the workhouses have an even worse lot in life. I'm hoping that the reform movement that is sweeping Parliament will help them all."

Jason stared at her for a long moment. "You know, you truly are a remarkable woman."

"Oh, I do not think so," she quickly denied.

"But you are. You think of others constantly, and never of yourself."

"You are exaggerating, I'm sure."

Jason lifted an eyebrow. "I am exaggerating? Let's see—giving money to orphans, inviting me along on your Yule activities." Gazing at her intently, he added meaningfully, "And marrying Stephen to please your father."

She glanced at him quickly. "Is that what you think, Mr. Burke?"

"You all but admitted it earlier."

She fingered the nosegay of flowers. "Well, I must confess that I've never tried to place my own needs first. That seems an exceedingly selfish way to live."

As Annie turned to select some spices at a stand,

Jason pondered her reply. In the late 20th century, where selfishness was vogue, Annie's attitude might well be deemed foolish. Here, he found her outlook far too endearing. Again he reflected on how refreshing she was, how different from the self-absorbed women he had known in his time. She was truly an old-fashioned delight. Yet Jason was also left struggling with the reality that Annie's very self-sacrifice might well prove her undoing—especially if she persisted in her plan to marry Stephen.

Annie made the rest of her purchases, and they left the marketplace together. They headed back toward the Strand, where the coach was parked.

Jason caught Annie's sleeve next to the doorway of a quaint shop with expensive cheeses and hams displayed behind leaded glass windows. "Annie?"

She regarded him shyly. "Yes?"

He smiled. "Thank you for today."

"You are most welcome."

He touched her hand. "Will you think about something for me?"

"What is that?"

Carefully, he said, "I think that sometimes, when we try so hard to please others, we may end up bringing unhappiness not only to ourselves, but to everyone. Do you understand what I'm trying to say?"

She chewed her lower lip. "I suppose."

"Then perhaps you could start thinking of yourself just a little more?"

All at once, Annie would not meet his gaze. She turned her head to watch an elderly couple, laden down with packages, emerge from the shop doorway.

Jason cupped her chin in his fingers, forcing her to look at him. "Annie? What is it?"

With a guilty smile, she admitted, "I'm not above thinking of myself."

"Oh, you're not?" he teased. "In what way?"

Her expression bordered on mischievous as she admitted, "Well, when I invited you to come along for the Yule activities, I was actually being—"

"Yes?"

She gazed up at him raptly and whispered, "Rather selfish."

"Oh, Annie."

Jason would not even notice until later that he had dropped all her packages. With a groan, he pulled her close and kissed her ardently. She did not resist; indeed, he heard a tiny sigh escape her as his mouth claimed hers. Her lips were warm and sweet, trustingly parted, on his. Her softness, her heat, seemed to seep into his very blood as he clutched her tightly and inhaled the heavenly essence of her—lavender and woman. Never had a woman thrilled him so, touched him so deeply, and he cherished her against his hammering heart.

After a moment, he could feel her hands reach around to stroke his back, caressing him, even as her lips eagerly moved against his. Her surrender ignited such a firestorm in his blood that he crushed her to him and thrust between her lips with his tongue. Even as he yearned to plunge deeply into the sweetness of her warm mouth, he felt a shudder rack her and he pulled back, afraid he had gone too far.

For a moment, they stared at each other, both breathless and wide-eyed following the moment of intimacy and discovery. Annie, too, had been left reeling. She felt vulnerable, bewildered, tremendously shaken. Never had any man stirred her as Jason just had with his kiss. She realized that her father had been right. She was behaving imprudently—and couldn't seem to stop herself!

At last, Jason said hoarsely, "I'm sorry. I was out of line, wasn't I?"

Annie didn't answer, but stared up at him with a tenderness and uncertainty that twisted his heart.

He stroked her flushed cheek. "Annie? I just feel you are selling yourself short. I want you to realize that there are other men in this world besides Stephen."

Then he saw the tears brim in her beautiful, golden eyes, and the sorrow and poignancy there lanced him like a knife in the heart.

"Unfortunately," she replied in a voice so low he could barely hear her, "at the moment, there is only one."

CHAPTER SIX

Over the next ten days, Jason became better acclimated to 19th century London. He started his job at the *Bloomsbury Times*, writing nostalgic pieces about the city amidst Yule preparations. While it was an adjustment to write the stories by hand, without the aid of a modern computer, he did have Annie Simmons to thank for the wealth of material he was able to draw upon for his articles. She insisted that Jason be included in all the Yule events she attended with Stephen and her father—much to the exasperation of the two other men, Jason was certain. Yet both Annie's father and her fiancé were obviously consummate British gentlemen whose innate sense of good manners forbade them to exclude the American guest who so obviously needed assistance with his new duties. And Annie often invited along on the excursions an unmarried friend of hers, Harriet Pierce, whose presence lent a more balanced effect—and no doubt somewhat appeased Stephen regarding Jason's continued presence.

Together, the five attended church, watched bell ringers and mummers perform in the London streets, and delighted at the colorful wares of the toy vendors, as well as the beautiful Christmas cards, greenery, and lovely gifts displayed in the various shop windows.

They viewed a glorious pantomime of Aladdin at the Drury Lane Theater, as well as a *tableau vivant* at the Royal Opera House. Jason even helped Annie hand out small mince pies to the jolly carolers who seemed to appear nightly on the stoop of the hotel.

The highlight of the activities for Jason was an evening the five spent at St. James' Hall, hearing Charles Dickens perform a public reading from *A Christmas Carol*. For Jason, never had history so sprung to life before his very eyes than when he watched the stately, energetic author read his own brilliant descriptions of London at Yule. Jason could even feel something of Dickens's message of inspiration and hope seeping into his own blood.

Daily, Jason recorded his observations for the newspaper, in a manner Mr. Spencer found fresh and lively. Annie, too, was thrilled with Jason's progress. One morning at breakfast, with Jason, her father, and the two spinsters present, she read from his new column, "An American in London."

As the others listened and Jason sipped his tea self-consciously, Annie quoted, "This American sees in London a time of great misery, but also a time of great hope. A spirit of reform is sweeping the country, as evidenced by the many fine proposals being presented to Parliament. Yes, there are children slaving away in the factories, or selling flowers for pennies in the markets, but there is also concern and caring. An innkeeper and his daughter took in this stranger from America who arrived here without a farthing in his hand, and with no one to recommend him. Women such as the innkeeper's daughter are busy this season preparing baskets for the poor. This reporter finds here in London a very human time, compared with the impersonal world he left behind. Perhaps Charles Dickens summed it up best when he recently read publicly from *A Christmas Carol*, which is itself a tribute to the redemption of the human spirit. To quote Tiny Tim, 'God bless us, every one.'"

Annie finished her reading and flashed a bright smile at Jason. The two spinsters clapped and oohed and aahed with delight, while Jason tried to hide his embarrassment. Annie's father responded with a subdued nod toward the younger man.

"Your article is splendid, Mr. Burke," exclaimed Media.

"And do you indeed find America much more impersonal compared with Great Britain?" Mary added.

Jason nodded, turning to smile at Annie. "To tell you the truth, America seems a world away right now."

"A world that we are glad you left, so that you can bring us your beautiful insights, Mr. Burke," Annie replied sincerely.

"Well," Annie's father added, clearing his throat, "I am pleased to note that your employment is progressing so well, Mr. Burke."

With reluctance, Jason drew his gaze from Annie and nodded to her father. "And for that, I must thank you and your daughter."

Jason had not again kissed Annie, although he sensed that she felt the same tension and attraction that stirred him each time they were together. Being around her was, in so many ways, torture for him. She was so bright, so full of life and vitality. She seemed to take delight in every minute of the Yule activities. To Jason, she represented all the hope and optimism and zest for life that he himself had lost. He feared he was more than a little in love with her, and he had no way of knowing whether that love would ultimately save her or destroy her. He was frequently tortured by doubt. In wanting to rescue her from Stephen's clutches, was it possible that he was pushing her farther toward disaster—at his own hands?

While Annie was often nearby, she was also frustratingly untouchable. The solid barrier of her engagement to Stephen continued to loom between them. Watching Prescott perpetually hover about her, holding her hand or even kissing her cheek, was almost more than Jason could bear. He remained determined to disabuse Annie of her desire to wed Stephen, but he still wasn't completely sure just how he would accomplish his goal. If only he could arrange for more time alone with her—but, aside from the one excursion they'd taken together, her father, Stephen, or Harriet was always present.

At the same time, Christmas Eve—the very night on which Stephen would supposedly desert Annie, and she might well die—loomed ever closer. A sense of frustration bordering on desperation nagged Jason as he wondered if he could do anything at all to stop the coming disaster. Each time he glanced at the lovely Annie—watched her eyes sparkle with joy, her cheeks dimple with laughter—and then thought of her dead, his blood ran cold. And he could not even resolve to protect her on Christmas Eve, when he had no idea if he would still even be here in Victorian London then. He could not begin to understand the mystical forces that had brought him here—or to know whether, at any moment, he might be swept back to his own time again. Often, he remembered the ominous last line on his invitation, "You'll come back on Christmas Eve."

On an evening a week and a half before Christmas, Annie invited Jason and Harriet to accompany her, Stephen, and her father to a Christmas dinner given by her father's cousin. Using the better part of his weekly wages, Jason bought himself a new black suit for the occasion. Glancing at himself in the mirror, he had to admit that he looked rather dapper in the black cutaway, matching trousers, and ruffled linen shirt. Picking up his silk top hat and ebony walking stick, he felt like an authentic Victorian gentleman.

He went downstairs and paused outside the drawing room at the sound of voices. He could hear Annie and Stephen inside—and clearly, they were arguing.

"Must you drag along Burke again?" he heard Stephen ask irritably. "He is behaving rather like a stray dog who refuses to quit following us about."

"Why, Stephen, what a cruel thing to say!" Annie cried. "Mr. Burke is our guest. He is a newcomer from America, with no contacts in London, and he needs our help. Haven't you read his marvelous articles in the *Bloomsbury Times* each day? Why, if we hadn't taken him about with us, he never could have published those articles—or provided for his own livelihood."

"Why do I have the feeling that you are far more fascinated with the man than with his writing?"

"Stephen, that is simply not the case. And you are sounding jealous."

"I am jealous!"

"Mr. Burke may only be here for a fortnight longer. You and I will marry in the spring, and then we will be together. In the meantime—"

"In the meantime," Jason heard Stephen cut in, "I must remind you that I have no one else in my life—not even a casual lady friend. I'm simply asking the same level of devotion and commitment from you."

As Annie and Stephen continued to bicker, Jason silently seethed with anger. Oh, the cad, he thought, feeling incredulous over Stephen's lie. How could Prescott claim to Annie that he had "not even a lady friend," when the scoundrel kept a mistress on the side? How could he blatantly deceive Annie, then demand that she end her friendship with him?

Silence had fallen in the parlor, and Jason, fearing that Stephen was kissing Annie, felt jealousy shoot through him. He strode into the room, only to draw a breath of relief. The two were yards apart. Stephen stood scowling with his elbow resting on the fireplace mantel, while Annie had wandered over to pick up a small doll ornament that had fallen off the Christmas tree.

"Good evening," Jason said, flashing a cheery smile to both. "Are we ready to leave?"

Annie, looking gorgeous in a green silk evening dress with a low neckline and gigot sleeves, turned to smile a greeting at Jason. "Of course, Mr. Burke. And don't you look dashing. Father should be down any moment now, and then we shall all go pick up Harriet."

"Great," Jason said.

"Ah, yes, splendid," Stephen added with a sneer. "There is nothing I like better than courting my fiancée by committee."

The four left the hotel in Stephen's elegant custom coach. Heading into the city, they crossed London Bridge to the South Bank and picked up Harriet Pierce at her parents' charming Queen Anne town house on St. Thomas Street. Harriet, a vivacious creature with dark brown hair and green eyes, took the only remaining seat, next to Jason—and then greeted one and all with effusive hellos.

"Well, I must tell you, dears," Harriet said brightly as the carriage rattled off, "I have been running myself ragged today on Bond Street, trying to complete my Christmas shopping." She smiled at Stephen. "Mr. Prescott, I simply must get by your haberdashery to get Papa a new cravat."

"We have some very nice silks, just in from the Orient," Stephen replied.

"Oh, and Papa does so love those fancy things." She turned her glowing smile on Jason. "And what of you, Mr. Burke? Have you gotten around to Bond Street as yet? If you need more background material for your series of articles on our city, I should be delighted to assist you in any way."

Jason smiled at the young woman. Harriet was lively and pretty, and he suspected she was already rather enamored of him. The problem was, she wasn't Annie. He did often wonder why Annie so frequently included Harriet in their outings—and he fervently hoped it was to appease Stephen regarding his own presence, rather than to interest him romantically.

"You are very kind," Jason murmured.

"Why don't the three of us go over to Bond Street tomorrow afternoon?" Annie suggested. "I've shopping to complete myself—then we could go by Stephen's haberdashery, and perhaps the four of us could have tea together."

"Ah, a wonderful idea," agreed Harriet, clapping her hands.

Stephen, meanwhile, scowled darkly, but was evidently too much of a gentleman to veto Annie's suggestion.

They soon arrived at the home of Oscar Simmons's cousin, Catherine Holcomb, who lived with her husband, William, in a modest Georgian town home in the East End. Yet, while the Albert Gardens address was unpretentious, the cozy home was as festively decked out for Yule as the most lavish mansion in Regent's Park. As Catherine and her husband received Jason and the others, he glanced about the hallway, which was festooned with holly, and decorated with the traditional candlelit "kissing bunch" suspended over their heads, as well as angels, tambourines, trumpets, a gingerbread house, and a Nativity scene gracing the various tables.

Several other family friends, as well as Jason's employer, Mr. Spencer, had been invited for the dinner, which was held in the homey, paneled dining room. The table was set with the finest Irish linen and Paris china. A boar's head, stuffed with an orange, served as the centerpiece. The main course was roast turkey with chestnut stuffing, served with fresh vegetables, hot bread, and white wine. By each plate, the hostess had placed a "Christmas cracker" for the guests. The crackers were rolled cylinders of colorful paper cinched near each end. The cylinders made a loud popping sound when pulled apart, and the laughing guests cracked them open to find tiny treasures—toys, small bells, paper flowers, or hats. Annie toys, small bells, paper flowers, or hats. Annie exclaimed over the paper rose found in hers, while Jason was amused by the paper crown in his.

The conversation was convivial, several of the

guests congratulating Annie and Stephen on their engagement. While Stephen and Annie accepted the fond wishes graciously, Jason noted a mood of tension between them that had been present ever since they had all left the house in Stephen's carriage. There was mention of the current clash in Parliament over Disraeli's new budget, and the rumors that even the queen and Prince Albert were growing concerned over the escalating crisis.

Several of the people complimented Jason on his recent articles. Their host, William Holcomb, said to Jason, "Mr. Spencer here tells me that you may not be staying long here in England."

Jason nodded. "That is true."

"But your pieces in the *Bloomsbury Times* are fascinating," put in Catherine, "and you seem to favor this country over your own. Have you not considered staying here permanently?"

Before Jason could answer, Stephen cut in rather sardonically, "Perhaps Mr. Burke might better seek his fortune back in his own country. It is not that easy making a life for oneself here on a newspaperman's salary." He glanced meaningfully at Harriet, then at Annie. "I should think that if Mr. Burke remained here, he could never hope to support a wife and children."

Harriet, not about to be baited, winked at Stephen and said, "I should wager that Mr. Burke feels as I do. Why worry about being rich if one can be happy?"

The guests seemed to agree. A couple even murmured, "Hear, hear," and raised their glasses.

Then, with a twinkle in his eye, Mr. Spencer spoke up to Stephen. "You know, you might be speaking precipitously, Mr. Prescott." He nodded proudly to Jason.

"As talented as young Burke is, and as old as I'm getting, I wouldn't be at all surprised to see him running the *Bloomsbury Times* before too long."

At this pronouncement, both Annie and Harriet beamed at Jason, and he grinned back at both. As other appreciative murmurs drifted down the table, Jason could have sworn that he heard Stephen's jaw grinding.

After a lavish dessert of plum pudding served with hard sauce, the guests gathered in the parlor to sing the traditional carols—"The Holly and the Ivy" and "Silent Night"—while Catherine accompanied the hymns on the piano. Soon, Stephen suggested that their hostess play a few waltzes so the guests could dance. As the others looked on raptly, Stephen waltzed Annie about the parlor to the strains of a Chopin waltz. Old Mr. Spencer joined in with his wife, and Jason dutifully asked Harriet.

Staring at Stephen's smug smile as he held Annie close and whirled her about, Jason knew that Prescott was deliberately staging a scene, trying to prove a point. Meanwhile, Harriet tried to make pleasant conversation with Jason, but he responded in distracted monosyllables. When the music stopped, he muttered an apology to her, strode up to Annie, and bowed before her.

"May I have this dance?"

Annie glanced questioningly at Stephen.

"By all means," Stephen muttered less-than-graciously.

Jason was chuckling as he drew Annie in his arms and swept her about to a Strauss waltz. He felt deeply thrilled to be close to her—to watch the light play over the beautiful honey-brown curls piled on her head, to see her eyes sparkling with gaiety, her pink lips curving with happiness.

Jason glanced at Stephen, who stood scowling formidably at the side of the room. Teasingly, he confided to Annie, "Stephen was too much of a gentleman to refuse my request, but I'll bet he would like to call me out about now."

She dimpled. "Oh, he will get over it."

Jason felt a frown drift in. "I heard the two of you arguing earlier. It was over me, wasn't it?"

She shot a furtive glance at Stephen, then murmured, "Please, you must not concern yourself. It will pass."

"If I were truly unselfish," Jason admitted, "I would stop going out with all of you, in deference to Stephen." In a huskier tone, he finished, "But where you are concerned, my lovely Miss Simmons, I'm afraid I find myself feeling more selfish with each passing day."

Seemingly amazed, Annie stared up at him.

"I was wondering something earlier," Jason went on.

"And what is that?"

He nodded toward Harriet, who was laughing as she sipped eggnog with Oscar. "Do you keep inviting Harriet along for my sake, or to keep Stephen off-guard?"

She paled. "What do you mean?"

Jason pulled Annie slightly closer. Inhaling the sweet, feminine scent of her, he stared down into her wide, vibrant eyes. "Do you want Harriet along to distract me, or as a foil to distract Stephen from the fact that I'm interested in you?"

Appearing flustered, Annie responded, "I—I want Harriet along because she is my friend."

Her nearness, even her endearing confusion, were

playing havoc with Jason's senses and his good judgment. Leaning toward Annie's ear, he whispered, "Do you want Harriet to distract me, Annie?"

Now she appeared adorably flustered, avoiding his gaze and stammering, "I—I'm not sure."

"Or is it you who is in need of a buffer?" he pressed on. "Do you like having your friend along because I make you feel things you'd rather not feel?"

"Perhaps," she admitted in a whisper.

"Doesn't that tell you something?"

She glanced up, frowning slightly. "What do you mean?"

"I don't think you should marry Stephen."

"And why not?"

"I just don't think he is right for you. I sense something false about him."

She smiled quizzically. "And are you offering an alternative, Mr. Burke?"

"Jason."

"Jason."

"Why must there be an alternative?" he argued. "Why should your life revolve around any man?"

She shook her head slowly. "Mr. Burke, now you are toying with me."

"In what way?"

"You want me to feel things, don't you?" she challenged passionately. "Feelings for you. But it is a game to you. You are hardly prepared to follow through with any kind of commitment, are you?"

Jason could only groan. "Annie, I'm sorry. There are complications—problems I can't tell you about. I don't know how long I'll be allowed to stay in England." With both fervor and uncertainty, he added, "But even if I were prepared to follow through, would you break things off with Stephen?"

"I—I don't know," she admitted honestly.

"I just don't want to see you selling yourself short for the sake of your father—or simply to have a home and security."

"Simply to have a home and security?" Her laugh was incredulous. "But Mr. Burke—"

"Jason."

"Jason." Earnestly, she said, "My purpose in life has always been to have a home and a husband—and children."

Jason stared at her—so determined, so naive, so beautiful. All at once, he desperately wanted to have all those things—with her.

It was hard for him to speak, but at last he said, "If such is your heart's desire, then I think you should pursue it. But with a finer man than Stephen."

She laughed. "You are saying I am too good for him?"

"Oh, yes."

"And what of you, Mr. Burke?" All at once, she took the offense, smiling and edging slightly closer to him. "Am I too good for you as well? Will you not be pleased until you see me canonized?"

Jason broke into a grin. "Miss Simmons—"

"Annie," she corrected.

"Annie, you are teasing me. That can be perilous."

"And I would like an answer."

As they spoke, Jason had maneuvered Annie out into the hallway. He glanced over their heads and pulled her to a halt, suddenly feeling quite devilish.

Nodding toward the ceiling, he murmured, "Isn't this the kissing bunch you once told me about?"

"Did I?" She stared up at him raptly.

He lowered his face toward hers and whispered, "What I have in mind for you, Miss Simmons, hardly involves canonization."

Jason pulled sweet Annie closer and kissed her. He moaned as the taste of her lips excited him unbearably. He crushed her to him and pressed his tongue hungrily against her wet, warm lips. She opened to him eagerly and Jason reeled with desire. She tasted so delicious, and felt so vital, so soft and warm in his arms. His heart pounded with the need to possess her. He could have devoured her on the spot. He realized she was perfect for him—his old-fashioned lady. He ached to make her his, forever.

Annie was equally mesmerized by Jason's kiss. It seemed like forever since he had held her thus, and his male strength, his scent, the heat of his mouth, set her senses aflame. She realized achingly that she had been deluding herself about Stephen. Never had any man excited her as Jason Burke did!

"What have we here?" demanded an angry voice.

At the sound of Stephen's harsh question, Annie and Jason sprang apart like lovers caught in the act. They turned to confront a furious Stephen, a scowling Oscar, and a white-faced Harriet, all of whom now stood beyond them in the hallway.

Not giving Jason a chance to reply, Stephen stepped forward and grabbed Annie's arm. "I think it is time for all of us to leave."

"But, Stephen," she protested, glancing helplessly from her fiancé to Jason, "you mustn't become angry at Jason. The kissing bunch is a Christmas tradition here in England—"

"That we'll all doubtless read about in Burke's article in the *Bloomsbury Times* tomorrow?" Stephen cut in furiously. He hurled a glare at Jason. "Mr. Burke, I think Miss Simmons has taught you quite enough about Yule customs here in England. Learn whatever else you need to know from someone else besides my fiancée!"

As Stephen led her off, Annie could not protest further. Jason helped Harriet into her cloak, and the five proceeded back to the Simmons Hotel in tense silence.

Half an hour later, after Stephen dropped Jason, Annie, and Oscar off at the Simmons Hotel, Annie's father turned to Jason in the downstairs hallway.

"Mr. Burke," he said coldly, "you are no longer welcome to stay at this hotel."

Annie was aghast. "Father, how can you say such a thing?"

But Jason held up a hand. "Annie, it's all right." He turned to Oscar. "You are right, sir. I acted out of line tonight, and for that, I must apologize. I have also imposed on your family quite long enough. I will settle up accounts with you in the morning and seek lodgings elsewhere."

"Very good," Oscar said gruffly.

Meanwhile, Annie threw her father a look of confusion, hurt, and anger, and rushed off up the stairs.

Jason watched her helplessly, then turned to Oscar, who had also watched his daughter's flight with an expression of anguish.

"I didn't mean anything by my actions, sir," he reiterated. "I suppose I simply became caught up in the spirit."

"And in setting Prescott in his place after he insulted you at dinner?" Oscar finished with biting cynicism. "He was right, you know."

"What do you mean?"

Oscar regarded Jason with contempt. "You would never make my daughter a proper husband. You are an American upstart, a drifter. Stephen is a successful haberdasher, and well-established in this community."

"And you think he is what Annie needs?"

"Yes! Leave my daughter alone! You have taken advantage of her kindnesses quite long enough. Stephen Prescott is the right man for her."

CHAPTER SEVEN

The next morning, feeling dispirited, Jason packed his few meager belongings, settled up his account with Annie's father, and then left the Simmons Hotel. He let a room at a boarding house near St. James. He did not see Annie for several days, and he felt at something of a loss regarding her. He still very much wanted to protect her, but he did not want to cause her pain, or especially, to provoke an alienation between her and her father. Oscar Simmons obviously remained convinced that Stephen was the right man for Annie.

Jason sensed disaster hovering closer to Annie with each day that passed. He agonized about how he might help her in the scant days remaining before tragedy would surely strike her. Worse yet, he continued to experience the nagging fear that he might be snatched away from his new existence on Christmas Eve—and what would happen to Annie if he couldn't alter her destiny before then?

Then surprisingly, on a morning a week before Christmas, Annie appeared at the newspaper office. He glanced up to see her standing in front of his desk, dressed in a cloak, bonnet, and muffler, with her cheeks bright pink from the cold.

The sight of her filled him with both joy and relief.

He stood and smiled. "Why, Annie. What a pleasant surprise."

"Are you doing well, Jason?" she asked awkwardly.

"Yes, of course."

"We haven't seen much of you since you moved out of the hotel."

He sighed. "Annie, you know how it has been with your father and Stephen."

"Are you getting settled in your new surroundings?"

"Yes—I like my room in the boarding house near St. James. I have a nice view of Westminster Abbey." Catching her dismayed expression, he quickly added, "Still, it is not the same as the Simmons Hotel."

She smiled. "Jason, I've come by to invite you to go on an excursion with me, my father, and Stephen tomorrow."

"Annie . . ." Helplessly, he shook his head. "I can't be responsible for causing any more bad feelings."

"But you must come along this time!" she protested. "You see, our friends the Youngbloods have invited us to a gathering at their farmhouse in the country. In her note, Mrs. Youngblood specifically urged us to bring you along as well. This would be the perfect opportunity for you to do research on how an English country Christmas is celebrated. Not only that, but Father has hired a sleigh and coachman for the occasion. It's a fairly long drive, so we'll be gone from before noon until the wee hours of the morning."

Jason felt very tempted, but he was also feeling skeptical. "What about your father and Stephen? What are their feelings on this?"

She lifted her chin. "They have both consented to your coming along."

Jason was astounded. "They have? But why?"

Annie glanced away, avoiding his probing gaze.

"Annie?" He grinned. "What did you do—apply the thumbscrews?"

She giggled, then flashed him a conspiratorial smile. "Really, Jason, such extreme measures were hardly necessary. I know Father feels badly for so precipitously banning you from the hotel following Cousin Catherine's dinner party, and I think I have managed to convince Stephen that he, too, overreacted to our kiss that night."

"You have?"

She flashed him a near-impish smirk. "And besides, I warned both Father and Stephen that I would not attend the Youngbloods' gathering unless you were included."

"Annie! You didn't!"

"I did," she admitted unrepentantly. "When I pointed out to them both that it would be the height of ill manners to exclude you when you could write about the occasion in the *Bloomsbury Times*, they both finally relented."

Jason shook his head. "My, you are determined. And count on a British gentleman ultimately to bow to good manners in all things." Rather hesitantly, he added, "What about Harriet?"

Annie sighed. "I invited her as well, but she claims to have a touch of the ague. However, I suspect that in reality—"

"Yes?"

She regarded him with mingled sadness and longing. "That Harriet is quite taken with you, Jason, and that she misinterpreted what she saw beneath the kissing bunch."

He felt a stab of regret. "Oh, Annie. I've been

meaning to send her a note of apology." He reached out to stroke her soft cheek. "But was it a misinterpretation on Harriet's part, or did she simply view the truth, and find that too painful?"

Annie glanced away, obviously acutely discomfited.

"I'm sorry," Jason hastily added. "I didn't mean to put you on the spot. It's just that . . ." His voice trailed off as he stared at her wistfully. "I really can't offer Harriet any encouragement."

"Oh, Jason," Annie whispered, staring at him with equal yearning. Before he could comment further, she added quickly, "Will you come with us tomorrow?"

He frowned. "You are very kind-hearted, but I fear my being along will cast a pall over the entire occasion."

"Nonsense," Annie said briskly. She regarded him with touching tenderness. "Besides, I've missed you."

Jason felt bittersweet emotion twisting his own heart, and could not contain the fervency of his reply. "Oh, Annie. I've missed you, too."

The visit to the Youngbloods' farm did turn out to be a strained occasion in many ways. The sleigh ride saw the group divided into separate camps—Jason seated on one side, with Stephen, Oscar, and Annie on the other. Their journey passed mostly in silence.

Jason did enjoy the sights and sounds of the sleigh ride—the cold wind and the flakes of snow in his face, the jingling of the horse's harnesses and the sounds of the coachman's shouts to the team as they glided over the Great West Road toward Chiswick. The countryside was a fairyland—trees swathed with snow and dripping with icicles, farmhouses winking with warm, welcoming lights in their windows, smoke curling from their chimneys.

The Youngblood farmstead was equally picturesque. The roofs of the farmhouse, as well as the barn, well house, dairy, and dovecote, were caked with snow. The paths, corrals, and fields lay blanketed in deep drifts.

Jason and the others stamped their feet against the cold as they made their way to the door of the Tudor cottage with its high-pitched roof.

A smiling John Youngblood, with pipe in hand, greeted them and beckoned them inside. "Come in out of the cold, all of you."

Jason was amazed by the rustic farmhouse, with its soaring sawn timber roof, puncheon floor, and rustic country furnishings. The large main room swarmed with people, and the scene was one of near-chaotic revelry. John and Emma Youngblood had six children ranging in age from two to twelve, and the couple had also invited over friends from neighboring farms. At least a dozen youngsters scurried about, laughing and shouting, half of them playing a wild game of hoop-and-hide, while the others were chasing down a quartet of frisky kittens that bounded about everywhere, knocking over baskets of fruit, climbing the pants legs of guests, and chewing on the furniture. The smell of baking bread curled out from the bake oven, mingling with the aromas of spiced ham, sweet potatoes, steaming cabbage, and stewing pears that drifted out from the kitchen. On the open hearth, a crane supported a stock pot, steaming with mutton stew, and a whistling tea kettle.

Annie made a point of introducing Jason to everyone and explaining about the series of articles he was writing. A couple of the farmers really warmed to the subject, spinning yarns of Christmas memories from their childhood. Jason noted that Stephen made a point of trying to keep Annie out of reach of his American rival as much as possible. He also noticed Prescott drinking generous portions of the apple cider one of the farmers had brought along.

Dinner was a sumptuous feast. The adults were served at the large table before the blazing fire, while the children sat near the hearth with plates in their laps. Jason found the ham wonderfully spiced and flavored with oranges, the sweet potatoes delectable with their brandy glaze, the cabbage delicious with its tang of apples and thyme. The conversation was lively, especially when Oscar Simmons informed the others of the rumors of the pending resignation of the earl of Derby's ministry. There was much speculation regarding what coalition the queen might now form to run the country. Then the discussion turned more provincial, with the farmers voicing their hopes for an early spring, while the children down on the hearth whispered excitedly about the coming of Father Christmas. The kittens, meanwhile, were also feasting, having found their way back to their basket on the hearth, and to their mother's milk.

Throughout the meal, Jason had to struggle not to stare at Annie. She sat across from him next to Stephen, looking so beautiful with the fire dancing highlights in her hair and gleaming in her eyes. The shy smiles she occasionally cast his way made his heart ring with joy as he realized that she was indeed very happy that he had come along. Meanwhile, Stephen, seated beside her, looked on broodingly and paid much more attention to his cider than to the meal.

As Mrs. Youngblood was serving up the dessert of mince and pumpkin pie, the Youngblood baby awakened, wailing loudly in her cradle across the room.

Annie hastened to go get the child and rock her. Jason could not take his eyes off her as she rocked the infant and hummed her the sweet, lulling strains of "The Coventry Carol." At that moment, watching Annie made him want desperately so many things that seemed forbidden to him here—a wife, a home, children of his own—the very things he had once scoffed back in the present. He realized that the spirit of Christmas, of family, hope, and joy, was in his soul tonight, even as his love for Annie was burning in his heart. And it seemed incredible to him that only two weeks past, he had been an unmitigated cynic who had greeted the 20th century Yule celebration with Ebenezer Scrooge's typical "Bah, humbug."

After the dishes had been cleared and the baby put back in her cradle, Mrs. Youngblood suggested that they all play games. The men arranged chairs in a circle, and adults and children alike played several riotous rounds of Hot Cockles and Hide the Slipper. The atmosphere grew really rowdy during the game of blindman's buff. Jason was even impelled to spring up and grab a rambunctious, blindfolded child who was charging about dangerously close to the fire.

As the guests were laughing, taking a break from the games to sip berry wine, John Youngblood glanced at Jason and said, "Perhaps our guest from America would like to suggest a game."

Jason pondered that a moment, then grinned and snapped his fingers. "How about charades?"

Several of the guests murmured their approval, while Stephen piped up in a slurred voice, "We do not play French games here, Mr. Burke."

Mr. Youngblood waved Stephen off. "Oh, nonsense, Mr. Prescott. I think we need not tremble in fear of

Louis-Napoléon tonight. Indeed, England may prove the emperor's ally in his dispute with the Russians." He nodded to Jason. "A game of charades sounds splendid, Mr. Burke."

Oscar Simmons volunteered to be scorekeeper, and Jason suggested that the theme of the game be famous couples from history—an idea heralded with great enthusiasm by the others. Mr. Youngblood paired the guests off into two groups, and Jason was thrilled when he and Annie ended up on the same side, opposite the group that included Stephen.

Much fun followed. Two of the children did a splendid job of portraying Martha and George Washington—the boy pretending to chop down a cherry tree while the girl went through the motions of washing. Mr. and Mrs. Youngblood sent the guests into gales of laughter as they portrayed Antony and Cleopatra, especially when Mrs. Youngblood performed a wildly histrionic version of the queen's death by an asp bite.

Jason's group selected him and Annie to do the next charade. He whispered a suggestion in her ear, and she nodded happily. Taking her hand, he led her across the room to the Youngbloods' candlelit Christmas tree, which sat resplendent on a small table near the window. He extended his arm as if to present the glittering, star-topped spruce to her. He then went down on one knee and kissed her hand, while she affected a pleased, if imperious, pose.

"Queen Victoria and Prince Albert!" one of the children cried.

Before Annie and Jason could even turn to confirm the correct guess, a red-faced Stephen came charging across the room and literally yanked Annie away from Jason.

"Keep your damned hands off my fiancée!" he blazed to Jason.

A collective gasp of horror rippled over the room, followed by a terrible silence. Jason shot to his feet and glowered at Stephen; this time the man had gone too far! When he glanced at Annie, he found to his dismay that she appeared mortified and very hurt.

Oscar Simmons rose and came over to join them. Seeming to recognize that Stephen was indeed out of control, he laid his hand on the younger man's shoulder and said quietly, "Stephen, you are letting the cider speak for you. This is only a game. Mr. Burke meant no harm."

Stephen hurled a contemptuous glance at Jason. "It is far more than a game to him and we all know it. He is playing for keeps!"

While Annie trembled with hurt and outrage, Oscar continued to speak to Stephen in low, firm tones. "This is not a matter to be settled here, in front of everyone. You will not embarrass us in front of our friends—nor will you humiliate my daughter this way."

Stephen seemed to remember himself then. He nodded resignedly to Oscar, then turned to Annie. "I'm sorry. Perhaps this time I overreacted."

Annie glared at Stephen and said nothing.

Oscar turned to address John Youngblood. "John, we've had a splendid evening, but we do have a long drive back to London."

"You could stay the night—we have plenty of room," Emma offered generously.

"Thank you, but we really must get back."

The foursome rode back to London, again divided into separate companies—Annie, Oscar, and Stephen sitting across from Jason. The night had grown bitterly cold, with a thousand bright stars glittering in the clear black skies above them. All four passengers were covered with many layers of quilts. Soon, both Stephen and Oscar drifted off to sleep, and Annie and Jason were the only ones awake. They stared at each other achingly, their stark faces illuminated by the silvery light of the moon.

To Jason, it was as if no one else in the world existed but the two of them. He watched in anguish as a tear trickled down Annie's cheek. The sight of her sorrow seemed to drive a lance deep into his very heart.

"Sweetheart, please don't cry," he whispered tormentedly.

"I'm going to break off my engagement with Stephen," she whispered back, choking on a sob.

Jason could not help himself then. Staring at her with his heart in his eyes, he said, "Darling, come here."

Even as she was drawing back the quilts, Jason was reaching out for her, drawing her across the sleigh and into his lap. He covered her with the quilts, cuddled her close, and then his ravenous lips took hers.

Their kiss blazed like fire in the freezing cold night. Jason devoured Annie's mouth, plunging deep with his tongue, possessing and savoring her. She clung to him and kissed him back with equal ardor. To Annie, the moment was pure paradise—this man was everything she wanted, her destiny. She felt a part of him, as if they were truly one, inseparable. Jason, too, felt the love, the deep bond between them, and only wished he could hold her this way forever.

At last their lips parted on a sigh. He kissed away the tears on her cool cheek and slipped his gloved hand inside her cloak, pressing it to her slender waist.

"You were right about Stephen," she said brokenly. "He is shallow. He is a cad."

Jason felt guilt assailing him. "He is a man who feels threatened on a very basic level. He fears that another man is trying to steal his woman."

"Are you?" she asked achingly, lifting her brimming gaze to him.

"Oh, God, Annie, when you look at me that way . . ."

"Are you?"

A long, thorough kiss followed before he could answer. "I'm afraid I am," he admitted with a groan. "And I can't say I wouldn't react much the same as Stephen under similar circumstances."

"I know why Stephen got angry tonight," she said poignantly. "He saw the way I looked at you."

"Oh, Annie." Jason's voice was agonized. "Darling, you are making the right decision about Stephen. He is wrong for you. But please do not make this about me. It mustn't be because of me."

"But it is," she cried. "How can it be otherwise?"

"Annie, please, I could hurt you," he pleaded. "I may not be able to stay here—"

"I don't care! I want to be with you now, even if I must lose you later. I think I'm falling—"

"No, don't say it," Jason implored. "Please, you mustn't say it."

But she *would* say it—and thus Jason silenced her the only way he could, kissing her again and again and again, until both of them were feverish with desire.

CHAPTER EIGHT

A couple of days passed for Jason, and Christmas was now only five days away. Memories of the glorious time he and Annie had spent kissing and caressing in the sleigh continued to haunt him. He knew he was in love with her, and the anguish of his newfound love was tearing him apart. He kept telling himself that he had accomplished his purpose; he had convinced Annie to reject Stephen. Now he need not worry that Stephen might somehow hurt her on Christmas Eve, and thereby precipitate her death.

As for himself and Annie, as much as he missed her, he rationalized that it would be best if he put a halt to their budding relationship; otherwise, he might well risk becoming the man who would destroy her, especially if what he suspected came true, and he was somehow whisked back to the present on Christmas Eve. He had put into effect the delicate balance he had sought—now he had best leave well enough alone.

Only Annie would not give up on him. When she came by the newspaper office to invite him out for tea, it broke his heart to refuse her, to tell her that he was too busy. When she sent him a letter—a bewildered note asking him why he was avoiding her—he managed to restrain himself from rushing to her at once.

But then he came home from work one evening to find her sitting in his room!

Jason was mystified as he walked inside his room and saw Annie seated across from him in a chair by the window. A pale golden light spilled in from outside, outlining her lovely form. She had removed her cloak, bonnet, and gloves, and she looked so beautiful in her blue velvet dress, with her shining hair piled on top of her head. Her features mirrored a stark anguish that slashed at his heart, and it took all Jason's self-control not to rush over and pull her into his arms, crush her to his heart.

"What are you doing here?" he cried.

She rose and came over to stand before him. "I had to see you again, Jason."

"But how did you get in?"

She smiled. "I convinced the landlady that I am your cousin from Kent."

Jason clenched his fists helplessly. "Annie, you shouldn't have done that. You shouldn't be here."

An anguished cry escaped her. "Why are you treating me this way—so coldly, so cruelly? Ever since we went to the country, you've been like a stranger."

He avoided her bewildered gaze. "Annie, I'm sorry, but I just feel that it is best if we don't see each other."

"Then why have you stolen my heart as you have?" she cried.

"Oh, Annie." As much as Jason knew he was doing the right thing, the raw anguish on her face clawed at him and he could only hate himself in that moment.

"You have gotten your way now," she went on in a tortured voice. "I have broken things off with Stephen. Yet still you are holding yourself apart from me! Why, Jason? Is it because you know you must leave?"

"Yes, I doubt I can even stay beyond Christmas." He touched her cheek gently. "And I simply cannot face hurting you."

"But don't you know that you are hurting me terribly now, this very moment?"

When he saw her tears, it was more than Jason could bear. He pulled her into his arms. His lips took hers with ravenous need.

"Oh, Jason, Jason," she whispered, kissing his chin, his neck. "Please say you are mine. Please love me, if only for today."

Fighting for control, he broke away. "Annie . . . My God, we mustn't! You simply don't understand. What I feel for you could well doom you, destroy you."

"I don't believe that!" she cried, stepping forward and wrapping her arms about his waist. "I could never believe that your feelings could harm me in any way. And furthermore, I don't care."

He groaned in agony as her nearness battered his resolve. Helplessly, he stroked her hair. "You simply have no idea of the forces at work here. Somehow, I must make you understand."

"Understand that you have my heart," she whispered, staring up at him with tear-filled eyes. "That is all that matters now."

When Annie stretched on tiptoe to kiss him so sweetly, so trustingly, Jason's control snapped. His mouth ravished hers and his fingers pulled the pins from her hair. At the back of his mind, he knew that he was surely giving in to madness, but he didn't care. All at once, nothing mattered to him but this moment, this woman he loved with all his heart. Surely what he felt could not hurt her—what he felt seemed so strong, so right. In his anguished soul, he knew that he would soon leave her, perhaps lose her forever. But they would be together now, today, in every way. And he would cherish that memory in his heart for the rest of his life.

He swept her up into his arms and carried her to the bed. He fell on her, covering her face with hot kisses, and she laughed with joy, kissing him back and hugging his neck.

"Oh, Jason! I knew you felt as I do! I just knew it!" she cried exultantly.

"Oh, Annie, Annie," he cried hoarsely, his lips against her lovely throat. "We really shouldn't. But you are right, my darling—you truly are in my heart, and I cannot resist you!"

Jason's mouth claimed hers voraciously, while his fingers worked at the tiny pearl buttons at her bodice, then undid the ties of her corset and camisole. She responded with equal fervor, pulling loose his cravat and undoing the studs on his shirt. He moaned as her warm fingertips caressed his muscled chest; she sighed as his hand cupped her firm, warm breast. When his lips and tongue followed to tease her nipple to unbearable tautness, she cried out with delight and dug her fingernails into his strong shoulders.

Again, they kissed ardently, making love with their lips and tongues until their mouths felt melded. Jason pulled off Annie's dress and petticoats, then pulled back to stare at her in her lacy camisole and bloomers. Desire roared through his veins, settling in his loins with tortured intensity. Never had she looked so irresistible, so adorable! Her honey-brown hair cascaded in lush waves about her face and shoulders. Her eyes were dark, large with passion, her cheeks hotly flushed, her lips wet and bruised by his kisses. Her breasts were bared, the beautifully rounded globes rising and falling so sweetly as she sucked in her breath in ragged gasps—gasps of desire for him!

The sight of her—wanting him, open to him—excited him beyond reason. "Oh, Annie," he whispered with rough ardor. "I wonder how I have ever managed to resist you!"

She smiled and stretched upward to press her lips to his chest, and violent spasms of need consumed him. He covered her breasts and her stomach with kisses, then raked his hungry gaze lower, reaching down to untie the ribbon at the waist of her bloomers. He felt her trembling and pressed his hand to her belly, caressing gently as he stared into her fevered eyes. He burned to join himself with her, but first took a moment to kiss her tenderly as he slipped his fingers inside her bloomers and stroked the warm center of her.

When he heard her soft cry of passion, when he felt her wetness, it was more than he could bear. His heart was pounding with his obsession to possess her, and he was aroused far past endurance. He positioned himself over her, pressing the heat of his chest to her warm breasts, and the hot steel of him to her tenderest parts. She moaned and arched against him eagerly.

Jason's control broke. His mouth took hers, smothering her low sob as he moved to embed his rigid length in the warm tightness of her. The fiery rapture of possessing her was like nothing he had ever felt before—exquisite pleasure. All of him became a building explosion centered in her heat. He felt her tense with pain as he broke through her maidenhead, and he murmured an apology into her mouth. When he felt her relax to take his deep thrust, he could have wept with joy.

Indeed, Annie was heedless of the pain as she felt Jason move deep to possess her. Her heart was brimming with the overwhelming joy that at last, he was hers. Never had she known such shattering, beauteous ecstasy as she did with his hard, hot body crushing into hers, his mouth fusing with hers, and the solid length of him at once tearing her apart and making them one. When he began to move gently within her, she encouraged him with wild, wanton kisses. He quickened his pace, impelling her to cry out and arch upward to meet him, until both of them were hurled into the searing cataclysm of rapture. They clung to each other as the powerful waves of ecstasy propelled them ever closer, ever deeper into each other's bodies and hearts.

A long moment later, Jason gently withdrew from Annie and stared down at her with concern. "Are you all right, darling?"

"Wonderful," came her joyous reply as she kissed him.

Though he kissed her back with equal fervor, inwardly, Jason was already feeling bedeviled by guilt and doubt, especially as Annie lay beneath him—so beautiful, so vulnerable, so fragile—and bound to him by the wondrous joining they had just known. Releasing her, he sat up in bed and raked his fingers through his hair.

Oh, Lord, what had he done? He had placed his own needs, his passion to possess her, over her best interests. He feared that Annie was falling in love with him. He knew he was in love with her, and he had no way of knowing whether that love would bless her or doom her. What if they did become involved in an intense love affair and then he was whisked back to the present on Christmas Eve? Would he be the one who would end up hurting her badly, and even causing her death? He had to consider what was best for her and act accordingly—as painful as it might be for him.

She sat up next to him, touching his shoulder. "Jason, what is it?" When he didn't answer, she added, "Don't tell me you already regret our lovemaking?"

At once he was contrite. He pulled her into his arms. "Of course not, darling. Get dressed now. We must talk."

After both were dressed, they sat down across from each other at the window, both wary as strangers.

Jason leaned toward Annie, lacing his fingers together. "Annie, this has to stop."

"Jason—"

He held up a hand and pinned her with his dark, tortured gaze. "Hear me out. We can't go on like this. Sooner or later, I'm bound to hurt you. I doubt I can even remain here in England, or ever provide you with an adequate future."

"Do you think I care about money?" she cried. "And I think you are making excuses."

"Perhaps I am." He stared at her in anguish.

"But why?"

"I just . . ." He gestured helplessly. "There are complications. Forces that are too frightening, too dangerous, for us even to talk about. I . . . just can't give you what you need."

Her eyes flared with bitterness. "It sounds to me as if you won't."

"Perhaps so," he conceded.

"Then give me what you can," she pleaded.

"No!" he cried.

Jason stood and began to pace, staring at Annie in anguish. She regarded him with hurt and bewilderment.

"Don't you see?" he asked distraughtly. "We can't risk this happening ever again. In the end you'll only get hurt—and you could even become pregnant."

Listening to him, Annie was in torment herself as she realized at last that Jason could not possibly love her. If he did, how could he spurn her this way?

"Do you think I would try to trap you into marriage?" she asked angrily, getting to her feet. "Do you presume that this is why I came to you today?"

He stepped toward her. "Of course not, darling, but—"

"I came to you because I—"

He quickly crossed the distance between them and grasped her by the shoulders. "Don't say it!" he pleaded. "Please, you must never say it. You will only make things much worse in the end—for both me and you."

Now she shoved him away and regarded him with anger and disillusionment. "After what we just shared, you won't even hear my feelings?"

"I can't," he said hoarsely. Though it killed him to say these things, he knew he must bring her to her senses. "The truth is, I think we are wrong for each other and I can't ever marry you."

"Then what just happened between us?" she cried. "The passion of the moment?"

He could only groan.

Despite the tears now gleaming in her eyes, Annie drew herself up with pride. "I see that I have deluded myself about you, Jason. Perhaps Father was right. You and I are too different. I may have felt a certain passion for you, but that was only a fleeting thing. What I really need is someone trustworthy and solid—someone like Stephen."

"Annie! You can't mean that!"

"I do!" she flared. "With Stephen, I have elements in common, and we can build a good future together." Her expression was one of intense disillusionment. "You are not the man I thought you were, Jason. This was—only an infatuation."

"Annie—are you sure?" he asked in anguish.

"Yes. I am sure. After being with you today, I know now that it is Stephen I truly love."

Jason was in hell. He still did not trust Stephen with Annie—and yet how could he know that with him, she would fare any better? He seemed damned every way he turned!

"I—I'm sorry things turned out this way," he said helplessly.

"Of course you are." Her words were cutting as she headed for the door.

"Annie, please," he pleaded, following her. "I truly am sorry. Can't we at least try to part as friends?"

She turned to him, her face eloquent with her emotional struggle. At last she sighed and said, "You are right, Jason. After all, you never made me any promises. You never said you would stay. It is not your fault that I threw myself at you today."

"Annie, I'll not have you speaking of yourself in such a manner!"

Tears glistened in her eyes. "But it is the truth, isn't it? It is not your fault that you . . ." Brokenly, she finished, "Don't love me."

Jason almost lost all control then, almost cried out his love for her and rushed over to beg her forgiveness. In the nick of time, he managed to remind himself that such a reckless, selfish action might well cause her death.

"I—I don't know what to say," he murmured at last, clenching his fists.

"Will you be leaving for America soon?" she asked.

"Most likely, yes," he admitted.

"Will you at least come celebrate Christmas Eve with us at the hotel before you go?"

He was incredulous. "Annie, you must be joking. Your father and Stephen will roast me up with the Yule log."

"No, they won't," she insisted. "I won't allow it. And didn't you just say you wanted us to part as friends?" Thrusting her chin high, she added, "You *will* want to see how happy I'll be with Stephen, won't you?"

Jason could have died on the spot.

She stepped closer and spoke more gently. "At least drop by, so we shall both know that we part without ill will." Almost helplessly, she added, "Jason, it's Christmastime, and you mustn't be alone. And you can't simply disappear this way. Our boarders—particularly Miss Mary and Miss Media—keep asking about you. You must tell everyone good-bye."

Jason felt too defeated to protest. "Very well, Annie."

His heart felt broken as he watched her leave. He told himself that he had made the only right choice. Still, his agony brought him to his knees and tore an anguished sound from his lungs.

Annie, too, left Jason with a heavy heart. While she knew now that she would never have Jason's love, she could console herself with the remembrance of their glorious lovemaking, and the knowledge that she had acted in his best interests, that she had assured his happiness, even if at the loss of her own.

At least the two of them would get to spend Christmas Eve together. With that memory to treasure in her heart, perhaps she could get through the bleak years ahead.

And Annie couldn't deny that she had been just a little perverse, a little selfish, in her final invitation to Jason. She could not help but cling to the hope that, when he saw her with Stephen on Christmas Eve, he would have a change of heart and come back to her forever. . . .

CHAPTER NINE

Jason did not know which way to turn.

Following his emotional encounter with Annie, he was besieged by heartache and indecision. The memory of making love to her was so beautiful to him that he wanted nothing more than to rush to her and beg her forgiveness for his seemingly callous rejection of her afterward. Yet how could he know that such a move would not bring disaster hurtling down upon her?

On the other hand, she now seemed determined to wed Stephen, and this possibility filled him with equal fear and dread. If only he could know for certain whether it was to be himself or Stephen who was destined to hurt her on Christmas Eve! And that day was now almost here!

On the day before Christmas Eve, Jason decided to visit Stephen in his haberdashery in Mayfair. Sweeping through the front door of the elegant establishment, Jason noted that the gaily decorated shop swarmed with noisy customers and the air was redolent with the mingling smells of Christmas greenery, male toiletries, and new cloth. Both male and female customers were present, many of them sitting on plush ottomans sipping hot, spiced tea as clerks scurried about, showing the latest gentlemanly fashions.

Jason managed to flag down a clerk who was racing by, trying to juggle at least a dozen hats. The harried employee showed Jason to Stephen's office in the back. As expected, Jason's reception there was cold. On spotting Jason in the portal, Stephen arose from his desk and spoke with hostility.

"Burke—what are you doing here?"

Jason faced down the other man unflinchingly. "I came to speak with you because I am concerned about Annie."

"Hah!" Stephen scoffed. "That did not stop you from doing your best to put Annie and myself asunder."

Jason nodded grimly. "Obviously, that was a mistake on my part."

"Indeed!"

Jason offered a gesture of conciliation. "Please, can't we put aside our mutual antagonism for a moment and think instead about Annie's best interests?"

Now Stephen appeared both insulted and perplexed. "Of course, I am always solicitous of Annie's welfare. But what, specifically, is your concern?"

"Have you seen her?" Jason asked anxiously.

After hesitating a moment, Stephen admitted, "We have been very busy with the Christmas crush. But yes, I did see Annie briefly a few days ago when she stopped by the shop." He flashed Jason a triumphant smile. "She told me she is willing to renew our commitment."

Jason sighed. "She loves you, you know."

Stephen appeared pleasantly surprised. "She does?"

"That is what she told me."

Stephen frowned darkly. "Then it puzzles me that she would confide such intimate feelings to you, rather than speaking with me."

"Sometimes it is easier to confide in a friend," Jason stated carefully. "And what of your commitment to her, Prescott?"

"What do you mean?" Stephen countered defensively.

"Are you going to give up your mistress now?"

Stephen turned as white as some of the papers on his desk. "What makes you think I have a mistress?"

Jason laughed ruefully. "Don't be coy, Prescott. It's unbecoming. On the night we all met, I overheard some gossip in the hotel drawing room, and that's when I became aware of your shabby little affair. Have you never considered how hurt Annie may become if she ever learns of your betrayal? What if the next time, she is the one who overhears such a rumor?"

"Have you told her of your suspicions?" Stephen demanded angrily.

"Certainly not. Believe it or not, I want what is best for her. She loves you—and therefore, I would not deliberately try to sabotage her happiness."

Stephen nodded. With surprising humility, he said, "Listen, Burke, as much as I have resented your presence here, I must admit that your romantic competition has taught me a lesson."

"In what way?"

"I almost lost Annie. This is something I will never forget, for whether you believe it or not, I really do love her. As for my mistress—I have already ended the liaison. And I promise you that I will never again do anything to hurt Annie or compromise her happiness."

Jason regarded Stephen with surprise and some lingering doubt. "If what you say is true, then I must congratulate you on coming to your senses."

"You have my solemn word that I have."

"Are you willing to shake on that?"

"Of course."

After the two men shook hands, Stephen asked, "What of you, Burke? What are your plans?"

"I . . ." Awkwardly, Jason related, "I'll most likely be returning to America right after Christmas. In the meantime—I did want to warn you that Annie has invited me to attend the Christmas Eve gathering at the hotel. She wanted me to stop by and tell everyone good-bye—and I think it is also important to her that she and I part as friends."

"Burke . . ." Stephen shook his head resignedly. "Leave it alone, will you? Let her go. I assure you, she is in very good hands."

"I suppose she is," Jason felt impelled to admit as he left.

He had accomplished his purpose here. This realization brought Jason both joy and sorrow. He knew now that he must have been brought here to bring Annie and Stephen together, and especially, to make Stephen realize that he could never toy with Annie's affections, or betray her.

He realized, too, that Stephen was right that he needed to bow out now. Why prolong things by spending Christmas Eve with Annie when it was even possible that he might be whisked away to the present right before her very eyes? Again, he remembered the prophecy, "You'll come back on Christmas Eve." His mission here was completed, and he had the feeling that he might indeed soon return to his own world, his own time. He would have to cope with the heartache of losing Annie—but never would he lose the new hope and positive outlook on life she had given him.

But he also knew that he had to see Annie one last time to make certain that she was content in her decision to wed Stephen, and also to bid her good-bye.

Early on Christmas Eve morning he stopped by the Simmons Hotel, taking with him a Christmas present he had bought for Annie. In the downstairs hallway, he was greeted by a stern-faced Oscar Simmons.

"I am glad you've stopped in, Burke," Simmons greeted him coldly. "You have saved me a trip by the newspaper office."

"Sir, I would like to speak with Annie," Jason stated firmly.

"My daughter does not wish to see you," came the contemptuous reply. "If you will join me in my office, she asked me to give you something."

Bemused, Jason followed Oscar into the office. Oscar handed him an envelope. Jason opened it and, to his surprise and keen disappointment, he found inside a ticket for a steamer bound for New York.

The steamer was scheduled to depart the London docks tonight!

Jason glanced skeptically at Oscar. "Annie asked you to give me this?"

He nodded. "As I said, my daughter does not care to see you again. She is far too busy planning her wedding to Stephen."

"But—she asked me to spend this evening with all of you," Jason protested. "Indeed, she made me promise I would attend your Christmas Eve gathering."

Oscar gestured toward the ticket. "I think you have the answer to that right there." Vehemently, he added, "For God's sake, man, leave well enough alone! Haven't you done my daughter enough damage already? Let her enjoy Christmas Eve in peace—with her father and her fiancé."

"Will you at least give Annie my present?" Jason asked, extending the box.

Oscar Simmons took the gift without comment, and Jason left.

Jason went back by the newspaper office and handed Mr. Spencer both his final column and his resignation.

The old gentleman appeared keenly disappointed, saying, "I had such high hopes for your future here with us."

"I must apologize for leaving so suddenly," Jason replied. "But I've now finished my 'American in London' series, and I think it is time that I head back where I belong."

"If it is a matter of money," Spencer said, "I was already thinking of giving you an increase. Also, I was not speaking idly at the Holcombs' dinner party when I said that one day you will likely be running this place."

"I know, Mr. Spencer, and I really appreciate your faith in me. I simply feel that my destiny lies elsewhere."

The two men said their good-byes, and Jason returned to his boarding house to pack.

That night, as Jason stood on the deck of the steamer looking out through the fog at the cluttered St. Katherine docks, he could hear the church bells tolling in the distance, their joyous tones seeming to mock him now.

Eight o'clock. Annie's gathering should be starting.

Would she regret sending him away? Would she miss spending Christmas Eve with him, just as he was filled with anguish to be apart from her now?

He wondered idly what would happen to him. It didn't seem to matter that much, now that he knew he could never have Annie's love. Would he indeed travel on to America—where he might look up his ancestors, as well as the mysterious Finias Fogg—and start a new life there? Would he be whisked back to his own time before the steamer even left the London docks?

Did he care? What mattered was that Annie's happiness, her future, had been secured. He ached more than ever to go to her, yet he could not risk upsetting the delicate denouement he had established in her life.

Then, all at once, Jason was stunned to watch Stephen Prescott hurry up the gangplank!

Jason crossed the deck to confront the other man. "What in God's name are you doing here? Why aren't you with Annie?"

"Burke." Stephen was huffing from the cold and exertion. "Thank God I've caught you in time. It was pure hell getting Oscar to tell me which steamer you were taking."

"But why did you wish to find me?" Jason asked incredulously.

Regret and anguish tightened Stephen's features. "I may be a cad, but I'm not that much of a cad. You must go to Annie immediately."

Jason remained flabbergasted. "And you must explain what you are talking about."

Stephen nodded. "As I told you yesterday, I've only seen Annie once during the past few days. I really had no idea the situation had gotten so grave. . . ."

"For heaven's sake, man!" Jason burst out impatiently. "Out with it!"

"I went by the Simmons Hotel two hours ago to ask Annie out for an early supper. That is when Oscar admitted to me that she has been crying in her room almost nonstop for days now—ever since you broke things off with her."

"What?" Jason cried.

"Oscar is furious at you for hurting Annie," Stephen continued in a rush. "He admitted to me that he bought the steamer ticket and gave it to you, claiming that it had actually come from Annie."

"You mean that—"

"Annie has no idea of what has truly transpired. And Oscar told me he cannot wait to tell her that you have left."

"Oh, my God," Jason muttered. "But why have you come to me now?"

Stephen drew a heavy breath. "Because, whether you believe it or not, I too want Annie to be happy. I've been deluding myself ever since you appeared here in London. I know now that it is you who she really loves. And when Oscar tells her that you have left her on Christmas Eve, without even saying good-bye, it is going to kill her."

It is going to kill her! Jason was left reeling as Stephen's ominous words reverberated through his brain, along with Annie's dire warning from the present: *I died on these steps on Christmas Eve in 1852, when I learned that my true love had deserted me.*

Oh, merciful heavens, what had he done? He realized that Stephen was right! Through trying to act in Annie's best interests, he had instead doomed her! He had brought about the very calamity that he had struggled so hard to prevent. For *he* was Annie's true love, and now he had deserted her—on Christmas Eve! And, when her father told her that he was gone, that he had broken his promise, she would die!

"Well?" Stephen prodded impatiently.

Jason was already bounding off for the gangplank, yelling over his shoulder to Stephen, "We must hurry to the Simmons Hotel at once—and pray that we are not too late!"

CHAPTER TEN

Let there be time. Please, God, let there be time.

This was Jason's fervent prayer as he and Stephen rushed in the doorway of the Simmons Hotel half an hour later.

At once, he spotted Annie conversing with her father at the top of the stairs. He saw the shattered look on her face, and his heart went cold. Oh, God, Oscar must be telling her that he had deserted her.

He saw her begin to collapse. Desperately, he bounded up the stairs.

"Annie!" he cried.

He watched her turn, saw the look of raw joy on her face as she spotted him. But it was too late, for she had already lost her balance. He saw her ashen-faced father reach for her, too late. . . .

With a strength that astounded him, Jason sprinted upward and swept Annie up into his arms in the nick of time.

"Annie! Oh, Annie darling!" he cried, clutching her close.

"Jason—you have come back!"

You'll come back on Christmas Eve. All at once, Jason laughed aloud as at last, he realized the rhyme's meaning. He had come back—to save the woman he loved!

"Yes, I've come back—to stay, darling, if you'll have

me," Jason said passionately. "Please, Annie, say you'll forgive me!"

Her reply could not have delighted him more. "I love you, Jason," she whispered.

"I love you, Annie," he said.

Followed by Stephen and Oscar, Jason carried Annie up to her room. Stephen bid her a happy Christmas and tactfully took his leave.

Jason sat in the chair next to Annie's bed, holding her hand. Oscar stood in the doorway, looking much sobered.

Annie glanced over at her father and smiled. "I'm going to marry Jason."

Oscar nodded and stepped inside. Torment twisted his voice. "Annie, I too must beg your forgiveness. Because I foolishly believed that marriage to Stephen was best for you, I interfered in your life and almost caused your death. Why, I wasn't even going to give you the Christmas present Jason brought you earlier today."

"Jason came by here—today?" Annie cried. "And you did not tell me?"

Oscar sighed heavily. "You see, my dear, Jason didn't desert you. I bought a steamer ticket and gave it to him, telling him that it came from you." Shuddering, he glanced from Annie to Jason, then back to his daughter. "Then, moments ago, when I watched you almost tumble to your death—and even in the midst of that peril, saw you looking at Jason with such love . . ." His voice breaking, Oscar paused to wipe a tear. "Why, 'tis the same look that was on your dear mother's face the day she first told me she loved me."

"Oh, Father." Annie's face reflected her poignant joy.

"Can you ever forgive me?" he asked abjectly.

"Of course, Father." Annie held out her arms.

Oscar rushed to his daughter, and the two embraced for a long moment. Then a much-relieved Oscar stood, offering his hand to Jason.

"I'm trusting you with my daughter's future, you know," he said sternly, shaking the younger man's hand.

Jason nodded soberly. "I'll do my best to make her happy, sir—and to provide for her."

"Very good. I'm sure you will." Abruptly, he smiled. "Indeed, right before you arrived, I was speaking with Old Spencer downstairs. He's distraught over losing you. In due course, I'm sure you will be running the *Bloomsbury Times.*"

An awkward silence ensued, and Annie caught her father's eye. "Could you leave Jason and me alone a moment?"

Oscar appeared taken aback. "But daughter, that would not be—"

"You may leave the door ajar. And I promise you that Jason and I will come down and join the rest of you in only a moment or two."

Oscar nodded. "Very well. But are you sure you are up to entertaining tonight?"

"Oh, yes."

Oscar left, and Jason sat down on the bed, hugging Annie tightly to him. "Darling, I'm so relieved that I arrived in time," he whispered against her hair.

She laughed. "Believe me, so am I."

He drew back to stare at her questioningly. "But I do wonder something. . . ."

"Yes?"

"Why did you tell me that you loved Stephen, that you wanted to marry him, when none of it was true?"

A guilty smile curved her lips. "Because I wanted to do what was best for you. I thought that if I could convince you that I truly was happy with Stephen, then you could return to America with a clear conscience and peace of mind."

"Oh, Annie!" Jason was shaking his head at the irony. "In wanting what was best for each other, we almost lost everything."

Annie regarded him with adoring eyes. "Still, in my heart, I always hoped that you did love me, that you would come back to me tonight. And I was convinced that you would at least stop by to say good-bye. That is why I was so stunned when Father told me . . ."

He kissed her hand. "I know, darling. And I'm so sorry for putting you through so much grief."

"We are together now, and that is all that matters." She regarded him curiously. "What changed your mind, Jason? What brought you to your senses—and back to me?"

There, Jason had to chuckle. "My darling, that is a very long story."

"But one you will tell me?"

"Oh, yes, when the time is right. However, for the moment, I think we had best join the others downstairs—before your justifiably irate father comes charging up here."

"Very well. Only, you've forgotten something."

"I have?"

Her smile was joyous as she curled her arms around his neck. "You have yet to give me a proper kiss."

He did.

A few minutes later, Jason and Annie joined the guests in the parlor. One and all were thrilled to see Annie and Jason there together, and Old Spencer in particular was delighted to hear that Jason was prepared to return to his post.

Jason helped Mr. Holcomb drag in from outside the giant Yule log, and a cheer went up from the guests as the two men dropped the huge chunk of wood into the fire. There followed wassail for all, served up with the traditional Christmas Eve "dumb cake" that the two spinsters, Miss Media and Miss Mary, had baked. The refreshments were accompanied by several rounds of "Merry Old Christmas."

Later that night, after the guests had departed, Oscar, Jason, and Annie left in the coach to go to midnight candlelight services together. The cold London night was ablaze with a million stars and alive with the sights and sounds of Christmas—pipers playing in the streets, carolers singing outside the ancient Tower of London, Christmas trees glowing in the windows of homes, and everywhere, the beautiful church bells tolling out the coming of Yule. Sitting close to Annie and holding her hand as they clattered through the streets, Jason had never felt happier or more filled with joy and hope.

At St. James Church, they listened with awe and reverence as the vicar read the story of the coming of the Christ child. Then the three held their candles high and sang together, "Joy to the World."

It was well past one when they returned to the hotel. A heavy snow was starting to fall. As the three navigated carefully up the slippery front steps, Oscar said to Jason, "Stay the night with us, why don't you? You must not head home in this blizzard."

Jason was only too eager to agree.

Inside the warmth of the hallway, Annie turned to her father and said, "I want to marry Jason right away."

Both Annie and Jason glanced at Oscar expectantly. Jason added, "Sir, I would be delighted to arrange for the license immediately after Christmas."

Oscar nodded. "Of course."

Then Oscar hugged them both. After Annie's father went upstairs, Jason pulled her close beneath the kissing bunch—and the two lovers long-savored that glorious tradition. . . .

Early on Christmas Day, Jason joined Annie, her father, and several of the hotel guests in the drawing room. A mood of great gaiety consumed all as they ripped open their presents. Jason was thrilled when Annie presented him with a blue sweater she had knitted—she was equally delighted with the fur muffler he had given her. Annie and her father were mystified to open a package from America which contained a fruitcake from none other than the mysterious Finias Fogg, who had also enclosed a brief note apologizing because neither he nor one of his representatives had been able to travel to London!

Her expression astonished, Annie turned to Jason. "Isn't it odd that Mr. Fogg never even mentioned you?" she whispered.

He leaned over and whispered back, "Don't worry, darling. One day, I'll explain all about how I got here—and we may even go to America to meet Mr. Fogg!"

At noon, Mrs. Chandler served up a sumptuous feast—roast turkey with sausage stuffing, candied sweet potatoes, English peas in cream sauce, and hot yeast rolls. Afterward, everyone clapped as the smiling cook brought in the flaming plum pudding. Everyone savored the rich, brandy-flavored dessert.

Following coffee, the yawning guests retired upstairs to nap off the feast. Jason left to go by his boarding house and pack his things.

That night, when all was quiet, Annie came to Jason in his third-floor room. He answered her knock to find her standing in the corridor in her gown and wrapper—and gazing at him with so much love!

"Annie, you shouldn't be here," he scolded in trembling tones.

Wordlessly, she shut the door and moved into his arms.

With a groan he clutched her close and kissed her. "Oh, Annie." He felt as if he held heaven itself in his arms.

"I wanted to wish my husband-to-be a proper Merry Christmas," she murmured, kissing his jaw.

He stared down into her beautiful, golden eyes. "Oh, my darling! You've already given me the most joyous Christmas gifts ever. You've given me back hope—and joy, and love in my life."

Taking Annie's hand, Jason drew her over by the fire. They knelt together on the rug, kissing and caressing in the gilded light.

"Someday," he murmured, kissing her soft neck, "I shall tell you how a lovely ghost brought me to you."

"A ghost?" she retorted, dimpling adorably. "And a pretty one? Now I am jealous!"

"You shouldn't be, darling," he teased back tenderly, "for it was you. You are my beautiful ghost of Christmas past, Annie."

"I am?"

"Yes, indeed."

Annie regarded him with awe and delight. "And you are the light of my life—now and forever."

Soon their clothing lay discarded in a pile on the floor, and Jason carried Annie to his bed, pressing her beneath him. They lay with bodies tightly coiled, their fevered kiss burning with all the love they felt. Jason tenderly kissed Annie's breasts while she caressed him boldly, wrapping her fingers around the warm steel of him until he groaned with unbearable need. When he pressed to bring them together, she took him eagerly, deeply.

"Oh, Jason," Annie cried, feeling filled to her soul with ecstasy and love. Running her fingers through his hair, she murmured, "I want one more Christmas gift from you, my soon-to-be husband."

"And what is that, my soon-to-be wife?"

"I want your child."

"Oh, Annie."

There in the glow of the fire, the last Christmas gift was lovingly given—and, with love, was received.

LISA CACH

A Midnight Clear

To Bill Yeaton

CHAPTER ONE

Woodbridge, Vermont
December 1, 1878

Her breath misted before her, a faint drifting ghost in
the cold night air. The train platform looked empty, illuminated by a yellow gaslight that was dim and soft
against the winter darkness. All was quiet but for the
hiss of the engine's steam and the rumbling of a freight
door. Catherine stepped down from the train onto the
wooden planks, her heeled shoes thudding on the hollow surface. She was used to the frantic rush of New
York, and had forgotten the slower pace of home. Only
a few others were disembarking at this station, already
walking toward the exit, leaving her alone beside the
blackened steel wheels.

With each stop the train had made, each familiar
place-name called out, her excitement had built, and
she had peered blindly out the window at the depths of
the night, searching vainly for some known landmark,
restraining herself from telling the others in the carriage that this was where she was from, this was where
she was born and raised. And here she was at last,
standing on the planks of the Woodbridge platform,
unable to believe she had finally arrived.

"Catherine!" her father's voice called.

"Papa!" she cried, her nearsighted eyes searching
him out, and finding him at last, a figure that became
clear as he moved toward her. She hurried to close the

distance, the long back hem of her velvet skirt, with all its folds and flounces, dragging fashionably across the wood, the opening of her silk-and-mink coat flapping. She was showing unseemly enthusiasm, she knew, and Aunt Frances would not have approved.

Her father caught her in a hug, enveloping her in the scents of wool and pipe tobacco, reminding her for a moment of her childhood. He patted her on the back, his broad hand over-strong in his enthusiasm, and then released her. He blinked rapidly, a suspicious sheen in his eyes.

"Did you get something to eat? Was the trip comfortable?" he asked. "Did you have any problems switching at White River Junction?"

"I'm fine, Papa, just tired. Two o'clock in the morning is a weary time for a train to arrive." Her original train had left New York at four in the afternoon, and she was stiff and sore from sitting on the poorly padded seats, her tight, elegant travel ensemble a constant reminder to sit straight and not lean back. She was exhausted, and the space between her shoulder blades ached with tension.

"Your mother is waiting up, and I shouldn't be surprised if Amy is still awake as well," he said, leading her into the station, where porters would bring in her trunks. "Your visit is all Amy's been able to speak of for weeks."

"I've missed her."

He glanced at her, the sheen still in his eyes. "We've missed you, too," he said, then looked away. "Porter!" he called, his voice loud in the quiet station, and went to fetch her luggage.

"Good gracious, where did you get *that?*" Amy asked, staring with wide green eyes, the plumed purple hat in her lap forgotten. The young girl was sitting cross-legged atop her bedcovers, clad in a white nightgown.

Catherine looked down at herself, at the red French corset and white silk chemise she'd just revealed by removing her bodice and camisole. "In Paris. There are dancers there who wear nothing but scarlet corsets and short petticoats, and they lift even those up to show their legs to the men."

"You saw them?" Amy asked, incredulous.

"Once. Aunt Frances thought it would be educational to go to such a dance hall show. She says that one can on occasion be daring if one is sure to behave like a lady whilst doing so. Of course, she also said it is even better if one can count on the silence of one's friends."

"What was it like at the dance hall? Were there *ladies of the night* there?" Amy half-whispered, eyes widening on the forbidden words.

Catherine laughed. "And what would you know of them?"

"I would know much more if anyone thought I was old enough to discuss them."

"You'd find them more sad than fascinating." She went to hang her bodice in the wardrobe. Talking with her younger sister was increasing the sense of unreality she felt, back in the room in which she had grown up. Amy in person was somehow different than Amy in letters, where Catherine had let her imagination fill in her sister's spoken intonation and expression. Was this Amy the same girl she had thought she had stayed close to through the mail? Even Mama had been altered, more gray in her hair, her cheeks a little fuller than Catherine remembered, her figure a little heavier. It was a surprise to realize that her family had been living their own lives while she had been away, growing up and growing older.

"So there were such women there?"

"I don't know for certain. Aunt Frances forbid me to gawk, and it was too dark and smoky to see much, anyway."

Amy's eyes went once again to the corset. "Mama doesn't have anything like that."

"Do you like it?" Catherine asked, striking a pose with one hand on her hip, the other lifting her skirts to show a bit of stockinged leg.

"Do I! I got my first corset this year, you know, but it's a plain thing, all white cotton without any trim or lace or anything. I don't even need it yet," she complained.

Catherine smothered a smile. "You wouldn't remember, but I was the same shape as you at thirteen. In two years you won't recognize yourself." She remembered as well her own young fascination with pretty underthings, and how they had seemed both forbidden and unattainable, things that belonged to a very adult world. In her trunks was a pink, beribboned corset for Amy, and a chemise and drawers "combination" trimmed with Valenciennes lace. They were innocent enough for a girl, but pretty enough for any woman. She would give them to Amy in private, though, as she hardly thought her sister would enjoy opening such gifts in front of Papa.

"Truly, you looked like me?"

"Truly. But you'll be much prettier than I, with your eyes."

"I like your brown ones," Amy said. "They look like weak tea in white china cups."

"Do they?" Catherine laughed, and turned to look at

herself in the mirror. Her eyes were slightly bloodshot, her pale skin showing the shadows under her eyes. Her irises did indeed look the same color as weak tea. "I suppose you're right." Her dark brown hair was still piled up at the back of her head, the large loose braids pinned over small cushions to give the arrangement the great mass that was fashionable. Her scalp and every muscle atop her skull ached with the weight.

She heard Amy moving behind her, the bed creaking as she climbed off.

"Cath, look! It's snowing!"

She went to the window, where Amy was already raising the pane, heedless of the additional chill to the room. Catherine stuck her head out beside her sister's, watching the fluffy flakes fall silently in the light from the window.

"It's the first snow of December," Amy said. "Do you remember what that means?"

"Of course I do. Wasn't I the one who told you in the first place?" Catherine said, remembering the myth her grandmother had told her. "With the first snow of December, the snow fairies come to celebrate the Christmas season. They grant the wishes of those with pure hearts, and then with the ringing in of the New Year, they return to their lands in the north."

"I'm too old to believe it anymore, but I like to pretend it's true."

"I do, too," Catherine admitted. She put her hand out, catching a cluster on her palm and watching it melt. The breeze picked up, and she shivered. "It's too cold to be hanging out a window in my underthings," she said, and withdrew into the room.

Amy lingered a moment longer, then followed, pulling shut the sash. "I'm glad you're back, Cath."

"I am, too."

The clock in the hall below was striking half past three when she finally blew out the lamp and pulled up the covers against the cold of the room. Amy slept in the bed next to hers, her final "good night" followed quickly by deepened breathing, her gray cat, Quimby, nestled at her feet.

Home, at last. It had been nearly two years. Catherine had been living and traveling with Aunt Frances, her mother's wealthy, artistically inclined sister, since shortly after Catherine's graduation from Mount Holyoke. Last Christmas had been spent in London, there had been months in Paris, long stays with friends in Italy, and weeks at a spa in Switzerland. For the past several months they had been in New York, in Aunt Frances's large town house, entertaining poets, painters, writers, and the more daring of the New York social elite, all while Uncle Clement had happily busied himself with his business affairs, remaining in the background of his wife's social world.

Aunt Frances had wanted to give her an education of a different sort than the scholastic one offered at Mount Holyoke, and Catherine had to admit that her aunt had succeeded. Perhaps she had succeeded too well, and home would now seem small-minded and provincial in comparison to such grand sights as the canals of Venice and the palace of Versailles, not to mention the dancers of Paris. Maybe she would no longer fit in here.

She stared into the darkness, listening to the faint creakings of the house and to Amy's breathing. There were no sounds from the street, Woodbridge asleep for the night. She was tense despite her exhaustion, the room feeling less familiar than the opulent bedchamber she had left behind in New York, with the mementos from her travels on the walls and strewn about on small tables. Would this house ever feel like home again?

She scolded herself for even thinking the thought. Surely she would feel more a part of things in the morning, after a good night's sleep, and after a few days she would find herself once more in step with the rhythms of her family's life. She would cease noticing the changes, and would forget that she had been away.

After all, if she didn't belong at home, then where *did* she belong?

CHAPTER TWO

"No, Mrs. Harris, it is $9.32 that you owe. It says so right here," Will Goodman insisted, showing the older woman the accounts ledger where he kept track of how much credit had been extended to his customers. He brushed back the lock of brownish-blond hair that had fallen into his eyes.

"I was certain it was $14.32," Mrs. Harris protested, her brow drawn into ridges of confusion. "With the sausages from last week, plus the new shoes for Joshua and Ann, and then there were the five pounds of sugar . . . I thought I had kept track. I'm not forgetful; you know that, Mr. Goodman."

"Of course not. Much as I would like to take $14.32 from you, especially if you were to offer it in part as cookies and pies, I'll have to settle for the $9.32."

"I'm afraid all I have at this time is—"

"I was thinking," Will interrupted, as if he had not heard her, "that I might be needing some help around here through the month. I know this would be asking a great deal, but do you think that I could steal Joshua and Ann away from you for an hour or two after school every day?"

"I don't think they'd be much use to—"

"I know it would be an imposition, what with all the

chores that I am sure wait for them at home, but I would pay them well."

Mrs. Harris blinked at him, her frown growing deeper. "What would you be wanting them for? What use could a ten- and an eight-year-old be to you?"

"Well, Mrs. Harris," Will said, leaning over the counter and taking on a confidential air. "You might not believe this, but other children are not so well-behaved as your Ann. At this time of year, what with all the shopping people are doing, they tend to let their little ones run round loose, knocking over displays, getting dirty fingers on clean goods, and making a god-awful amount of noise that distracts the other customers and affects my bottom line."

Mrs. Harris "mmmed" in sympathy, nodding her head.

"Now your Ann, she's a gentle, clever child. I was thinking that I would have her sit over by the woodstove there, with a stack of storybooks. When those rambunctious sorts of children come in, I can send them over to Ann, where she can read to them and keep them out of trouble while their mothers shop."

"She's very good with the young ones at home," Mrs. Harris agreed.

"And Joshua, well . . ." Will scanned the front room of his general store, his eyes lighting on the solution to this problem. "Besides for sweeping and dusting and keeping an eye out for thieves who pocket my goods—there are some who come in here, you know—"

"Ahhh?" Mrs. Harris breathed, eyes widening.

"Besides that, I have a rather daring advertising campaign in mind. I have some new sleds that have come in," he said, nodding toward the bright red sled on display in the front window. "Very high-priced, and they are not selling like they should. Now that it has begun to snow, I'd like to send Joshua out with one of those sleds. When the other kids see how fast it goes, they'll be begging their own parents to buy them one for Christmas. I need an athletic boy like Joshua to show it off to its best advantage."

"And how much would you be paying for the services of my children?" Mrs. Harris asked, her eyes taking on a speculative gleam.

"Let's see what we can work out, shall we?"

Will was putting his fake public account book away when Tyler Jones, his senior shop assistant, shuffled over to him, wrinkles set in disapproving lines.

"You go easy on her again?" the man asked, shaking his graying, balding head in disgust. "You're going to run yourself right out of business, doing things that way."

"Mr. Jones," Will warned flatly.

"*Shhhhh*," Jones said, eyes wide, hushing himself dramatically with a finger against his lips. "I didn't see a thing. I know nothing."

"Good man."

"As long as I'm not a jobless man. Yours is not the only general store in town, you know. You have to stay competitive, or they'll drive you out of business."

Will just looked at him until the old man threw his hands up, shrugging his shoulders up around his ears.

"But you're the boss! You know what you're doing!"

"It's good to hear that you remember that."

Mr. Jones rolled his eyes and began to shuffle away. "Ignorant pup," he muttered under his breath. "Practically *gives* things away. What type of way to run a store is—"

"And which of us owns this place, old man?" Will called after him, then cut off the rest of what he was about to say as the bell rang over the door, and business captured his attention.

Mr. Jones's complaints did not concern Will, knowing as he did that they had no basis in truth. He was a partner in the glass factory downriver, a shareholder in an ironworks, and had invested in an import/export company that had grown to pleasingly profitable dimensions. His ties to these businesses and others helped him to stock his store at minimal expense. Few in Woodbridge knew of the extent of either his investments or his philanthropy, which was how he liked it. It went against his nature to draw attention to himself, and there was a subtle pleasure to be had in keeping his true self secret, as if by doing so he maintained some element of freedom.

The day went quickly as he, Mr. Jones, and his other clerks helped customers, stocked shelves, carried parcels, measured out cloth, fitted shoes, weighed out butter, and balanced books. They sold gloves, candy, shaving gear, pots, dye, sheet music, irons, rolling pins, toys, stockings, winter coats, eggs, and pork. He sold anything and everything that would fit inside one of the large connecting rooms, and if he didn't stock something someone desired, he would order it for them. He loved his store, and the work of running it.

All considered, it seemed that he had everything he could desire. Work that he loved, money invested to guard against misfortune, a large house newly completed on Elm Street, and the goodwill and regard of his fellow businessmen and customers. Life, he reflected as he closed up shop that evening, was complete.

* * *

"So tell me, are there any young men who have caught your eye?" Catherine's mother asked, sitting down in her accustomed seat at the end of the dining table, a cup of tea before her. She was a tall woman, more stately than slender, her dark hair dusted with gray, and she had large, warm brown eyes of a deeper shade than Catherine's own. She wore a high-necked blouse and a cinnamon-brown skirt, bustled at the back in a style slightly out of date, but that nonetheless looked fitting on Mama.

"Perhaps one or two," Catherine replied obliquely, and looked at her mother from the corner of her eyes, checking for how well the bait was being taken. She knew that Mama liked nothing better than a tale of romance. She picked over the sausages and eggs in the warming dishes on the side table, slowly filling her plate.

"That viscount you wrote to us about, in London? Is he one of them?" Mama asked.

Catherine added a few slices of toast, then brought her plate to the table, setting it on the white lace cloth and taking her place to the immediate right of her mother. "I think he has become engaged to a Boston heiress."

"Oh. How very disappointing."

"Of course, the British are not the only ones with an aristocracy," she said, and paused to take a bite of food, remaining silent while she chewed.

Mama pursed her mouth impatiently, then made a noise of frustration. "Catherine Linwood! You're teasing me. You know very well I've been waiting all morning for you to get out of bed and come tell me all about your social life. A dozen times I almost went up those stairs and woke you myself."

Catherine laughed. "I'm sorry. I know how much you want to hear about my being courted, but there really isn't much to tell. There have been flirtations, but most have not amounted to much. The young men my own age all seem so . . . foolish. And the older ones are boring, with big bellies," she said, arching her back and arranging her face to match that of a self-satisfied businessman, thumb in watch pocket.

Mama's lips curled up in reluctant amusement. "You're a naughty girl."

"The best ones, of course, are already taken," Catherine said, dropping the pose.

"Did you say *most* flirtations have not amounted to much?"

She had known her mother would catch that small discrepancy. She chased a piece of egg around her plate with her fork. "There is one man who seems to have a certain interest in me."

"For heaven's sake, who?"

She gave up on the egg, and lay her fork down in the correct four o'clock position. "Stephen Rose. His family is filthy rich: They have money in railroads and shipping and ironworks and who knows what all else. Aunt Frances would scold me for speaking of their money, of course. She says it is not genteel to do so."

"It's not genteel only so long as you have enough money not to care. My sister cares about money and who has it, you can be sure, no matter her artistic airs. You'll notice she did not marry a poet," Mama added dryly.

Catherine had noticed that herself. It was amusing to think that Aunt Frances, with her elegance and sophistication, had once been a little girl having hissy fights with Mama. Although she knew they loved each other very much, Mama and Aunt Frances had always shared something of an abrasive relationship. "Mr. Rose must have enough money even for her standards, as she allows his visits and is always most eager to see him. I have the impression she arranges to throw us together."

"Is he handsome?"

"Terribly. He's all dark hair and black eyes, tall, and has the most graceful manners. He can charm anyone he has a mind to."

"And has he charmed you?"

She recalled the white flash of his smile, as he would lean down close to whisper something to her while listening to a concert; the skill with which he would sweep her around the dance floor in a waltz; the small thrill of pride when he led her in to dinner, and the other young women, more beautiful than her, watched in envy. "I suppose he may have," she admitted.

Her mother looked at her, eyes evaluating. "Are you in love with him?"

A nervous laugh escaped her lips. "Aunt Frances says I must be! There's no reason not to fall head over heels for Mr. Rose: He's handsome, rich, charming, and quite clever. He's considered an excellent catch."

"Mmm."

They were both silent for several moments. "Mama, how do you know if you are in love with a man?" Catherine asked, all trace of jollity gone. "It's true that my heart beats faster when Mr. Rose comes in the room, and his is the first face I look for in a gathering. I miss his company when he does not come to call for a number of days. Does that mean I love him?"

Mama reached out and squeezed her hand where it lay in her lap. "If you're not in love, then at least you are on the path toward it."

"I suppose I don't need to worry about the question now, though, do I?" she said brightly, trying to escape thoughts of her confused feelings for Mr. Rose. "I'm home, and he's far away in New York. I have all of you to think about now."

Her mother just raised her eyebrows.

The Linwood house was alive with the murmuring voices of guests, punctuated by bursts of laughter. The rooms, always chilly in winter, were growing cozy with the heat of bodies, the happy exchange of greetings adding an additional, intangible warmth to the evening air as friends and family gathered to welcome Catherine home.

"Will, this is my sister, Miss Catherine Linwood," Robert said. "Catherine, William Goodman."

"It's a pleasure to meet you, Mr. Goodman," she said.

Will took her gloved hand, her palm down, her fingers long and delicate as they rested lightly over the side of his hand. "It is a great honor to make your acquaintance," he said hoarsely, performing an abbreviated bow over her hand and earning a brief, puzzled look from her glorious eyes.

"Catherine will be with us through the holidays," Robert said. "She's been traveling the world, seeing sights that make Woodbridge look like a country backwater in comparison."

"And meeting men that make you look like a positive cave dweller," Catherine said to her brother, mischief in her eyes, and laughing at his falsely affronted expression. The sound was warm and melodious, sinking through Will's chest and wrapping around his heart.

A commotion at the door drew her attention. Will

wanted to say something, but was tongue-tied, his lips parted and silent as Robert said something else to his sister. She laughed again, and then her eyes went back to the door with delighted recognition.

"Robert, Mr. Goodman, do forgive me," she apologized, and left them abruptly, hurrying toward the front hall, the scent of lily of the valley hovering faintly behind her.

Will stared after her retreating figure. She was wearing a burgundy silk gown, trimmed in black velvet and lace, the sleeves mere strips of material across her upper arms. She wore a velvet choker, the darkness of it emphasizing the creamy expanse of exposed bosom, and the gentle rounded curves of her shoulders. Her body was tightly corseted, the horizontal folds and gathers of her skirt around her hips making her waist look minuscule in comparison, the gathers at the back of her gown trailing yards of rich burgundy that dusted the floor in a short train.

Ludicrous, to be struck dumb by a pretty woman! He was thirty years old. He was no longer a giddy young boy. He was beyond adolescent embarrassments. He didn't believe in love at first sight.

And yet . . . In the space between one heartbeat and the next, when she had met his eyes and said, "It's a pleasure to meet you, Mr. Goodman," in a voice like mulled wine, Catherine Linwood had sparked to life a fire inside him.

The pleasure of meeting her was all his. But why? *Why?*

Earlier today he had congratulated himself on his life being complete. God had heard him and laughed, placing this woman down before him to prove his ignorance.

She was laughing, her gestures animated, her hand touching briefly on the coated arm of the visitor at the door. Will took his eyes from Catherine long enough to examine the newcomer, and felt a flush of jealousy run through his blood.

He'd never seen such a handsome man—the word *dashing* came ridiculously to mind—and dressed in a manner that bespoke such careless wealth. This man came from money. He'd been born to it, and had the air of one who had discovered that anything he wanted could be had for a price.

"Will? Will!" Robert said, stirring him from his staring.

"Huh?" he grunted, articulate as an ape.

"Good lord, man, you look like you've been kicked in the head."

Will blinked, frowned, and tried to focus on his friend. Robert Linwood was a few years younger than he, but he and the Linwood family had become good friends over the past few years. Robert was a lawyer, who like many others in Woodbridge relied on the town's position as the county seat—and thus the home of the county courthouse—for his business.

"There is a saying amongst shopkeepers," Will said, still half-dazed, "that customers do not know what they want. A man may come into a store seeking only boot black, but then his eye lights upon a pocket watch and suddenly he must have it. He did not know he wanted a pocket watch. He got along fine without one for many years. But now he must have it, and if he cannot afford it he will leave the store with that watch haunting his thoughts until he finds the money to buy it."

"Are you feeling quite well?" Robert asked.

Will looked back to Catherine, who was introducing the stranger to her parents. Her excitement was palpable, even from across the room. "No, not quite."

Dinner was its own unique agony. The dining table was crowded, all its extra leaves put into use. Catherine was at the other end of the table, the newcomer, Mr. Rose, seated next to her and making himself the cynosure of the gathering.

"'Well, I never!'" Mr. Rose was saying, imitating the voice of an affronted woman of the upper classes, to the great amusement of those guests seated near him. "And then she tripped on the train of her gown, falling into a servant and sending his tray of glasses crashing to the floor!" A drumming of laughter followed the denouement to the story.

Will did not laugh, watching instead how Catherine smiled, as if she had heard the tale before, and then glanced quickly at those near her, gauging their reactions as if seeking communal approval of this man. Her eyes flicked briefly down to his end of the table, squinting a bit, but then her attention went back to Mr. Rose, who had begun another anecdote about life among the upper crust in New York.

"I don't like him at all," Amy whispered at his side.

Surprised, Will turned to the girl with whom he had developed a small friendship during his visits to the house. She would not normally have been allowed to partake of a dinner party at her age, but an exception had been made tonight. "Do you speak of Mr. Rose?"

"I don't think he's a nice man."

"He appears to be entertaining everyone very well."

"All he does is mock people. I don't think that's a kind thing to do, do you?"

At the moment, Mr. Rose was doing a wicked impression of an Irish maid who did not understand the workings of water faucets. "No, not especially."

"I don't trust people like that."

"Did he say something cruel to you?" Will asked, catching the fiery look of resentment Amy cast at the man.

"No, it's just . . . There's just something about him. When we were introduced he said what a 'little doll' I was, and treated me like I was still in short skirts. I think he was even considering giving me a pat on the head. Then he ignored me completely."

"He and your sister make a handsome pair."

"Don't say that!" Amy grimaced, and gave a theatrical shiver of abhorrence. "I shouldn't like to have him as a brother-in-law." She was silent a moment, her dark brows frowning as she stared down the table at the object of her loathing. Then her gaze switched to Will, and her lips curled in a mischievous smile that was a younger version of her sister's. "I would much rather have *you* for a brother-in-law. Then Catherine wouldn't go off again to New York. She'd stay right here."

Will choked on the swallow of wine he'd just taken, and after he finished coughing, tried to sound nonchalant. "Do you think I'd stand a chance against Mr. Rose?"

"You're a decent-looking fellow, and much nicer."

That didn't sound a ringing endorsement. "Nice" and "decent-looking" had not been known to win female hearts away from the "dashing" or "amusing." "I think your sister is barely aware that I exist. She never looks this way."

"That's because she's half-blind," Amy said.

"What?"

"She's nearsighted. Everything beyond about six feet gets blurry, and she refuses to wear eyeglasses. Even if she did look away from that man, she wouldn't be able to tell who was who down here. I do think that if she got to know you, she'd see that you were a much better choice than Mr. Rose. You think she's pretty, don't you?"

He swallowed, and suddenly found the plaster moulding on the ceiling to be of absorbing interest. "Uh . . ." he said noncommittally.

"You must. I think she's beautiful. And you need a wife. There's no one else you've got your heart set on, is there? Wouldn't Catherine do?"

He brought his eyes back to her intense green ones. "I suppose she might," he admitted.

Amy beamed at him. "I would be aunt to your children. Isn't that wonderful?"

Will blinked at her, thinking of the necessary steps to producing children with Catherine Linwood. "That would be . . . remarkable."

Voices from below were audible through the floorboards, the party continuing even as Amy got into her nightgown, shivering in the chilly bedroom. More guests had arrived after dinner, friends stopping by to welcome Catherine back. If she hadn't had school in the morning, Amy knew she would have been allowed to stay up, but she couldn't say she particularly cared to as long as *he* was here.

She couldn't put her finger on why, exactly, she did not approve of Mr. Stephen Rose. He seemed to have charmed most everyone, and she should have thought it romantic that he had followed Catherine home, taking up residence in the inn next to the courthouse so that he could be near her. Instead she found herself wondering why the man couldn't go and impose his foul presence on his own family.

Worst of all had been the glow in Catherine's cheeks as Mr. Rose paid court to her. She deserved better than someone like that. She deserved someone kind and thoughtful, like Mr. Goodman. Even though Catherine was ten years older than Amy, she had never made Amy feel the age difference. She sent gifts from her travels, and wrote letters assiduously. Amy knew she couldn't have asked for a better sister—unless, that is, she had a sister who lived in Woodbridge, instead of in New York and over half of Europe.

If Catherine married Mr. Rose, she would never settle here, that much was plain. Mr. Rose would be quickly bored and dissatisfied with life in Woodbridge.

Her only hope was Mr. Goodman. She'd marry him herself if she were old enough, but she loved Catherine enough to sacrifice him to her. He wasn't as tall or handsome as Mr. Rose, and probably nowhere as rich, but he had kind, soft blue eyes that crinkled at the corners with humor. He didn't say much, but one always felt he thought you were important when you spoke to him, and deserving of his attention.

Not like Mr. Rose.

But Catherine, she couldn't see the truth of the two men, just as she couldn't see more than six feet in front of her. Mr. Rose had blinded her heart, with his funny stories that made you feel a bit ashamed of yourself for laughing, and with his romantic good looks. How could she ever get her sister to see the pure, hidden light of Mr. Goodman, when Mr. Rose was busy burning like a bonfire?

A wave of laughter rose up from the parlor below. Amy wanted to stomp her feet in frustration, get all their attention and tell them to throw Mr. Rose back on the train to New York.

She went to the window, looking out at the snow that had begun to fall once again. The lantern at the end of the front walk was lit, creating a pool of yellow light in which to watch the flakes, blowing in the wind. The neighboring houses, large and white like their own, were dimly visible, one or two windows glowing with lamplight.

If only the snow fairies were real, she'd ask them for help. She had a pure heart, after all, didn't she? She might know about ladies of the night, but she'd never been kissed, and wasn't that supposed to be part of the contract? Wishes were always meant for virginal young girls, and what use was being a virginal young girl if the legends were not true?

A figure appeared beneath her, coated and hatted, walking down the path away from the house. She knew somehow that it was Mr. Goodman.

What did it matter that the fairies weren't real? She could still wish, couldn't she?

She left her room and went to the nursery, long since turned into a work and sewing room for her and her mother. She found a piece of white paper and scissors, and took them back to the slightly warmer confines of her bedroom.

She folded and snipped the paper, tiny triangles and diamonds of white falling onto her writing desk. Minutes later she unfolded a paper snowflake, airy and delicate. She dipped her pen into ink, and very carefully, in tiny script, wrote her wish upon the spines and crystals of the flake:

"*I wish that Catherine could see Mr. Rose's and Mr. Goodman's characters as they truly are.*"

There. That was an honest wish, one that had Catherine's fortune at heart, and not Amy's own selfish desire to have her sister live in the same town. Amy loved her birth place, and intended to marry and raise her children here, when the time came. Life would be perfect if Catherine were living here, too.

She went to the window and raised the sash. The wind blew and blustered, sending flakes dusting into the room, then quickly changed direction, pulling at her hair and dragging tendrils across her cheek.

She kissed her paper flake, and threw it into the swirling snow. For a moment it dropped, and then it was caught in a gust and danced out away from the window, rising, rising, and she stuck her head out to see it go. Up it went, beyond the reach of the lantern's light, and then she could see it no more. She stayed hanging out the window for a moment more, silently asking the snow fairies to answer her wish.

Somewhere, in the distance, she could hear the faint jingling of sleighbells.

"Are you asleep?" Catherine whispered, sitting on the side of her own bed, feeling weary now that the party was over. The lamp on the dresser across the room was turned low.

Amy's eyes opened, and she smiled, her young features barely visible in the dim light. "What time is it?"

"Nearly one A.M. Everyone has gone."

"Mr. Rose, too?"

"To the Woodbridge Inn. He says he'll stay there through New Year's, although he'll have to go see relatives in Boston for a bit."

"Why did he come, Cath?"

"What a silly question!" Catherine said. "To see me, of course."

"Doesn't it seem a bit strange to you, his following you here? It makes him seem like a dog without a home of his own."

"Of course he has a home of his own, and family, too. Don't you like him?"

"Are all the men in New York the same as him?"

"The same, how?"

Amy shrugged.

"Come, you needn't worry about hurting my feelings," Catherine said. "You don't have to like him just because I do. What's wrong with him?"

"He's not right for you. I don't think he's a good man."

Amy's words touched a deep, hidden doubt about Mr. Rose that Catherine had harbored for weeks, and she reacted against them. "You don't even know him. He's very attentive to me, and there is no scandal attached to his name. Why should you not think him good?"

Amy gave another shrug, barely discernible beneath the blankets humped over her shoulder.

"I think he's quite delightful, really," Catherine said crossly, and went to the dresser and began to remove her jewelry. "It was terribly romantic of him to come all this way to be near me. He charmed everyone who met him tonight. Even Papa seemed to like him."

"Papa seems to like everyone, but if you ask him, it's not always the case."

"I *shall* ask him," Catherine snapped. She tried to reach the buttons running up her back, and after a few futile tries gave a little huff of frustration and went back to Amy. "Give me a hand with these, will you?" she asked, presenting her back.

"Don't be angry with me," Amy said softly, as she sat up and went to work on the fabric-covered buttons.

Catherine's head bowed under the weight of that gentle plea. "I'm not, darling," she said quietly, and when the last of the buttons came free she turned and sat on the edge of Amy's bed, meeting her sister's eyes. "I'm tired of waiting, is all. I don't know if you can understand that. I like Mr. Rose better than I've liked any other suitable gentleman I've met, and I want to believe that he is the one for me, so I can finally stop looking. I want all of you to like him, so that I will know I made the right choice if I marry him."

"I only want you to be happy," Amy said.

Catherine smiled, and couldn't explain why Amy's words put the sting of tears in her eyes.

CHAPTER THREE

"Catherine, you have a package!" Amy exclaimed, bounding into the kitchen, still wearing her coat and hat. The cold, clear air of the outdoors came with her, caught in the folds of her coat, streamers of it invading the warmth of the kitchen.

"Who's it from?" Catherine asked, setting her rolling pin aside and wiping her floury hands on her apron. She was wearing a blouse and skirt, but the skirt's train had become such a trial in the kitchen that at last she had pinned it up, the peacock-blue material twisted into an awkward pouch behind her knees. The heat from the ovens had brought out a fine sheen of perspiration on her skin, and tendrils of hair stuck to the sides of her face and neck. She was enjoying herself thoroughly, her mind having been lost for hours in the immediacy of dough and spices, fruit and sugars as she worked alongside the family's taciturn cook, Mrs. Ames. There was a French apple tart cooling on the racks, as well as a variety of cookies.

"It doesn't say. Here," Amy said, extending the small package toward her. "Ginger cookies!" she then cried, spotting her favorites, and quickly nabbed one off the cooling racks as Mrs. Ames raised a wooden spoon in mock warning.

Catherine took the package, examining the neat

copperplate writing addressing it to herself. There was no other mark on the brown paper wrapping, nothing to say from whence it had come. "Where did you find it? The mail has already come today."

"Perhaps he forgot this, and came back. It was on the front step."

Catherine turned it over in her hands, then with a facial shrug took a knife and cut through the string. She unwrapped the paper, and into her hand fell a flat box about six inches long, and less than half as wide. It was padded on its outside, and covered with a pale blue silk that shifted to silver when she tilted it. There were silver hinges at the back. "Curiouser and curiouser," Catherine said, then opened the lid.

On a bed of white satin sat a pair of spectacles. She pursed her lips, then slid her gaze sideways to Amy, who was standing beside her, eagerly peering in, cookie held to her lips.

Amy looked up at her, catching her suspicious stare. "I didn't send them! Honest!"

Catherine looked back at the spectacles. No, Amy would not have had the money to buy them. The frames were gold, and so finely wrought that Catherine doubted their practicality. It would take barely a nudge, surely, to bend the ear pieces out of shape. The lenses themselves looked too thin to withstand a puff of air.

There was something written on the inside of the lid. She tilted it, and brought it closer to her face. Spelled out in gold embroidery she read:

See far
And see near
But let your heart's
Sight be clear

She repeated it aloud for the benefit of Amy and Mrs. Ames. "What do you suppose that means?" she asked, genuinely puzzled now.

"Put them on," Amy said, her voice tight.

Catherine glanced at her, noting the intensity of her expression. "My eyesight is not half as bad as you think it is. I assure you, I can see well enough to make my way around the kitchen without falling into the fire."

"Please, let me see them on you," Amy asked, pleading.

"My hands are dirty. I'll try them later," Catherine said, and shut the box with a snap. Why was her family forever after her to wear eyeglasses? She could see what was in front of her, and wasn't that all anyone needed? It wasn't like she was a hunter who needed to spot a deer two hundred yards away. "Perhaps Aunt Frances sent them," she mused aloud.

An hour later, with the last batch of cookies in the oven, Catherine went up to the room she shared with Amy. She opened the pale blue box and looked down at the spectacles, frowning, wondering if they truly were from Aunt Frances. The more she thought about it, the less likely it seemed. Her aunt was as eager as she to let vanity overrule practicality in the matter.

She set the box down and took out the spectacles, carefully unfolding the ear pieces. She had her own pair of eyeglasses, but they were graceless, heavy things compared to these. With a glance at the door to check that Amy was not waiting and watching, she put them on.

And took in a startled breath.

The room around her was crisp and perfect. She blinked, and stared, and turned her head left and right.

Her own spectacles improved her vision, but only slightly. They were nothing like this.

Good heavens, she thought, *is this how everyone else sees the world?* It was no wonder her family implored her to wear eyeglasses, if so.

She went to the window, and looked out across the narrow front yard and the street, to the large white houses opposite, with their black shutters and doors, and the brass knockers surrounded by green wreaths. The bare trees were frosted with snow where the wind had not blown it off, and above it all the clouds were delicate streamers of candy floss across a blue-white sky. She felt tears start in her eyes. She had never in her life seen the details of real clouds, only how artists had chosen to depict them in paintings.

These spectacles were magic, pure and simple.

She would never take them off. She would sit here until the stars came out, and the moon, and she would see its shadowed craters for herself. She would walk in the woods, and see birds fly from tree to tree. She would go into town, and read shop signs from a block away. She would see everything as it was for the first time in her life!

She had been staring awestruck at the drifting forms of the clouds for she didn't know how long when a movement from the corner of her eye caught her attention. She turned, and coming down the sidewalk was Mr. Rose, in his elegant topcoat and hat, swinging an ebony cane.

She pulled away from the window, her hand going to her hair. She went to the cheval mirror, and when she looked into her own face saw something she wasn't expecting. Her eyes were sad and uneasy, not at all the way she thought she felt at this moment. She leaned closer to the mirror, looking into her amber-brown eyes, and as a knock came at the door below something of panic flared deep within them.

It was the eyeglasses, it had to be. She took them off, and immediately she looked like her usual self again, cheery and at ease. There must be something in the shape of the frames that gave her that illusion of looking like an unhappy mouse. She could not have Mr. Rose seeing her that way.

She snapped the lid shut on the spectacles, tucked up the straying wisps of her hair, and went down to greet him.

"You must find Woodbridge very quiet after New York," she heard Mama saying as she came down the stairs.

"There is a certain rustic charm to the village, almost as if it were caught in a past century," Mr. Rose said. "It's quite restful. One needn't worry that one is going to miss anything of interest."

"Indeed," Mama said.

"Mama is a director of the Woodbridge Drama Club," Catherine said, coming into the sitting room. "Everyone looks forward to the plays they put on. Many would be sorry indeed to miss one of their productions."

Mr. Rose made a half bow of apology toward Mama. "I can only imagine that the plays must be a great delight to the audience, with such a mistress at the helm. You bring elegance to all that you touch."

Mama's cheeks pinkened, and Catherine wondered if it was in pleasure or because Mama found the flattery a trifle fulsome. "Thank you, Mr. Rose. Now if you'll both excuse me, I must talk with Mrs. Ames about dinner," she said, and left them alone.

"Now why are you frowning at me, my precious lily?" Mr. Rose asked, coming to her and taking both of her hands in his own. "Are you not happy to see me?"

Catherine smoothed away the frown she had not known she was wearing, and gave him a smile. "Of course I am. I just hope you are not finding Wood-bridge to be terribly boring."

"I look upon it as an adventure into the wilds, worth enduring for the pleasure of one native's company," he said, looking deeply into her eyes.

She laughed nervously, and broke the gaze. "Did you notice the portrait on the wall, there?" she asked, seeking to divert his attention.

"The watercolor? Yes, I could not help but recognize your inimitable style. Was she truly cross-eyed, or was that your own special touch?"

Catherine tried to smile at the jest, going over to get a closer look at the portrait she had done of her grandmother when she herself was twelve. At the time she had not yet mastered the three-quarter profile of a face, and her grandmother did indeed look as if her eyes were not in concert with each other. One shoulder was higher than it should have been, and the hands were in an unnatural posture. Her grandmother had died a few months after the portrait was painted, though, and she knew her mother treasured it for reasons other than its artistry.

"It doesn't show much promise for my future as a portrait painter, does it?"

"Don't tell me you still intend to dabble?"

She shrugged. Mr. Rose, she sensed, would not be one to put one of her artworks on the wall for senti-mental reasons. He'd likely be embarrassed for his friends or family to see such a thing, for they might doubt his aesthetic sensibilities. She wondered if he was thinking a little less of her, now that he saw she came from a town that was uncultured and provincial in comparison to the great cities of Boston and New York, from whence his own ancestors had sprung.

Mr. Rose's superior sense of what was fashionable and in good taste had been part of what had drawn her to him. He was so much more cultured and finely bred than she, she had gladly relied upon his aesthetic opinions to guide her, and had trusted his judgment as being more discerning than her own. She was afraid of appearing lacking in his eyes, an object worthy of his mocking ridicule, and in New York had constantly, subtly, sought his approval. She was surprised by the stab of resentment she now felt toward him, at his dismissal—however warranted—of her watercolor painting.

"I was thinking we might take a stroll. You can explain to me this fine metropolis where you were raised," he said, and waggled his eyebrows comically at her, lightening the mood, and sweeping away the shadowed thoughts that lurked in her mind. "Only, I do hope it is not the fashion here to go about in public with one's skirts pinned up behind."

She felt a burn in her cheeks, and excused herself to go let down the train of her skirt.

CHAPTER FOUR

The air was bright and chill, her breath freezing in her nose. A light dusting of snow last night had renewed the sparkling beauty of winter, concealing the dirty slush that had been accumulating along sidewalks and roadsides. Catherine pulled the door of the house shut behind her, and felt her heart lift at being outside and alone. Mr. Rose, who had danced attendance on her almost every day, had gone to Boston to pay a visit to cousins, and would not be back for a week. Amy was in school, Papa at the lumberyard. Mama was planning meals with Mrs. Ames, and training the new maid. She was on her own.

Once out of sight of the house, Catherine reached into her reticule for the box that held her spectacles. Mama and Papa had denied buying them, as had her brother, Robert. Mr. Rose she had not even asked, knowing instinctively what the answer would be. She had put them on once for Amy, and it had almost broken her heart how clear the hope and youth were upon her sister's face.

She had not yet come to terms with wearing them regularly. It was something she had resisted for so many years, she could not bring herself to give in so quickly to the seduction of that crystal vision. At least, she could not give in before her family, who had been pestering her for so long to wear eyeglasses. In private was different, and so was alone in public. Half the faces in Woodbridge might be familiar to her, but with the exception of her lifelong friends, no one else knew of her battle against ocular assistance.

The street her family lived on was only a five-minute walk from the center of town. She put on the spectacles, and felt a thrill race across her skin as the world leaped into focus. The picket fences, the bare maple and oak trees, the brook that was visible at the backs of several houses, running down to join the Ottauquechee River, it was all perfectly etched in sunlight and snow.

Her skirt swished along the sidewalk, the train and underskirt gathering matted clumps of snow. She knew she was smiling like a fool as she turned onto Elm Street and headed toward town. Houses gave way to shops, and then she was at the intersection with Central Street, where the tall iron fountain for watering horses stood like an island in the middle of a stream. The water was frozen now, she could see that even from the edge of the road.

She was about to turn right, to make a circuit of the village green, but her eye was caught by bright colors in the nearest shop window. She stepped closer, putting up her hand to the glass to cut out the glare, and peered in at the Christmas cards on display. They were a reminder that she had yet to buy any, and that her Christmas shopping was only half done. She went in.

Cinnamon-scented warmth greeted her, and for an instant she wondered if she had stepped into someone's kitchen. A woodstove sat at the center of the room, and on the braided red rug in front of it sat four or five children, all listening raptly as a girl only a few years older read to them from a picture book. The girl sat in a rocker, her black-booted feet several inches above the floor.

Catherine moved closer to the stove, and saw that a vat of spiced cider sat simmering there, cups and cookies on a tray to the side, apparently for the customers to take as they pleased. She realized then that she had been in this store once before, a summer a few years ago, but only for a few minutes. It had been lemonade on offer at that time, and meringue cookies.

She moved away from the stove, listening with half an ear as the girl read her story, and gazed at the goods stacked upon the shelves and arranged under the glass counters. She had seen goods in stores before, but never all at once, the sheet music twenty feet away as plain to her vision as the roll of ribbon in front of her. There was a young clerk helping a woman across the room, and up on a ladder a boy was arranging cans. A few other shoppers milled about.

Catherine wandered through a doorway into a room displaying housewares, then into another with dry goods. She heard an odd, irregular rapping sound coming from behind a curtained doorway, and idly wandered toward it, her curiosity prompting her to pull the edge of the curtain aside and see what was making the noise.

A man stood in a storeroom, facing half away from her. In his hand was a can of peaches, and as she watched he turned it slightly, then with a hammer whacked a dent into the side of it. He set it in a box along with several others, then searched the shelves. It was potted beef this time that fell to the hammer.

She stared, transfixed by the odd behavior. He was slightly taller than average, his frame strong, his hair a dark brownish blond. When he turned the right way she could see part of his face, and could not help but think that it was a good countenance, something level and steady in his features that spoke of a well-grounded man. The impression made it all the more difficult to understand what he was doing.

"Pardon me, sir," Catherine found herself saying, and the man tensed. "Is the owner of the shop aware that you are damaging his goods?"

He turned around, and she met the loveliest pair of soft blue eyes she had ever seen. It was as if the first warmth of spring resided within them, and she was struck speechless.

"Miss Linwood," he said, his cheeks taking on a faint tinge of pink. "You've surprised me."

"I beg your pardon—" she began, then stopped herself. "Mr. Goodman?" she asked, astonished, and not at all certain the name she had dredged out of her memory was the right one. Surely if she had been introduced to this man once before, she would be more certain of it. She could not have forgotten him!

"Did Robert not tell you that this was my store?" he asked.

"Oh! I see!" But she did not see. Her eyes went again to the box of canned goods.

He grimaced. "I don't suppose you could pretend not to have seen me doing that?" he asked.

"It is no business of mine what you do with your goods," she replied. "I should not have disturbed you in the first place. My apologies, Mr. Goodman. Good day." She started to let the curtain fall back into place.

"Wait!"

She opened the curtain again. "Yes, Mr. Goodman?"

He put his hammer down atop a box. "Was there something you were looking for?"

"Excuse me?"

"In the store," he said, gesturing vaguely toward the room behind her.

"Oh. Well, yes. Christmas cards. I have suddenly recalled that I have yet to write a single one. Those in your window are quite lovely."

He came toward her, and she stepped out of the way, feeling suddenly a trifle embarrassed that this man she had met in her own home was now going to wait on her in his shop. It felt a peculiar and awkward situation.

"I ordered them from Louis Prang, the lithographer in Boston. I wasn't certain they would sell well. Not so many here have caught on yet to the fashion of sending them."

She let him lead her back to the front room, and to the small collection of cards. One was of a girl lighting candles on a tree, one of a striped stocking stuffed with toys, there was a trio of trumpeting angels, and last a row of tiny toddlers alternating with songbirds on a branch, with the title "A Christmas Carol." Mr. Rose would have chosen the trumpeting angels, she was certain, but the silly, sentimental toddlers made her smile. "These will do, I think," she said. "Could I have sixty?"

His eyebrows went up. "You'll have cramped fingers when you're done with that lot."

"I suppose I shall."

He began to count out the cards, but was interrupted by a raw female voice.

"Mr. Goodman! There you are. Where is my order? I've been waiting these past twenty minutes, wondering where you'd gone off to."

He paused in his counting, casting a wide-eyed look at Catherine.

"Go ahead," Catherine said. "I'll count them out myself."

"I'll be back in a moment. Do forgive me."

She nodded, and took his place at the drawer of cards, her mind only partially on what she was doing. From the corner of her eye she watched him hurry to the discontented woman, confer with her for a moment, and then disappear into one of the back rooms.

She had her cards counted out by the time he came back, carrying the small crate with the dented cans and placing it on the wooden counter next to several other goods, most of which were already wrapped in brown paper and string. Catherine moved slowly closer, keeping her eyes averted, her ears straining to catch their exchange.

"It's a good thing there are people like me who are willing to take damaged goods off your hands," the woman was saying.

"Indeed I am fortunate in that regard," Mr. Goodman said. "Every shopkeeper knows that it would not do to have such as these sitting on the shelves, giving an impression of poor quality. You, however, are a Vermont woman through and through, and know the value of your money."

She sniffed, her chin going up. "A pretty can makes no difference to me, so long as the contents are as they should be. Half off, you say?"

"One third."

The woman grumbled, then nodded her consent. Catherine surreptitiously looked the woman over, noting the faded fabric of her skirt and her aged coat, the seam at the corner of the pocket having clearly been mended. Her eyes went back to the woman's face, and the tough-jawed pride evident there, and finally comprehended Mr. Goodman's peculiar behavior with the hammer.

Mr. Goodman called over one of the younger clerks to finish wrapping the woman's parcels, and then he came back to her.

"I've taken half your cards," Catherine said as he came up to her.

"No matter," he said, pulling out a sheet of paper and stacking the cards neatly in the center. He would not meet her eye, his attention all upon the engrossing task of wrapping her Christmas cards. She thought she could detect a tinge of red color in his neck and cheeks, contrasting with his white collar. A lock of his hair fell forward over his brow.

He doesn't like anyone knowing what he does, she intuitively understood. *He'd rather people thought him a poor businessman, than that they be aware of his charitable nature. How very peculiar.*

"I'll put these on your family's account, then," he said, tying the string and finally looking at her.

"Yes, thank you." It would save the awkwardness of handing him money, turning him into a clerk who waited upon her. "I must congratulate you on your store, Mr. Goodman. The stores in New York may be larger, but they have not half the atmosphere of congeniality as yours."

"Thank you, Miss Linwood," he said, and favored her with a smile that transformed his face, taking his regular features for a moment into the realm of masculine beauty. Coupled with that warm gaze, it was a powerful combination.

Something stirred deep within her, a gentle shifting

of she knew not what. She gave an uncertain smile, and picked up her package, suddenly feeling ill at ease and eager to be gone. "Good day, Mr. Goodman."

"Good day, Miss Linwood. I do hope we meet again soon."

Will watched her as she left his store, the sleighbells he had put above the door for Christmas jingling at her departure. He saw her pause outside the door for a moment, then turn to the right, toward the village green. When the last glimpse of her figure, gowned in dark chocolate brown and a coat edged in mink, disappeared from sight, his shoulders sagged. He gave a quiet moan and grimaced, hitting himself upon the forehead with the heel of his hand.

What a dolt she must think him. Hammering at his own cans, babbling on about Boston lithographers and Christmas cards—what did she care if his cards sold well, or where they came from?—then grinning like a simpleton when she had complimented his store. "I do hope we meet again soon," he'd said, eager as a puppy. "You'll have cramped fingers." "Did Robert not tell you this was my store?" Lord save him from himself. He must seem crude as clay in comparison to the urbane Mr. Rose.

"Joshua!" he called, and a moment later the ten-year-old appeared from a back room. "I think we're in need of Christmas greenery. Round up a couple of your friends, and we'll take the wagon into the woods to fetch some."

"Yes, sir!" Joshua whooped, and ran for his coat.

"Ann, do you want to stay or come with us?" he asked the girl who was sitting in the rocker.

"I'll stay if I may, Mr. Goodman."

He nodded, having expected the answer. He'd never known a child more in love with books. "Give Mr. Jones a shout if you need anything," he told her.

He barked orders to his clerks, desperate now to escape the shop. Heat burned his cheeks at the thought of his encounter with Miss Linwood, and it seemed the only way to extinguish it was to throw himself into the cold of outdoors. He couldn't stand to remain here at the scene of his humiliation, replaying it over and over in his mind.

"Did you want to make those deliveries, since you'll be out?" Greg, one of his clerks, asked.

"Yes, fine." It was an excuse to stay outdoors even longer, so he might as well.

It was half an an hour before the team was hitched, the orders loaded, and the boys all installed with blankets amidst the groceries, gunnysacks, pruning shears, and handsaws. Will pulled on his monstrous bearskin coat and matching hat, and climbed up onto the buckboard. Behind him, the boys were already bragging about what they'd buy with their wages from the outing, their daydreaming far outmatching their imagined income. Their enthusiasm brought a half-smile to his face. He remembered what it was like to be ten and fundless, and how exciting the prospect of earning pocket money could be.

As his mood lightened, his bumbling with Miss Linwood began to seem less of an irretrievable tragedy. She *had* said she liked his store. She had been quite complimentary on that score, and that was after all the rest, including leaving her to count out sixty cards herself. He clicked to the horses and gave them a light slap of the reins, and the wagon lumbered out from behind the store and onto Elm Street.

She had not recognized him immediately, but he imagined he must look different to her now that she was wearing spectacles. Perhaps Amy was correct, and Miss Linwood had never properly seen him at all. He thought she looked quite fetching in those fine gold frames, her liquid brown eyes gazing intently and, he assumed, clearly. He felt, somehow, that the spectacles made her a fraction more accessible to him, and a bit less an untouchable angel from another realm.

A bobbing set of feathers and a swishing brown skirt, dragging in the snow like the tail of an exotic bird, caught his eye. His heartbeat thundered, and perspiration broke out under the heavy bearskin. Ridiculous! He had but barely made her acquaintance, and he was mooning over her as if he were in love.

He slapped the reins again, the horses picking up to a trot. He eased them over to her side of the street, and slowed their pace.

"Miss Linwood!" he called, not giving himself a chance to think better of what he was about to do. "Miss Linwood!"

She turned, stopping, her expression one of utter surprise. "Mr. Goodman!"

He was calling to her on the street from a wagon buckboard. He knew it was not the behavior of a gentleman to a lady. He drew the horses to a complete halt. "Miss Linwood! We're going up to the woods to gather greenery. Would you care to join us?"

She gaped at him, eyes going to the wagon load of boys, then back to his bearskinned self.

He welcomed the gaping. Let her see that he was not Mr. Rose! Let her reject him outright, and avoid his company forever after, thus freeing him of any hope that she might someday greet his arrival with the same pleasure she had shown for her wealthy suitor.

"I—"

He waited. Let the ax fall swiftly, the stroke clean!

"I suppose I might," she said.

Oh, good lord. He sat frozen for long seconds, immobilized by those simple words of acceptance. What new hell had he bought himself, full of false hopes?

Dazed, he jumped down from the buckboard and took her parcels, handing them up to one of the boys. "Miss Linwood, may I introduce to you Joshua, Tommy, Eli, and George."

"My pleasure," she said, nodding her head to the lot.

The boys had fallen silent, shy where moments before they'd been swaggering young cocks. He remembered that feeling as well, and wished it were further in his past. Miss Linwood was neither sister nor classmate, mother nor teacher. She was a woman full-grown and lovely to look upon, and the boys were scared to death.

There was a mumbled, barely discernible chorus of "Nice to meet you." Will helped her up onto the buckboard, then climbed up beside her. He snagged a blanket from the wagon bed, and unfolded it over her lap.

She smiled at him, arranged her skirts, then settled her gloved hands atop the blanket, her back straight as if held by an iron yardstick. "I had been intending to see the woods," she said. "Thank you for inviting me to join your excursion."

"The pleasure is mine," he said, and put the wagon in motion.

Catherine swayed with the motion of the wagon, and held her chin up. As Aunt Frances had said, one could do the slightly scandalous as long as one behaved as a lady whilst one did it. She was chaperoned by four young boys, and Mr. Goodman was a friend of the family. There was no reason she should not be sitting here.

She felt her lips twitch. Aunt Frances would not have approved, however much she tried to persuade herself otherwise. One did not ride wagons into the countryside with men of brief acquaintance.

So why had she said yes? To see the woods through her new spectacles without her family to observe her, perhaps. Perhaps because she hadn't felt like returning home yet, despite the cold that had seeped through her thin boots and was numbing her toes. Perhaps, just perhaps, because Mr. Goodman had piqued her curiosity, and now that that instant of startled attraction had faded, she wanted to know a little more about him.

She turned her head slightly, trying to watch him without appearing to. He looked like a flustered bear, his blue eyes peering out with consternation from beneath his bushy black hat. He appeared, now that he had her in his wagon, to be not entirely certain of what to do with her. Mr. Rose would never have been at such a loss. It gave her a sense of power, to think that for once she was the one with the greater social ease. She was the one who was one step ahead, whereas she never was with Mr. Rose.

"Tell me, Mr. Goodman, how long have you been in Woodbridge?" she asked.

"Six years."

"Ah, indeed. And your family? Where are they?"

"I have cousins in New Hampshire." He looked like he wanted to say more, but was restraining himself. Perhaps he did not think she would find anything he said of interest.

"And do you come from a family of merchants?"

"My parents were farmers, not well off," he said, and when she nodded, making eye contact to show her interest, he continued. "It was never a life that appealed to me. One of my earliest memories is of going to the general store, and the wonder I felt looking at all those *things*, and all that candy. I thought Mr. Johnson, the owner, must be one step down from God to be owning all that. Even getting a peppermint stick into my hand was like a holiday to me. Plowing and sowing and mucking out barns seemed to me a foolish way to spend my time, when working in a store might be an option."

"What did your parents think of that?"

He shrugged his shoulders, the bear fur rising up to meet his hat. "Mother died when I was eight, and my father seemed to . . . fade after that. When I told him I'd gotten an after-school job at the store, he just muttered, and jerked his jaw forward in what I took to be acceptance."

He glanced at her. She nodded for him to go on.

"When I finished school, I went to Boston, working at a large store there for a few years. I thought I needed the experience of working in a large city. Then Father died, I sold what was left of the farm, and came here and bought a small dry-goods store that was for sale."

"I remember it. 'Cooper's Dry Goods,' wasn't it?"

"The very one."

"It seems you've made a success of your enterprise. Cooper's was not much of a store."

"I've been fortunate."

Catherine thought it was likely more than that. The man might have a soft heart, but he plainly had business sense. His merchandise was of good quality and

sold at fair prices, and the welcoming atmosphere of
the store made it the type of place one wanted to
linger and browse, even if there was nothing one
needed to buy. She well knew that was a circumstance
that had caused many of her own coins to flow through
her fingers.

They turned down a narrow lane, and followed it to
a farmhouse. He drew the horses to a halt, and called
over his shoulder to the boys, "Garfields'!"

Joshua stayed in the wagon while the three other
boys jumped down, then Joshua started passing goods
to them, which were carried up to the door in the pas-
sageway that connected kitchen to barn. An old
woman came out a moment later, and waved to Mr.
Goodman. He leaped down and went to talk with her,
and after a few words the woman—Mrs. Garfield, she
presumed—looked over at Catherine, met her eyes,
and nodded in silent greeting. Catherine nodded back.

Catherine sat and watched the rest of the exchange,
and watched the boys running to and fro with their
packages and burdens. She began to find herself feeling at a social disadvantage, sitting on the buckboard
of a wagon in her fashionable, frivolous clothes, the
jaunty, plumed hat atop her coiled hair ridiculously in-
appropriate to the occasion. Mrs. Garfield was wearing
a dark woolen dress, apron, and half-mittens, her hair
pulled simply back and covered in an outdated cotton
cap. She doubted Mrs. Garfield would walk in the
snow in thin leather boots with high heels.

When they were all back in the wagon and on their
way again, Mr. Goodman said, "I should have asked
before: Do you mind my making a few deliveries while
we're out?"

"Certainly not, I'm enjoying the ride," she said. He

seemed to sense her slight lack of conviction, his eyes on her for long seconds, and she felt a flutter of panic that he might actually turn the wagon around, drive back to town, and drop her at her house if she showed the least sign of wanting to return. She didn't want that, however out of place she might feel in her finery. She might look silly and useless sitting there, but her curiosity about Mr. Goodman was yet to be satisfied, and she would not leave until it was.

They rode in silence into the woods, the boys behind them having become accustomed enough to her immobile back that they had resumed their talk. She eavesdropped, smiling when one cursed and was abruptly hushed by the others in belated consideration of her presence.

"I must have come to Woodbridge at about the same time you left for college," Mr. Goodman said. "Robert tells me you went to Mount Holyoke, down in Massachusetts."

"I thought it was a huge adventure at the time," she said, and at his prompting told him of what it had been like, and talked as well of her travels with Aunt Frances. She paused when he halted the wagon and gave the boys instructions on what greenery to fetch, but then he prompted her to continue, staying with her in the wagon, as the snowy ground was too uneven and wet for her to walk upon dressed as she was.

It wasn't until the boys were coming back with their loaded gunnysacks and, surprisingly, a tree, that she realized she had been talking for at least three quarters of an hour. Mr. Goodman exclaimed over the unexpected spruce and climbed down, and she listened with half an ear to the boys' improvised explanations of how badly he needed a tree in his store. Her mind, however, was busy berating herself for talking on and on about herself and her travels.

He must think her a pretentious, self-absorbed braggart. He had coaxed her to talk, nodding and murmuring in the right places, making eye contact and giving her the sense that he *listened*, in a way that few men ever did, but any woman should know better than to take that at face value. Hadn't she herself gone through those very motions countless times with men these past few years, feigning interest in some stultifying tale, all the while wondering when the windbag would run out of air?

She half-turned and watched with a distracted smile on her lips as they maneuvered the spruce into the wagon, the top of it hanging well over the back end. Why was she so concerned about what he might think of her, anyway?

Because you admire him, a voice inside answered. Maybe she did. He was self-made, and yet maintained a kind and generous heart. He was free of pretension, and there was something honest and solid to him that she had found in very few men besides her father. He also looked, she thought, to be a happy man.

He caught her watching him, and smiled while cocking his head at the boys, as if to say, *See how they manipulate me?* She wondered how much extra the boys were demanding to be paid, for bagging such a large piece of greenery as a spruce.

Had Mr. Goodman ever married, ever been in love? It was not the type of question she could ask him on short acquaintance. She tried to imagine what it would be like to have him courting her, and failed. He was too far from the likes of Mr. Rose and the other men who had peopled her circle of late. Would he bring a small bouquet of flowers, that unruly lock of hair on his forehead ridiculously slicked back and subdued by pomade? Would he sit in the parlor with a cup of tea trembling on his knee, and try to make conversation?

He climbed back up beside her, the boys scrambling in behind. "Are you warm enough?" he asked. "There are more blankets in back."

"I'm quite comfortable," she half-lied, and felt a twinge of guilt for her thoughts on how he might court a woman. Whomever he chose to marry, she would be smart to count herself a fortunate girl.

CHAPTER FIVE

Catherine shoved the needle through a cranberry, then carefully pulled the dark red berry along the string until it nestled up against its twin. She reached into the bowl for another, shoving aside those that had black soft spots or were half white. Papa was hunched on a stool next to the fire, shaking the long handle of the popcorn popper, the seeds rattling across the bottom of the black mesh container. Amy sat with her on the floor, sewing small lace pouches that would hold candies for the tree.

"How late will Mama be?" Catherine asked her father.

"I'm to fetch her at nine, and none too soon, I'm sure. That drama club causes her more grief than joy."

"I think she enjoys complaining about them," Catherine said.

"It's worse this year. You know she and Maggie Walsch have written their own adaptation of Dickens's *A Christmas Carol* for the stage, don't you?"

"Dear me, no. Mama did not mention that part of it."

"Well. You can imagine the state she gets in when our local thespians question their lines."

Catherine pursed her lips and raised her brows, imagining the scene very well indeed. Mama was a lamb in the general course of things, but on the occasions that a creative project was put into her direct control, she became a field marshal who brooked no opposition. Those who questioned orders or threatened desertion were put to the firing squad. "Is Mr. Goodman in the play?"

"Mr. Goodman?" her father asked, eyes on the kernels that had just begun to pop. "Of course. He's Scrooge."

"*Scrooge?*" Catherine cried. "You cannot be serious."

Papa looked over his shoulder at her. "Who better than a shopkeeper? They're notorious for being tight-fisted."

"But Mr. Goodman! Or does Mama see it as a joke?"

Papa frowned at her. "I don't quite see what you're getting at, Catherine. He's an astute businessman, and living alone like he does in that new house of his, I think he fits the part rather well. It's easier to imagine him in the role than, say, Mr. Tobias, who has a wife and six children and is on the library board."

"Do people think him a miser, then?"

"I doubt that they think of him much at all. He's a bit of a cipher, our Mr. Goodman, and keeps himself to himself," her father said approvingly.

"Papa!" Amy cried, pointing at the fire.

"What? Oh, damn me," Papa said, turning back to his task and finding the popper full of flaming popcorn. He used the long handle to open the lid, and dumped the lot into the fire. "That's the third batch."

Catherine and Amy both giggled. Papa gave them a glare.

"Why are you asking so many questions about Mr. Goodman?" Amy asked her, as Papa refilled the popper.

"Who says I am asking 'so many'? I was curious, is all," she said primly.

Oh yes, she was curious, curious because at the second farmhouse where Mr. Goodman made a delivery he came back to the wagon with a pierced tin foot-warmer full of hot coals, knowing despite her denials that she was chilled. Curious, because when he had again prompted her to talk about herself, she had looked into his eyes and known that he truly was interested, and not merely feigning it out of politeness.

"Is he courting you?"

"Amy! What a ridiculous question. Of course not."

"I don't see what's so ridiculous about it. I like him, and think he would make an excellent brother-in-law."

"Oh, really," Catherine said, rolling her eyes, feeling a touch of embarrassment on her cheeks. Married to Mr. Goodman? She, the wife of the man in that enormous bearskin coat? How Mr. Rose would laugh!

"Did you ever ask Papa about Mr. Rose?" Amy asked.

"Eh, what?" Papa said, settling back onto his stool, casting another look over his shoulder at them.

"I wanted to know if Catherine had asked you your opinion of Mr. Rose," Amy said.

"No. Why? Did you want it?" he asked Catherine.

She busied herself with a cranberry, then glanced at him from under her brows. "If you were willing to give it."

"Things that serious, are they?"

"I wouldn't say that, Papa, but I trust your judgment and Mama's."

He gave the popper a shake. "He'd be able to provide for you, there looks to be no question of that. He's personable, and cuts a fine figure. He seems to have taken quite a fancy to you." He chewed the inside of his lower lip, eyes focused on the distance.

Catherine waited. "And?" she prompted.

"Hmm?" he said, pulled from his reverie.

"And what else?" she asked.

"And nothing else. He appears an eligible enough young man."

"But—What of his character? What type of husband would he make?" Catherine complained, unsatisfied. "Is he a good man? Would he be a good father?"

"I don't have a crystal ball, Catherine, and I barely know the man. You are the one who has spent time with him. You know the answers better than I would."

She gave a little grunt of frustration. Why was it a parent never had an opinion when you most wanted one, but was free enough with advice when you were in no mood to hear it?

"Damn me!" Papa cried again, and Amy shrieked in laughter as another batch of popcorn went up in flames.

"You have no idea how jealous I am of you right now," Melinda whispered into Catherine's ear. "I think he's the most handsome man I've ever seen." They were standing in the doorway to Melinda's house, Mr. Rose a few steps away on the short bricked path through the yard.

Catherine smiled at her friend, and at the baby she held bundled in her arms. "Nor have you any idea how jealous I am of you." Her childhood friend was married and a mother twice over. Her house was small and untidy, and she could only afford one maid-of-all-work, but she looked content.

"Hurry up and go now, or some Woodbridge spinster will lose her senses and kidnap him right before our eyes," Melinda said.

"I'll call on you again soon."

"Do. I can never seem to get out of the house when I have a baby underfoot."

Catherine pressed a kiss onto the downy forehead of the child, said her final farewells, and joined Mr. Rose where he waited, leaning his right hand atop his ebony-and-gold cane.

"Your friend is quite charming," he said as she took his arm and they began to walk.

"I am glad you think so. She was taken with you, as well."

"Such a sweet, simple girl. I can see how you would like her."

"I've known her since we were two, and she is not entirely as simple as she may seem," Catherine said, a faint touch of annoyance spoiling her mood. Was that a patronizing tone she had heard in his voice?

Mr. Rose laughed. "I've offended you! My dear," he said and, tucking his cane under his arm, he reached over to pat her hand where it rested in the crook of his arm. "I meant 'simple' in the best of all possible ways. She is unspoiled, and possessed of those 'simple' virtues that any man would wish for in a wife."

"Then I apologize," she said, and wondered what was wrong with her. If Melinda was to be believed, she was the envy of every unwed young woman in Woodbridge—and not a few of the married ones as well—and yet she was not entirely pleased to be walking beside Mr. Rose at this moment. He had returned from Boston the night before, and today when he came to the house had expressed his profound happiness to be once more in her company. He had made her mother laugh with stories about his Boston relatives, and then had readily agreed to accompany Catherine on her visit to Melinda. So why was it that she found herself ever so slightly irritated by his presence? Why, when he was so perfect a choice for a husband, did she find herself wishing he would go away?

"Your apology is most graciously accepted," he said playfully, and they turned a corner and began walking along the side of the village green. They had gone some distance in silence when he spoke again, somewhat puzzled. "Catherine, I do believe that man is waving to you," he said.

Catherine squinted into the distance, trying to make out of whom he spoke. She was not wearing her spectacles, and everything except the sidewalk a few feet in front of her was a blur. Her irritation rose a notch, for if Mr. Rose were not with her she *would* be wearing them, and seeing for herself who waved, thank you very much.

She knew it was her own vanity at fault, and not Mr. Rose, but that realization did nothing to improve her humor. "I cannot make him out," she admitted.

"He's stopped now. He's going into a store."

"Is he?" she asked, her grip tightening on Mr. Rose's arm. "Which one?"

"I cannot tell, the tree branches block the sign. Does it matter?"

"I thought it might have been a friend of the family, Mr. Goodman. He owns a general store at the corner of Elm Street," she explained.

"Did I meet him at your welcome-home party? Perhaps it was he. Shall we go say hello? I wouldn't like him to think you had cut him."

"No, that wouldn't do . . ." she said, her voice trailing off. Mr. Rose seemed not to notice, leading her briskly toward the store. She did not like the idea of seeing him in Mr. Goodman's store, the men speaking to each other and shaking hands. There was something to it that made the nerves in the back of her neck shrink in discomfort.

Mr. Rose opened the store door to the jingling of sleighbells, and stopped short when they had taken but a few steps inside. "Here now, this *is* quaint." The spruce from the woods was standing near one of the front windows, partially decorated with popcorn strings and paper figures. On a low table in front of it sat pots of paste, scissors, colored paper, popcorn, thread, and other materials for making decorations. Two small children, too young for school, were diligently snipping and pasting together a haphazard paper chain, as well as snacking surreptitiously from the popcorn bowl. "No one would believe this at home," Mr. Rose said. "Cookies and cider! And a rocking chair!" Someone's grandfather was sitting in the rocker, head on his chest as he snoozed near the warmth of the woodstove.

Catherine wondered what mocking stories Mr. Rose would tell his friends in New York about "quaint" Woodbridge when he returned. Would she have to sit and listen while he imitated Mr. Goodman and his quiet ways to the guests at the dinner table?

A figure approached, and even before he was clear to her eyes, she knew it was Mr. Goodman. "Miss Linwood, Mr. Rose. It's a pleasure to see you," he said, and as he came within her field of vision she saw that he was wearing a grocer's apron over his vest and shirt. His hair flopped down over his forehead as he shook hands with Mr. Rose, and Catherine could not help but think—and feel traitorous and small for the thinking—that Mr. Goodman suffered for standing next to Mr. Rose, tall and elegant in his well-tailored clothes, his wavy hair as black as midnight.

Mr. Goodman looked what he was, a shopkeeper in a town of middling size, shorter and broader than Mr. Rose, his coloring unremarkable. On the surface, there was nothing to set him apart from the dentist three doors down, or one of the innumerable law clerks at the courthouse.

Then his eyes met hers, and in an instant she found what she had seen before: kindness and understanding, humor that crinkled the corners of his eyes, and a quiet happiness in the soft blue depths that drew her with its promise.

"We saw you wave from across the green," Mr. Rose explained, then took a considering look around the front room. "I've never seen a store like this. I almost want to steal the rocker from that old man, and settle down for a nap myself. You should take your business to New York. Such a style of store would make shopping a great deal more pleasant for gentlemen forced to accompany their ladies. You would make a fortune!" Catherine felt certain Mr. Rose was offering false flattery. He preferred his shops to have marble floors, and clerks who fawned.

"Neither I nor my store are made for a large city. The pace here pleases me quite well," Mr. Goodman said, and then added with a straight face, "My only regret is that there is no front porch on which old men can whittle and play checkers in the summer."

Mr. Rose stared at Mr. Goodman for long seconds, and then burst out laughing, slapping him on the shoulder. "There's more going on than meets the eye with you, isn't there?"

Catherine found herself embarrassed for Mr. Rose and Mr. Goodman both, for what they must think of each other. She sensed a wire-thin tension between them, growing stronger by the minute. She shifted in discomfort.

"I am no more than you see," Mr. Goodman said. "I should very much like to continue our conversation, but I'm afraid I must man the counter. Miss Linwood," he said, bowing his head toward her. "Mr. Rose."

"Mr. Goodman," she said in parting, hoping he could see in her eyes that she regretted the subtle incivility of this encounter. The corner of his left eye twitched, in the bare hint of a wink, and she tightened her lips to keep from smiling.

"I'm in need of new gloves," Mr. Rose said to her as Mr. Goodman went back to his counter. "Do you suppose I might find some here that suit me?" he asked, and began to drift toward the glass-topped counters with their drawers of goods beneath.

"I told Mama I would not be gone long," Catherine said. "Would you mind terribly if we returned to the house?" She felt that Mr. Rose was but looking for the chance to find fault with the store, for no preordered gloves would pass the judgment of a man who had his sewn for his hands alone, at a cost ten times that of those to be found here. She could not bear the thought of standing by while he had Mr. Goodman bring out pair after pair, each found wanting, except for maybe one that he would deign to buy, if only to put Mr. Goodman more firmly in the ungentlemanly role of merchant by placing money in his hand.

"As you wish," he agreed amiably, and held out his hand for her to see the small place where the stitching in his glove had come undone. "I'll return later on my own."

She closed her eyes, shamed by her own thoughts about Mr. Rose and his motivations. She could no longer tell what was real, and what was imagined from her own doubts.

They walked back to her house, the sidewalks shoveled clear of snow but slick spots still making her glad to have Mr. Rose's arm for support. She wished she could wear her spectacles, and enjoy the light of the early afternoon sun on the snow.

At her door Mr. Rose stopped her when she would have reached for the latch, gently turning her to face him as they stood on the step. "You know that I care for you, don't you, Catherine?" he said, his gloved fingers touching lightly at the side of her cheek. It was the first time he had used her given name, and she was too struck by the look in his dark eyes to protest the familiarity.

Was this what love looked like? He gazed at her with pleading, as if she were the sun, and all his world would be winter without her. It seemed to her in that moment that despite his wealth and good looks, despite his social standing and charm, he needed her to save him from some dark emptiness hidden deep within.

She took hold of the hand touching her cheek, and squeezed it. "You have become a dear friend," she told him. Propriety limited her to such a gentle declaration, but she did not know if she could in truth have said more. She was thankful she did not have the option, and thus was not forced to reject it with him gazing at her in such a way.

"I brought you a gift," he said, and reached into a pocket inside his coat.

"I could not—"

"Please, Catherine," he said, taking out a small package wrapped in red paper. "Do not decline me this pleasure. Take it."

Reluctantly, she took it from his hand and held it against her chest, feeling that her acceptance was creating a tie by which she did not wish to be bound. "Thank you. Shall I open it now?"

He touched her cheek again, briefly. "Open it later."

She nodded. He smiled, and leaned closer. Her eyes widened and she tensed, sensing that he wanted to kiss her. A moment later he had leaned away again, and then was leaving, touching the brim of his hat to her as he sauntered down the path. She stared after him, and then, not wanting him to turn and catch her doing so, she quickly let herself into the house, shutting the door firmly behind her.

"Catherine, is that you?" Mama called from the small sitting room that served as her office.

"Yes, Mama." She followed her mother's voice, finding her sitting at her desk with various lists and Christmas cards spread over it.

"No matter how much one accomplishes in preparation for Christmas, there is always something more to do," Mama complained as she came into the room. Catherine dropped the gift and her coat on the small settee, then went to the fire and lifted the front of her skirts to let the heat reach her legs. "It seems I spend the entire month of December preparing, and then when it is all over I spend another month cleaning up. It gets worse every year. We didn't have Christmas trees when I was a little girl, you know. Things were much simpler. And now there are cards I must send as well! 'Twas an evil fellow who dreamed that up."

"You must let me help you more."

Mama waved her hand, shooing away her concern. "I have it all organized up here," she said, and tapped her temple. "I have your duties mapped out, do not worry yourself on that score. What's that?" she asked then, spotting the red box.

Catherine let her skirts drop and sat on the settee, lifting the box onto her lap. "A gift from Mr. Rose. He insisted I take it."

"Did he?" Mama said, brows raised suggestively.

Catherine undid the ribbon, pulled off the paper, then opened the flat box inside. "Oh," she said softly. Mama was craning her head trying to see, so she lifted the hair comb out of the box.

"Good gracious," Mama said.

"Indeed." The long comb was carved of tortoise-shell, and set with cabochons of a clear yellow stone. She did not know enough to tell what the stones were, but given Mr. Rose's wealth, she doubted he had bought her polished glass.

"It's lovely, and Mr. Rose has exquisite taste, but Catherine . . ."

"I know, Mama." Although neither Mama nor Aunt Frances had ever expressed any rules of etiquette specifically concerning hair combs, the item was per-ilously close to jewelry, and as such was far too personal a gift. Wearing it in her hair would, in some way, be like inviting Mr. Rose to touch her hair himself. "Should I return it to him?"

Mama was silent, a frown on her forehead as she considered. "He might take that as a rejection of more than just his gift."

"I know." She put the comb back in its box, and set it aside, then slouched down against the settee, her corset holding her torso straight even as her chin doubled, settling atop her chest. She let her hands flop to her sides.

"Catherine?" Mama said, coming over to sit beside her. "Has something changed since last we spoke of Mr. Rose?"

She flexed her hands in a minimal-effort shrug. "I don't know. Perhaps." She frowned, and rolled her head to the side to look at Mama. "I fear he is much more attached to me than I to him. He has put his heart on his sleeve, and I find myself wishing he would put it back inside his vest, out of sight. Why, Mama? Why should I feel that way? He is handsome and charming and rich, and I should be delighted that he has lost his heart to me. Is there something amiss with my own heart, that I do not respond as I should?"

"Perhaps he is not the man for you, and your heart knows it."

"I must be a very spoiled sort of girl if I am not satisfied with the likes of Mr. Rose. Perhaps the next man who catches my interest, I will grow tired of just as quickly. Mr. Rose has everything: Why have I lost my regard for him?"

"Catherine, you cannot force yourself to love someone simply because he seems to everyone else to be a perfect choice. If you do not love the man, then all the good looks and money in the world are not going to make you happy."

"I am not completely certain I could not love him," she said doubtfully. "And I do like him very much. Or I did. I do not understand why I have lately found myself so annoyed by his presence."

Mama patted her on the knee. "I think you will come to the right decision in time concerning Mr. Rose."

"What do you think I should do, Mama?"

Her mother smiled cryptically. "It would be of no use for me to say. Rest assured, when you come to your own conclusion, it will likely be the same I would have advised."

"Sometimes it is comforting being told what to do."

"And when have you ever wanted to do what you were told? No, I shall save myself the trouble and let you figure this out for yourself. If you want the comfort of being told what to do, you may smile prettily while I give you your chores tomorrow."

CHAPTER SIX

"Mr. Rose isn't coming with us, is he?" Amy asked, fastening the side buttons on her skating skirt. They were in their bedroom, dressing for the outdoors.

"I did not invite him, although I think perhaps I should have."

"Why would you have wanted to do *that?*"

"Amy! Because it would have been a small enough gesture, especially as the poor man has been alone here all this week, thanks to me." After giving her the hair comb, Mr. Rose had come daily to the house inviting her to walk or go for a sleigh ride, but each time she had put him off with protestations that there was too much to do in preparation for the holiday. She had not even let him in the house, or offered refreshments, her discomfort with the gift and all it implied making her uncomfortable in his presence, and yet she was too cowardly to be frank about her feelings. After several days of such treatment, he had ceased calling.

For the past few days Catherine had been free of either the sight or sound of Mr. Rose, but with his absence had come a sense of guilt and obligation toward the man, for he had only made the journey to Woodbridge because of her, and had held her in high enough regard to pour out the secrets of his heart. It had been callous of her to brush him off as she had, and with no explanation. She had formerly believed herself a friend to the man, and knew she owed him a face-to-face conversation on what could and could not be between them.

The guilt she felt over her unspoken rejection of Mr. Rose was only compounded by her growing attraction to Mr. Goodman. For the past week her only break from making wreaths, ornaments, centerpieces, and decorated cookies had been walks to Mr. Goodman's store to purchase items that she convinced herself were utterly necessary to the completion of the projects Mama had set for her. She had taken to dawdling there, chatting with him when he was free, or watching him help a customer from the corner of her eye if he was busy, as she pretended to page through the most recent *Harper's Weekly*. Yesterday she had made certain to mention, as if in passing, that she and Amy would be skating today.

She wondered if Mr. Goodman thought her a pest, or at least a trifle strange, to be spending so much time in his store. She was likely making a spectacle of herself to those who noticed her repeated, lingering presence, but Mr. Goodman himself showed no sign of thinking her visits remarkable. He treated her, she supposed, with the same kindness with which he treated everyone. When he looked at her, there was no hint of the needy-dog look that had haunted Mr. Rose's eyes as he declared his love to her. Mr. Goodman was self-contained, and for all that his character was clear to see on his face, his innermost passions were still private.

She pushed her spectacles up her nose. She had started wearing them earlier in the week, and after a few surprised comments, her family had largely forgotten them, acting after a day or two as if she had always worn them. Except for Amy, that is. Catherine thought her sister possessed of an obsessive fascination with the spectacles, and Amy had given a wide-eyed shiver of excitement when Catherine had let her try them on.

"Are you two ready, then?" Papa called up the stairs. "The horse will freeze to death if it has to wait much longer."

Catherine rolled her eyes, and caught Amy doing the same. Papa liked to blame an animal for his impatience or bad temper, whenever the situation allowed.

Papa dropped them from the buggy at the edge of the road, the pond no more than a hundred yards off. A dozen or more townsfolk, children and adults, were already there, skating round the oblong that had been cleared of snow.

They trudged down the path to the side of the pond, and sat upon the logs that had been arranged there for putting on skates. A fire had been built behind one of the other logs, to warm those who either tired or had come only to watch. Catherine searched the skaters for an upright bear, disappointed when there was none to be seen. The disappointment lessened when she took a moment to remind herself what a wonder it was to be able to see the faces of skaters thirty feet away. She was in danger already of taking her new clarity of vision for granted.

"Have I caught you coming or going?" a familiar voice asked, as a bulk of bearskin sat down next to Amy.

"Mr. Goodman!" Amy exclaimed. "We've just arrived. It's been ages since Catherine skated here, you know."

"Has it now?"

" 'Twould be best if you showed her which places to avoid." And then, all innocence, "Is that Becky over there?" she asked, peering across the pond. She finished fastening her skates onto her boots, and stood up. "You don't mind if I go join her, do you, Cath?"

Catherine raised her brows at her. "No, not at all," she said, and Amy skated off.

"Did that wire work as you wished, for the wreaths?" Mr. Goodman asked companionably as he bent down to put on his own skates. It was as if they were simply carrying on where their conversation had left off the day before in the store.

"It was just what I needed, thank you. Papa is using what was left for fastening the candles to the tree." Had Mr. Goodman come to the pond because she had told him she would be here, or would he have come anyway? she wondered.

"I don't suppose you have much opportunity to skate in New York."

"On the contrary, the ponds in Central Park are quite crowded with skaters throughout the winter. They are an especially popular place for courting couples," she said, and to her embarrassment found herself giving him a coy, sideways look.

"Are they?" he said mildly. "I would have to say the same use is made of the pond here." He nodded his head toward the skaters, and following his gaze she saw a young couple, the man taking great care as he guided his companion's efforts upon skates, reaching out to catch her when she seemed in danger of falling. The young woman shrieked and laughed as she stumbled awkwardly about, clinging to her beau's arm.

"I'd wager my best hat that she skates better than she lets on," Catherine said.

Mr. Goodman laughed. "But that's not the point, is it? Shall we?" he asked, standing and holding out his hand to her.

"I warn you now I am not going to slip and fall like that young woman, and neither do I shriek."

"I did not expect that you would, although laughing is not forbidden, so long as it is not at me," he said, giving that smile that turned his average face glowingly handsome, and made her heart contract.

She took his hand, gazing up at him and wishing he showed some sign of wanting to court her. From the way he behaved, she had no reason to think he thought any more of her than that she was the sister of a friend, the daughter of a family he respected, and perhaps a pleasant person with whom to converse. Had he even once looked at her as a potential sweetheart? she wondered.

Looking into his eyes, there was such understanding and interest, even admiration, it hurt to admit that he probably shared the same look with everyone. She knew somehow that he was a man whose kindness would not be limited to those he liked, and it ate at her that she could not tell if there was anything in that look meant especially for her.

"I shall have no limits placed upon my laughter, Mr. Goodman," she said, reaching the edge of the pond and releasing his hand as she glided out onto the ice. "If you fall, I shall laugh myself silly."

"Not if I pull you down with me," he said, and glided toward her.

She shrieked, then dashed away, and felt a flaming heat bloom on her cheeks. Had she truly just shrieked, after saying she would not? Oh, God . . . She glanced over her shoulder, and saw the bear was almost upon her. Another shriek pealed forth, and she dug her skates into the ice, racing to evade him. Her heart was beating wildly, perspiration breaking out, her muscles electrified by the thrill of being chased around the pond.

Will skated after Miss Linwood, the playful fun of pursuing her knocking up against the thought that she might be flirting with him. Might she be? It hardly seemed possible, but . . .

He caught up to her and grabbed her hand, swinging her around. She made another of those laughing shrieks, and he took her other hand as well, swinging her around him in a circle. "Stop! Stop!" she cried, laughing. "I'm going to fall."

He slowed, then brought her to a halt. She swayed, dizzy, and he pulled her closer, her feet motionless as she glided to him. She released his hands and grabbed higher up his arms for support, blinking her warm brown eyes at him as her vertigo passed.

"That was most unfair of you, Mr. Goodman," she said. "If I had fallen, it would not have counted, as it would have been entirely your fault."

"All's fair in love and war," he said, the words out before he could stop them.

She grinned mischievously at him. "And we both know which this is," she said, and skated away before he could respond, leaving him watching dumbly after her.

No, he didn't know which it was, not for her! And did she have any notion of what he felt for her, that it was deeply, desperately love, and not war?

She cast him one backward glance, as if daring him to follow and capture her again.

The shyness that had overcome him upon first meeting her was still with him, making it nearly impossible for him to show her that his interest was more than platonic. His natural reserve, which such a short time ago he had enjoyed, was in this case a torturous barrier that he did not know how to surmount.

The only way to prevent himself from gibbering like an ape in her presence was to pretend to himself that she was already a close friend. When she came to the store, he struggled to shut away his shyness into a dark, locked box, and refused to second-guess his actions and words. He coaxed her into talking about herself and her family's Christmas preparations, and as she talked he gradually forgot about his locked-away shyness. He teased her gently, making her laugh in those rich tones that grabbed at his heart. He helped her to find the goods on her list, discussions of each item wandering off into uncharted realms. The circuitous route of conversation led from ribbons to favorite desserts, from oranges to the time she had climbed Mt. Tom, from cloves to their mutual love of the novels of Wilkie Collins.

There was always one more topic to discuss, one more direction in which to take the conversation, and then she would take a glance at the watch pinned to her breast and give a start, apologizing for keeping him so long from his work. Each extra minute she stayed afterward was a victory, the visible reluctance with which she left him a boost to the morale of his advancing army.

He watched her figure gracefully moving through the other skaters at the opposite end of the pond, pausing briefly to skate a circle around Amy and her friend.

Miss Linwood's visits had given his attachment to her a deeper basis than a pretty face and infectious laugh. Her conversation was informed and perceptive, her mood usually one of quiet merriment. She was vivacious without being vulgar, mischievous without being cruel, intelligent without condescension. His heart had somehow known, at first sight, what it would find in her.

Even with her hints of flirtatious encouragement, though, the thought of openly courting her, exposing his heart for all to see, left him feeling ill. There was something within him that would not permit such a display.

He would not, could not try to persuade her to love him with sweet words and gifts of candy and flowers. He could not call on her, sitting like a lovesick fool in her parlor, while her mother hovered nearby as chaperone. By embarrassing himself, he knew that he would embarrass her, and put in jeopardy any fondness that she held for him. No, it was better to continue his attack of stealth.

"You shall become a snowman if you stand there much longer," Miss Linwood said, skating up beside him and scraping expertly to a stop. She had made the circuit of the pond while he stood frozen, contemplating his adoration of her. It had begun to snow, and glancing down he saw that a fine layer of it covered his coat.

"Of what were you thinking, to transfix you so?" she asked.

"Of how best to catch you, of course," he said, and raised his arms as if to do so. She gasped, and in her haste to back away lost her balance. He moved quickly, doing exactly as he'd said before she could fall. She was a welcome weight in his arms, her cheek pressed to his chest, her hands clinging to the fur of his coat, but he released her as soon as she had regained her feet. He skated away at a gentle pace, and after a moment she followed, gliding easily into place at his side as they circled the pond.

"You tricked me," she accused.

"I did nothing."

"Yes, and it was quite clever of you."

He smiled, but did not answer.

CHAPTER SEVEN

Catherine settled into her seat between Amy and Mr. Rose. They were in the McMahon family's old barn, converted two years ago into the drama club's theater. Doves and chickens were known to roost overhead, and the place would never completely escape the faint scents of its former use, but the fowl had been chased out for this night, and likely no one but Mr. Rose minded the smells of chickens and dust.

"My friends will never believe this," Mr. Rose said, shifting on his hard wooden chair and peering into the raftered gloom.

Catherine felt a spark of irritation invade her good mood. "Are you going to mock my mother's production to them?" she whispered fiercely, casting him a narrow-eyed glare.

"I would never do such a thing!" he exclaimed in a whisper, and grasped her gloved hand in both of his. "Catherine, you know I would not," he said, and gave her the wounded look that turned her stomach more each time she saw it.

"This play means a great deal to her," she said, and gently pulled her hand away.

"I know it does. And to you, too, so you may rest assured that I will applaud mightily at the final curtain."

Even those words annoyed her, sounding to her as if

he doubted the play could possibly merit such grand regard. She wished she had not invited him along, but guilt had made her do so. After returning from skating, she had found a note waiting from him, explaining that he had fallen ill with some manner of ague and was only now near recovery, and that he was more sorry than he could say that he had been unable to call on her those past several days.

She felt it was too sad for anyone to be ill and alone during the Christmas season, as he had been. And so, the invitation to the play. He had accompanied her, her father, and Amy to the barn theater.

She hoped for some point later in the evening to have a chance to speak privately with him. It was easy enough to see that he had not been well, although he claimed now to be fully back to health. His skin was colorless, his eyes bloodshot, and when he moved she sometimes caught a strange scent wafting from him. A devil in the back of her mind wondered if he had spent those days of "illness" drinking himself prone. She quashed the thought as unworthy.

The last of the audience straggled in, finding places in the seats that remained. The hard wooden chairs sat on risers that thumped hollowly under their feet, and the rustling and whispering began to settle as the lantern lights were lowered. When all had quieted to an expectant silence, and all eyes and ears waited for the curtain to rise, there came a deep, gutteral cry from off-stage: "Bah, humbug!"

Catherine put her hand to her lips, smothering the laugh that wanted to slip forth as she recognized Mr. Goodman's voice under the grouching exclamation of Scrooge. The curtain lifted upon the stark scene of Ebenezer Scrooge's counting house, the bare furniture and the meager coal scuttle, and she joined the others in applauding a welcome to the two actors sitting at their worktables.

Catherine rummaged in her reticule for her spectacles, slipping them on in the safety of the dark. She'd leave them on, too, and nevermind what Mr. Rose might think. She ought to have more backbone than to let his likely opinion of a pair of spectacles alter her behavior. If he saw fit to mock them, well, then, let him, she thought, lifting her chin and giving a little sniff. Perhaps he would find them so unattractive he would go back to New York and leave her to enjoy Christmas with her family in peace, with her having to say nary a word.

Mr. Goodman was all but unrecognizable in his costume, his hair colored gray and lines of miserliness drawn into his cheeks and under his eyes. He played the role of Scrooge with enthusiasm, being as sour and bad-natured as Dickens could have wished, if not more so.

Scrooge's nephew had come into the counting house, and for some minutes had been arguing cheerily with Scrooge about the worth of Christmas. "So 'a Merry Christmas,' Uncle!"

"Good afternoon!" Mr. Goodman barked, for the third time trying to dismiss the happy man.

"And 'a Happy New Year'!" the nephew gaily chirped, to the laughter of the audience. Catherine thought she even heard a reluctant snort of amusement from Mr. Rose.

"Good afternoon!" again, from Scrooge.

Catherine caught Amy's eye, sharing a smile with her. "He's good," Amy whispered. Catherine nodded. Seeing Mr. Goodman onstage, even playing the part of a despicable miser, had the curious effect of magnifying his attraction. She felt a queer sense of possessive pride over him.

The play progressed, flour-faced ghosts arrived and went, and then Mama was on stage, as Mrs. Cratchit serving the Christmas goose and pudding to her family as Scrooge and the ghost of Christmas Present watched from the side. Catherine and Amy both giggled to see Mama in costume, and then Bob Cratchit made his toast.

"A Merry Christmas to us all, my dears. God bless us!"

The Cratchit family repeated the toast, and into the following silence came Tiny Tim's voice, "Dog bless us everyone!"

Mama stared wide-eyed at the little boy, as did the rest of the Cratchit family. Scrooge winced in sympathy. The little boy's face turned scarlet, as he realized what he'd said.

"Mr. Goodman!" Mr. Cratchit said, trying to gloss over the boy's error by hurriedly raising his glass in the next toast.

Mr. Goodman, startled at hearing his own name on-stage, uttered an audible, "Eh?"

Suspicious coughing sounds rippled through the audience.

"Mr. Scrooge! Mr. Scrooge, I mean to say," Cratchit corrected, waving his glass and spilling his drink over both his hand and Tiny Tim, who looked on the verge of tears at this further insult to his pride. "I'll give you Mr. Scrooge, the Bounder of the Beast!"

"The *founder* of the *feast*, indeed!" Mama cried, to more muffled coughing. "I wish I had him here," Mama continued. "I'd give him a beast of my mind—*piece* of my mind, damn it!-" Mama swore, as the Cratchit family bowed their heads, their shoulders shaking, "—to feast upon, and I hope he'd have a good appetite for it!"

"My dear, the children!" Bob Cratchit reproached softly, covering Tiny Tim's ears, his face as tenderly disappointed as a saint's. "Christmas day."

Hoots and snorts of laughter burst out, both onstage and in the house. Catherine, Amy, and Papa joined in, safe under the cover of the crowd from the wrathful glare Mama sent out into the darkened theater.

"It should be Christmas day, I am sure," Mama said with vehemence and a withering look cast over the audience as she carried on with her speech. By force of will she seemed to settle them all, although Catherine heard a whispered, "*Piece* of my mind, damn it!" behind her, amidst shushing and giggling. She bit her own lips to keep from joining in.

The play made it safely to its conclusion with only minor mishaps, the cast all assembling onstage as a narrator read out the ending of the story, explaining how Scrooge became a good man, who kept Christmas well and avoided spirits ever after. Tiny Tim stepped forward and with extreme care enunciated the final line. "God bless us, everyone!"

Tiny Tim's real parents, in the audience, leaped up and shouted "Hurrah!" and applauded wildly as the curtain came down. Catherine joined them, and then the whole audience was on its feet, clapping and cheering as the curtain came up again upon an empty stage. The actors re-emerged, one by one, accepting their applause with great grins upon their faces.

When Mr. Goodman came out, the applause turned into as much of a roar as could be gotten from a crowd of such small size, and Catherine found herself stomping on the echoing risers in her approbation, and then she yanked off a glove and stuck two fingers in her mouth to give a piercing whistle.

"Good Lord, Catherine, control your enthusiasm!" Mr. Rose hissed beside her.

"Control your*self*, Mr. Rose!" she snapped back, and gave another whistle, twice as long as the first.

Mr. Goodman put his hand to his mouth, then threw a kiss to the audience, his eyes meeting Catherine's as he did so. She laughed, delighted, and was aware of Mr. Rose stiffening beside her.

The applause finally quieted, and the curtain fell for the final time. The lights were raised, and people began to leave, slowly, mingling near the exit and in front of the stage, talking about the performance as they inched their way outside. Some, like Catherine and her group, lingered inside, waiting for a cast member. Someone raised the curtain again, and a crew member appeared with a broom, quickly sweeping the stage and then disappearing behind the panels that formed the rear of the stage.

"She told me earlier she would need about fifteen minutes to change and put away her things," Papa said.

Mr. Rose touched Catherine's arm, lightly, and bent near her. "I'm going out for a breath of air. Would you care to join me?"

She shook her head, not looking at him, and pulled away just enough that his hand dropped from her sleeve. It would be a good chance to speak with him, but she was in no temper to do so civilly, after his attempt to shush her applause.

Mr. Rose hesitated, the answer plainly not what he had expected, then turned and pushed through the remaining crowd to the exit. Catherine saw that Papa was watching her, and she gave him a forced smile, trying to hide what she was feeling. He was usually obtuse to what the females of his family felt, but he had that look that said this was one of those rare occasions where his intuition and observations had come together to form a correct conclusion.

"Shall we take a look at the props?" Catherine asked Amy, for distraction. It was bad of her to snub Mr. Rose, after she had invited him here tonight, and yet she could not seem to help behaving coldly toward him.

She and Amy climbed the two steps up onto the stage, and inspected the furnishings of Mr. Scrooge's counting house. They could hear the excited chatter of the cast and crew behind the panels, as they changed clothes in the converted stalls and put all in order for tomorrow's matinee performance.

A few minutes later the cast began to depart, their earlier air of excitement subdued now as tiredness took hold. When Mr. Goodman came out, Catherine slid off Bob Cratchit's tall stool where she had been sitting, playing out the clerk's role to Amy's amusement. "You were wonderful, Mr. Goodman, wonderful!" she said. "I should never have thought you would make such a perfect Scrooge if I had not seen it for myself."

"That is high praise, coming from one who has likely seen the best actors that London has to offer."

"High praise, but deserved." She smiled up at him, her twinges of guilt about Mr. Rose vanquished for the moment by the warmth of Mr. Goodman's presence. "You seemed to be enjoying yourself onstage."

He ducked his head slightly, the lock of hair falling over his forehead. "I am surprised myself by my enjoyment. Except for in the theater, I do not like to be the center of attention. It is as if there is a side to me that only comes out upon a stage."

"Does that mean you aren't quite the reserved, noble man you seem?" Catherine asked in a purr.

He shot her a quick look, one that asked if that question was meant to be as flirtatious as it sounded. "We are none of us exactly as we might seem, nor are we as we might wish," he said.

She was about to ask him what he would change about himself—she could imagine nothing in him that was in need of alteration—when she felt a hand on her arm. It was Mr. Rose. She had not heard him come back in, so absorbed was she in Mr. Goodman.

"Come, Catherine," Mr. Rose ordered, and started to pull her away. "It is time you went home."

She jerked her arm out from under his hand. "Mr. Rose, I am not yet ready to depart," she said, and looked up at him from behind her spectacles. She did not like what she saw. Every suspicion she had had of his character was written more plainly on his features tonight than ever before. There was something wild and unstable in his eyes, something desperate and needy that repelled her. She sniffed the air, catching again that strange scent coming off him. "Mr. Rose," she asked as quietly as she could. "Have you been drinking?"

He took her arm again, pulling her away from Mr. Goodman and leaning down to whisper at her. "If I have, whose fault is that?" Mr. Rose said, his breath making her step back. "You have been playing games with me, Catherine, first enticing me to follow you to this backwater town, then snubbing my attentions and trying to make me jealous by making eyes at that sorry shopkeeper. And what manner of affectation are *these*?" he asked, and pulled the spectacles from her face. "I don't know what joke you're making, except on yourself by wearing them."

She couldn't speak for astonishment at his temerity, and then her chest filled with air as that astonishment gave way to hot, poisonous fury. "How *dare* you, Mr. Rose!" she accused, her voice louder than she had intended. She could not recall ever being so incensed, and in a distant way was astounded by the rising, angry pitch of her own voice. "You have no right, *no right*, to lay your hands upon my person so! You have *no right* to blame me for your drunkenness, and you *certainly* have no right to address me by my Christian name. *Mr.* Rose." Her next words were exactly enunciated. "Have I made myself clear?"

"You've made yourself clear enough, and shown your true colors, too," Mr. Rose said as angrily back. "Be careful, Mr. Goodman," he called past Catherine's shoulder, "if you allow such a one as this to lead you a merry chase. She has the heart of a whore, and won't be happy until she sees you grovelling in the dust for her favors."

Catherine heard her father give an angry shout, but it was Mr. Goodman who was first to respond, coming immediately to her defense. "No one may speak of Miss Linwood in such terms, sir," Mr. Goodman said in a steady, hard voice. "No one. You will apologize to her and to her family."

"Or what?" Mr. Rose sneered. "You'll make a play at chivalry and hit me? That will do nothing to change the truth."

"If you do not apologize," Mr. Goodman said lowly, "then we will all know that you are no gentleman, and a disgrace to your family's good name."

"No *gentleman*? Ha! And who are you to be judging who is and is not a gentleman? A shopkeeper! A peddler!"

"Do not make this more difficult than it has to be," Mr. Goodman warned.

"You want a fight, do you? You think you can best me?" Mr. Rose tossed Catherine's spectacles to the side, where they landed under a worktable and skidded along the floorboards. "I'll show you what gentlemen are made of." He lowered his head and charged.

Mr. Goodman stepped easily aside, and Mr. Rose, deprived of his target, stumbled past, unable to stop before running crown-first into a supporting post of the loft. He crashed down upon Scrooge's coal scuttle with a clamoring of metal and lay still.

Mr. Goodman bent and picked up the spectacles in the following silence, and wiped them carefully with his kerchief before handing them back to Catherine. "I'm terribly sorry about all this," he said. "I'll take him back to the inn."

"Oh no, Mr. Goodman, I couldn't ask that of you," Catherine said, and found to her surprise that she was shaking. She did not know if it was her own anger, Mr. Rose's unkind words, or the narrowly averted violence that had her trembling so.

"You do not need to ask. The man had too much to drink, and was not in his right senses. Please, try to forget what he said." He met her eyes, and the calm strength there helped to steady her, making her feel as if he held her safe in his arms. Her breathing evened out.

"You are being too kind," Papa said, coming up onto the stage and staring down at the sprawled form of Mr. Rose. "He deserves to be dragged to a snowbank and left there 'till spring."

"He's not worth the worry."

"Eh?" Papa asked.

"Of being hung for murder," Mr. Goodman clarified. "It would spoil my appetite for Christmas dinner. I do not think he is worth that."

Papa laughed. Amy went to Mr. Rose and glared down at him, with a look in her eye that said she'd very much like to kick him. Catherine felt her mother's hand on her shoulder. "It's time to go home," Mama said.

Amy came over and took Catherine's hand, squeezing it in silent support. The gesture put her on the verge of tears. The three of them left, leaving Papa and Mr. Goodman to deal with the unconscious Mr. Rose.

CHAPTER EIGHT

"Good gracious, Robert, what did you put in this?" Catherine asked her brother, after taking a sip of his eggnog. It was proudly displayed in an enormous crystal bowl surrounded by cuttings of holly, in the center of a lace-covered table. She would not have been surprised to see blue flames rising from the heavy yellow drink, for certainly there was more of the *nog* to it than the *egg*.

"I made it according to George Washington's own recipe. My friend from Virginia sent it to me. He says his family has made it this way for nigh on a century."

Catherine took another sip, her head filling with the fumes of brandy, whiskey, and God knew what else. "Then I am surprised they survived this long, and surprised as well that we were not left under British rule!"

Her brother laughed and filled a cup for another of his guests. He and his wife, Mary, had opened their house to friends and family for Christmas Eve, and the spacious rooms were crowded with New Englanders who had suspicions there was something irreligious in having a spirited Christmas party, but were reluctantly enjoying themselves nonetheless.

Catherine wandered over to where a fiddler was playing lively music, to which a few couples self-consciously danced. Children raced about from room to room, playing their own games, and in another room the more sedate sat and conversed near the tree, its candles lit and carefully watched by more than one eye, lest fire should break out.

Even as she watched guests and conversed with friends, part of her was constantly searching for Mr. Goodman. There was a small commotion at the door, and Catherine's eyes went to the figure entering there. Disappointment pulled at the muscles of her face when she saw the formal, well-tailored coat, but then the man turned and it was the face she sought above the wool muffler, bearskin nowhere in evidence.

After that embarrassing spectacle at the barn, she had become leery of any move that might be considered forward or flirtatious on her part. She did not want anyone thinking she had the heart of a whore, and so although every muscle urged her to go and greet him she checked the impulse, holding back with a shyness that was new and painful.

She stood half-hidden beside a potted palm, watching as the maid took Mr. Goodman's outerwear, and Robert went to welcome his friend. She willed him to look at her, to see her, and smile and come join her. She willed him to take her hand and lead her out to dance; to stand close and smile down into her eyes; to hold her hand against his chest and ask her not to return to New York, but to stay here with him, forever, as his wife and the woman with whom he would share his bed.

He looked her way, and their eyes locked. She knew that all she felt was writ plainly in her eyes. "*Heart of a whore*," she heard Mr. Rose say in her head. She glanced away and to the side, her lids lowered, and then long seconds later she looked toward him again. The entryway was empty.

The heat of embarrassment touched her cheeks. For all that Mr. Goodman had defended her in the theater, perhaps he felt that she had deserved Mr. Rose's insults. Part of her believed he would be right to do so.

Miss Linwood was even lovelier than the first time he had seen her, Will thought as she met his eyes from across the room. Her gaze was intense upon him, hungry and yet still. The dark green fronds of a palm formed tiger stripes across her breast, bringing to mind a great cat lurking in the jungle. She was wearing that same burgundy dress he had so admired before, its dark folds inviting touch like an animal's pelt.

She broke the stare, suddenly glancing away in a bashful gesture that was not in character with the woman he knew. It took only a moment to understand that it was the altercation with Mr. Rose that had done this to her, that had made her doubt her natural instincts.

For causing that moment of Miss Linwood's self-doubt, Will would gladly stuff Mr. Rose through a hole in the ice of the skating pond. He had wanted to do much worse to the man at the theater, but the stricken look on Miss Linwood's face had stopped him. Further violence would have served only to distress her more. No, far better to let Mr. Rose lie before her in his drunken stupor, knocked senseless of his own doing, and then gallantly volunteer to remove the offal from her sight.

"Will, you must say hello to Mr. Abernathy," Robert was saying, and pulled him away before he could protest.

Mr. Abernathy, the elderly president of a local bank, began yammering at him in words he could not understand. He saw the man's mouth moving, bits of spittle on his lips, but it was just noise to him, his thoughts obsessed with Miss Linwood and her hungry gaze. Countless impatient minutes went by as he sought holes in the conversation through which to bolt, and then at last he was free. He went in search of her.

She was no longer near the palm, nor was she in the crowd around the table with its great vat of eggnog. He went from room to room, searching, replying to the greetings of others with only a fraction of his attention. Where had she gone?

"Miss Linwood," a hoarse, low voice said behind her.

She turned, happily expectant, then stepped back when she came face-to-face with Mr. Rose. "What are you doing here?" she exclaimed, and felt a sudden queasiness in her stomach, her heart beating rapidly in what was almost fear. She was in a hallway, having just come from the washroom, and at the moment there was no one else about.

"Please, let me apologize," he said, grasping her hand. "There is so much I need to say to you."

"We have nothing left to say," she said, trying to control her voice.

"Please. Hear me out." He squeezed her hand, his eyes pleading. "You can give me that much."

She didn't want to talk to him, didn't want to be in his presence at all, nor did she want Mr. Goodman to come upon them together and think worse of her, but Mr. Rose did not look like he would be easily sent away.

"Please," he said again.

"Not here," she said brusquely. It was not physical harm she feared from him, but another raw, emotional confrontation. If it could not be avoided, at least this time it could happen in private. After a quick moment of thought she led him down a different, unlit hall to the sunroom that had been shut up for the winter, its wicker furniture covered in sheets. She could see her breath on the cold air, the room dark and forlorn out of season, illuminated only by the blue reflections of moonlight off the snow outside.

"Miss Linwood—"

"Mr. Rose," she interrupted fiercely, gathering her courage and going on the offensive. "I thought I made myself quite plain in the letter I sent to you with the hair comb. Our acquaintance is at an end."

"My behavior was unforgiveable, I know that, but I am asking you to please hear me out. Please. Miss Linwood, you cannot fail to know how I feel about you. I love you. There! I confess it! I love you, and I cannot live without you. If you were to deprive me of all hope of making you my wife, I think I should have to kill myself."

Catherine looked at him in horror. "You don't mean that. You can't!"

"But I do." He dropped down to one knee, and taking her hand began to smother it in kisses.

"Stop it, Mr. Rose! At once!" she ordered, jerking her hand from his grasp.

"Marry me, Catherine!"

"No." There seemed no other way to say it, no way in which to soften her answer. She was completely repulsed by him. Even his drunkenness had been better than this. "I will not marry you, and I shall never change my mind."

"I cannot live without you," he pleaded, tears in his eyes, his hands grasping at her skirts. "I'll kill myself."

She was furious that he would try to lay that guilt upon her. "I will not accept responsibility for your actions, Mr. Rose," she said harshly, trying to hide the quavering of her voice, hoping that her words were true. "You will leave this house, and never speak to me again. Good-bye." She yanked her skirts out of his hold and left the room, slamming the door behind her against the sound of his sobs.

In the empty hall she suddenly had to lean against the wall, her knees shaking and her breath short, nausea roiling her stomach. The muted sobbing quieted, and then she heard the outside door to the sunroom open and then swing shut, and she knew Mr. Rose had at last gone. She closed her eyes and listened gratefully to the silence.

Minutes passed, and then she heard a concerned male voice, its timbre familiar and welcome. "Miss Linwood, are you unwell?"

Catherine opened her eyes, and saw Mr. Goodman silhouetted against the faint light from the end of the hall. She released a shaky breath. "No, just a bit shaken. Mr. Rose was here. He asked me to marry him, then threatened to kill himself if I refused." She felt more than saw the sudden tension her words created in him, and quickly added, "I turned him down, and he left. He offered me neither insults nor harm." And then, the guilt she had said she would not accept crept in. "Do you think he will do himself an injury?"

Whatever feelings he was experiencing, Mr. Goodman held them under tight rein, asking only, "Was he drunk?"

"I don't think so."

"Then he should be out of danger's way for the moment. I'll send word to the inn to have someone keep an eye on him." She heard him take a breath, his hold on his temper apparently not quite as solid as she had assumed. "That was an unkind, manipulative thing of him to say to you, and I hope you do not allow it to trouble your thoughts. Mr. Rose is responsible for his own actions, and you are in no way to blame for whatever he does or does not do."

She touched her temple, brushing back a wisp of hair, feeling the dampness of perspiration on her brow. She tried to meet Mr. Goodman's eyes in the dim light, still not as certain of her innocence as she wished to be. "Have I behaved badly toward him?"

He came closer, to where she could make out his features. His expression showed no hint of judgment, his eyes telling her that he understood what she was feeling. "You did not behave badly. There is no way to save a heart from being crushed, when you cannot return its regard."

Did he mean the he would have to do the same to her? She gazed intently into his eyes, and suddenly knew it was not so, however much her fears may have tried to persuade her otherwise. This warmth in his eyes was meant for her alone, speaking of a desire that matched that in her own heart. A tingling awareness of his nearness ran across her skin. She wanted to touch him, and wanted him to touch her. She wanted to feel his lips pressed against hers, and his arms coming around her, enveloping her in the quiet strength that hid beneath his humble exterior.

She swayed toward him, one hand rising to lie against the broad warmth of his chest. He inclined his head to where their lips were a bare inch apart, her breath mingling with his. She caught a faint scent of spices and soap from his skin, and felt his heart beating beneath her palm.

They held the pose for an eternal moment, their breathing the only sound in the dark corridor, and then he reached up and clasped her hand on his chest, bringing it down. "Your family will be wondering where you've gone off to," he said, drawing back.

She ducked her head, disappointment cold upon her skin. At his prompting she slid her hand up to the crook of his arm, and let him lead her back to the party.

It was almost 2:00 A.M. and still Catherine could not sleep. Amy breathed heavily in her bed, only her face visible under the mound of covers, and the house was quiet. Despite the late hour, despite the eggnog from earlier in the evening, and despite the questionable relief of having made a final, irrevocable, face-to-face rejection of Mr. Rose, she could not rest.

It was not the anticipation of Christmas morning that had her tossing and turning. It was that long moment in the hall, when she had been on the verge of kissing Mr. Goodman. He had known what she wanted, and had wisely, honorably, chosen against stealing a kiss from her in the dark hallway of her brother's house, while she was yet vulnerable from the trouble with Mr. Rose.

Damn Mr. Goodman, and his noble heart. She had wanted that kiss.

And what if she had gotten it? What if she had squeezed a declaration of love from Mr. Goodman, what would she have done then? Would she truly be willing to stay in Woodbridge, to be Mr. Goodman's wife, if he would have her?

In a heartbeat.

The opera, the symphony, the theater, the artists and the writers, the bustle and sense of something new around the next corner that was New York; all that she would gladly give up, perhaps even without Mr. Goodman to go to. She was weary of New York, and the lifestyle in which she did not fit except with constant effort. She preferred unsophisticated Woodbridge, where her awkward watercolor could hang upon a wall without comment. She could be herself here, and most especially she could be herself with Mr. Goodman.

She heard a faint jingling of sleigh bells, *jing a jing a jing,* coming from outside, breaking into her thoughts. A reluctant smile sneaked its way onto her lips. Santa?

Jing a jing a jing.

Who would be out at this hour? She slipped from under the covers, and wrapping her robe around her against the chill, went to the window, picking up her spectacles on the way. She put them on, and moved aside the curtain to look at the moonlit night.

A sleigh was coming down the middle of the icy lane, drawn by two bay horses. As she watched, it came to a halt and a figure in a bulky bearskin coat hopped out, rummaged in the bags of goods piled in back, and then came toward her house.

She dropped the curtain, heart thumping, standing frozen for a moment, and then she threw off her robe and dashed for her clothes, cursing under her breath at all the fastenings it took to get them on.

Corsetless, her skirt half unbuttoned and her coat covering the equally undone state of her bodice, she dashed down the stairs in her socks and sat on the seat by the door, shoving her feet into her boots, wrapping the laces several times around her ankles in lieu of lacing them. She was out the door a second later, taking only a moment to notice the two small packages on the front step, running carefully on the icy ground to where the sleigh now waited, several houses down.

She reached it just as Mr. Goodman returned from another house. He stopped in his tracks when he saw her. Her breath was coming in gasps after her slippery sprint, and she hung onto the side of his sleigh.

"Miss Linwood!" he whispered loudly, "What in God's name are you doing out here?"

"As if you should be the one asking me such a question, Mr. Goodman! What are *you* doing out here, is more to the point," she whispered back, as conscious as he of how easily their voices would carry in the night.

"It's a secret. No one was supposed to see me."

"You might have thought to take the bells off your horses, if you were so anxious to go undetected."

"I did," he said with exaggerated patience.

"For heaven's sake, I heard them from my room," she said, moving toward the horses to point out his obvious error. She squinted, then moved her hands over the leather harnesses. There were no bells.

He raised his brows at her from over the backs of the horses.

"But . . . I *heard* them," she said. "Did someone else go by?"

"You're the only moving creature I've seen. You know, Miss Linwood, you have an uncanny knack for catching me at tasks where I would prefer to remain undiscovered."

"Poor you," she said, and gave him a mock pout. She climbed into the sleigh.

"Miss Linwood! Come down from there!"

"I am going with you. I couldn't sleep, and this promises to be much more entertaining than staring at the ceiling all night."

He hesitated a moment longer, then climbed up next to her and took the reins, setting the horses in motion with a light slap. "I'm going to be out all night, you know. You're going to get very cold."

She found the buffalo skin that was shoved to one side in a crumpled heap, and shook it out. "I shall be quite comfortable." As the horses trotted down the center of the street, it began to snow, light feathery flakes that fell gently around them. "Look, it's snowing," she said, then cocked her head to the side, frowning. "It's odd to see that, with the moon so bright."

He looked up at the night sky with her, to where the sky was nearly free of clouds. "Perhaps it is being blown off the trees and rooftops."

"Mmm," she said doubtfully. There was no wind.

The snow, as if possessed of a mind of its own, followed them in gently gusting flurries as they made their rounds of the town, and traveled out to the neighborhoods where the mill workers lived with their large families, Mr. Goodman stopping at houses where there were children and leaving gifts upon the doorstep. The snow swirled behind them as they drove out to farms, and it covered their tracks when they left, removing all traces of their passing. At the far edge of her hearing, Catherine thought she could detect the faint jingling of sleigh bells.

Catherine soon took the reins, leaving Mr. Goodman free to dig in his sacks for the right gift for the next house, and she did not feel the cold. They worked in silent concert, anticipating the needs and movements of each other. The hours of the night seemed to stretch into infinity, even as they flew by. It should not have been possible to make as many stops as they did, Catherine knew, yet somehow there was always time for one more, until the sacks were empty and the first faint light of dawn reached into the sky.

With dawn turning quickly to morning, she handed the reins to Mr. Goodman and he drove her back to her house. He helped her down from the sleigh, and led her up the walk to her front steps. During the night they had said nothing of what was in their hearts, and yet Catherine felt that an understanding had been silently reached, that during their early morning ride a bond had been formed between them that was meant to last a lifetime.

"Mr. Goodman," she said softly, looking up at him, as he paused with her atop the steps.

Silence held them, and Catherine felt a magnetic pull as he looked at her, the corners of his eyes crinkling, the soft blue loving and accepting her exactly as she was. He bent his head down and his lips gently took hers. She closed her eyes, feeling the warmth of his kiss move through her. His mouth moved over hers, nipping and caressing, and she happily answered with caresses of her own, her arms going around his neck as he in turn held her close, exploring her mouth, her cheeks, her brow.

She did not know how many ages had passed when she came to her senses, her face tucked into his neck as he held her, his cheek resting atop her head. She blinked and pulled back, still slightly dazed. He had the hint of a smile playing on his lips.

"Mistletoe," he said.

She blinked at him, and he nodded upward. She followed his gaze, to the ball of mistletoe she had forgotten, hanging above the steps.

"I should have brought you here sooner," she said.

Will smiled, watching the snow settle on Catherine's hair, still not quite believing that he had won her heart.

"Just what did you leave for us?" she asked, bending down to pick up the packages he had left in front of her door. "One for Amy, I see, and look here," she said, grinning mischievously, "one for me."

"You can open it now, if you like." It was a small, portable set of watercolors meant for use outdoors. Amy had once told him that Catherine liked to paint, and he knew she'd done the touching portrait of her grandmother, in the parlor.

She tore the paper off, revealing a flat box covered in pale, silvery-blue silk. She froze for a moment, then touched the silk and glanced up at him with a knowing look.

He was too stunned to speak. That was not the box he had wrapped yesterday afternoon. He had never seen it before, and yet that had been his wrapping paper, and his handwriting addressing the box to Miss Linwood.

She lifted off the lid, and there in the center of a bed of white satin sat a platinum ring. "Oh, Mr. Goodman," she sighed, and lifted the ring from its bed. It was studded randomly with tiny diamonds. "Snowflakes," she said, and there were tears shimmering in her eyes.

He bent closer, and saw that indeed there were small snowflakes etched into the surface of the platinum, between the glittering diamonds. It was a ring he would have chosen for her if he had had the chance, after their magical sleigh ride tonight.

She pulled the glove off her left hand, and then held out her hand, fingers parted. He stared at that white hand, and at the ring she held in the other. There seemed only one thing to say, only one thing to do.

"Will you marry me, Miss Linwood?" he asked, his voice gone suddenly hoarse.

"Do you love me?"

"Beyond words."

"Then yes, Mr. Goodman, I will marry you," she said, and a tear like crystal ran down her cheek. "For I love you, too."

He took the ring and placed it upon her finger as the snow continued to fall, soft and pure as the feathers from an angel's wings. She threw her arms around him, and he closed his eyes in thanksgiving to whatever heavenly force had put that blue box and ring inside his wrapping paper.

He held her, and in the distance he heard the faint, magical jingling of sleigh bells.

VICTORIA ALEXANDER

Promises to Keep

This story is dedicated to my dad,
who taught me to believe.

December 24, 1996

This was absurd. Ridiculous. If anyone spotted her here they'd lock her up and throw away the key. She shifted her weight impatiently from one foot to the other and summoned the composure born of a lifetime of wheeling and dealing in a man's world to keep her face expressionless, cool, and controlled.

The line in front of her proceeded at an agonizingly slow pace, feeding the joyous excitement of the youngsters before her and increasing her own sense of foolishness and embarrassment and, yes, perhaps a touch of fear. She was unaccustomed to lines, to waiting even a minute for what she wanted. And she was not used to fear.

The line moved ahead one space. Tension tightened her stomach. Did all women in their seventies act with this odd disregard for sense and sensibility? Did the realization that one was closer to the end of life than the beginning somehow trigger impetuous fits of irrational behavior? Was she succumbing to some irreversible geriatric disease? Dementia? Or worse? Or was she simply, finally, taking a hard look at a long life and finding the assets far overshadowed by the deficits?

Mothers with bright-eyed, stuffy-nosed charges in tow eyed her with mingled caution and curiosity. She ignored the impulse to return their speculative gazes with

the scathing, superior glare that had put many a recalci-
trant employee or bull-headed business rival firmly in
his place and instead drew a deep, steadying breath.

The line progressed. Her firm step belied the anger
spiraling within her. How dare these women stare at
her with such impertinence as if she were a doddering
old fool? Obviously these housewives and baby factories had no idea of who she was. Or rather, she corrected to herself, who she had once been.

Absently she stepped forward, her thoughts far from
the lush department store surroundings. Katherine Bedford had been a name in the world of business long before these women were born. In a day and age when
most women in the corporate arena had taken dictation
and the word "career" was synonymous with "husband
hunting" she had parlayed a tiny, regional company into
an international conglomerate. And eventually sold it
for millions. Her picture once graced the cover of *Time*.

"Ma'am?"

Her attention snapped to the man seated before her.
In spite of his red suit, masses of white, curly hair and
snowy beard, the face confronting her was that of a
young man in his thirties, no more.

Her heart sank. This was simply another department store Santa. A seasonal worker. A temporary employee. There was no magic here. Still . . .

She squared her shoulders and trapped his gaze with
hers. "I'm here to ask for my gift."

"Lady." The Santa's gaze slid to the teenage elf
standing off to one side in a silent plea for help. The
girl, who obviously would be more at home in a T-shirt
and jeans than elf ware, shrugged as if to say he was on
his own. "Lady," he said again.

She stepped closer and clenched her teeth. "Please."

Confusion colored the Santa's face. "I . . ." His voice lowered. "I'm just here for the kids."

Katherine bit back an irritated retort, annoyed more at herself than at him. This was a foolish, futile, last-ditch attempt to salvage something she'd lost long ago. To change what couldn't be changed. Perhaps she was in her dotage after all. Even so, she had come this far. Katherine Bedford never gave up on anything without a fight.

She leaned forward until her face was just inches from his and stared into uneasy, pale blue eyes. "Once, you offered me a gift, a Christmas present. And I didn't take it."

"Lady, I . . ." He hesitated and a subtle change washed through his eyes. They deepened, darkened to the hue of blue-black midnight. The shade of a winter evening. The color of Christmas Eve.

"You said you didn't need it." His voice came richer, wise and intense.

Her breath caught in her throat. The world around her, the line of children, the gaudy retail decorations, the junior elf all faded. She couldn't tear her gaze from his. She didn't want to.

"I was wrong," she said simply.

Compassion gentled his voice. "It's too late now, you know."

"Is it?" She fought back a rising sense of desperation. "Why?"

"You've lived your life. Made your choices." He raised his shoulders slightly in a gesture of inevitability. "You can't go back."

"You promised me a gift," she said, stubbornly refusing to succumb to sheer panic and outright failure. She was so close.

He studied her for a long, silent moment. "What do you want, Katie?"

Katie. No one had called her Katie in longer than she could remember. No one would have dared. Hope surged through her.

"Katie?"

"I want"—the words tumbled out of their own accord—"I want a second chance."

"A second chance?" Amusement danced in his eyes. "And do you deserve a second chance?"

Long years of ruthless deals and hardheaded decisions flashed through her mind. A lifetime of ambition and success. A lifetime alone.

"No," she said simply.

He laughed, a deep, genuine ho-ho-ho that somehow lifted her spirit and renewed her soul. "You never were a liar, Katie, I'll grant you that."

"I just thought . . . I had hoped . . ." She stared, speechless, unable to recall the last time, if ever, she had been at a loss for words. "You did promise."

He lifted a bushy white brow. "Santa always keeps his promises."

"Excuse me, ma'am."

Katherine shot the elf an angry glare.

"The other children are waiting," the teen said in that self-important way of people who abruptly rise to a position of power.

Katherine's gaze snapped back to the Santa. He shook his head as if waking from a dream.

"I am sorry, lady," he said, his eyes again pale, his voice immature and ordinary. "I just work here."

She stared for a moment, then nodded abruptly and turned, her position at once taken by an eager child.

She stepped away briskly, slowed, turned, and studied the scene.

Santa sat on his throne, children lined before him, a cheery elf by his side. Swags of red and gold cascaded around him and billowed above the aisles of the posh store. The final frenzied day of Christmas shopping was in high gear with only a few hours left to go. Crowds of last-minute gift seekers scurried past with expressions of panic or tired satisfaction. Had nothing changed at all?

Or had everything?

She walked through the quiet house and paused for a moment to listen to the sound of silence, of emptiness. Where was everyone? Of course, she chided herself, the staff was gone, given the day off. It was, after all, Christmas Eve. Annoyance shot through her at being alone, but she pushed the unworthy thought aside. The small number required to attend to her needs these days were excellent workers, loyal and competent. Good people. They deserved to spend the holidays at home with their families. It wasn't their fault she had no family of her own.

She wandered idly through the spacious house. Anywhere else in the country her home would be considered a mansion. But in this affluent Los Angeles suburb it was simply a big house.

Each and every room was pristine and perfect. Every feature, every aspect from sofas to art remained exactly as the high-priced decorator had arranged it twenty years ago. White on white. Unsullied, unspoiled, untouched. It struck her often lately how there was really nothing personal in her home. No photos of friends and family, no knickknacks picked up on fun-filled vacations, no out-of-place gifts cherished for the memory of the giver alone.

She climbed the stairs to the second floor and wondered why her thoughts turned more and more not to what she had but what she didn't. It must be *this* day, nothing more. Christmas Eve was an anniversary of sorts for her, one she had usually managed to ignore. But this year . . . this year things were different.

Katherine stepped into her bedroom, as impersonal as everything else in this house, and reached to turn on the television. No. She pulled back her hand in irritation. One of the hundred or so versions of that damned *Christmas Carol* might be on. She detested that blasted story. Once, years ago, an acquaintance had suggested that perhaps Scrooge wasn't all bad, just misunderstood. Why, wasn't the maligned creature merely a small businessman struggling to keep his head above water while coping with incompetent employees? She'd laughed at the time but privately thought there was some truth to the theory. Poor Scrooge was no doubt simply the nineteenth-century version of a workaholic.

Just like me.

She shook off the idea and cast a critical glance around the sun-filled room. Sunshine in December. Only in southern California. It was enough to make you laugh out loud. It never truly felt like Christmas here. What were the holidays without snow? Her only acknowledgment, or maybe concession, to the season these days was a wreath on the front door and an extravagant arrangement in the foyer, both from a very chic, very expensive florist.

Why was she so restless today? There were any number of things she could do to keep busy. She still retained her seat on several corporate and charitable boards. There was always correspondence or odds and ends to deal with. Today's issue of the *Wall Street Journal* still sat untouched. The latest nonfiction bestseller rested on the table beside her bed. Nothing appeared the least bit interesting.

It was that ridiculous visit. She shook her head in disgust. How could she have given into such an asinine impulse? It was sheer stupidity.

She grabbed the newspaper with newfound determination and settled into a chair. Past time to put that nonsense behind her. But the headlines made no sense, the words swam, the print blurred. All she could see were his eyes. Dark and deep. The color of Christmas Eve. She'd seen those eyes before.

He called me Katie.

The paper fell from her hands as if in slow motion.

He called me Katie.

The realization filled her with a kind of awe. Was there a chance then, after all? Could a woman who'd spent her entire life with her faith based firmly on reality, on statistics and balance sheets and bottom lines, now believe in miracles?

She rose from her chair and stepped quickly to the walk-in closet, afraid now to waste even a second. She knew where it was, had always known where it was, but never sought it out before today. Imagine—the irony pulled a smile to her lips—two impulses given into in one day. This must be some kind of record.

She pushed aside clear plastic boxes of neatly stacked shoes, seldom-used dress pumps, until she found an old-fashioned hatbox. She pulled the cardboard carton from its forgotten corner, ignoring the fine layer of dust that covered the faded gray and white striped design.

The eagerness of a child presented with a new toy or rediscovering a long-lost favorite filled her and she sank onto the plush carpet on the floor. Her hands trembled as she untied the dingy white cord binding the ancient box together. Her breath seemed to stop and she lifted the lid.

There was so little here. She knew, of course, before she opened the carton; still, the pitiful store of memories brought a lump to her throat. She grasped a handful of letters, tied with a string, all unopened, and relived the long-ago moment when she'd received them and knew exactly what they meant. She pulled out a delicate glass ball, frosted with glitter and the magic of Christmas, the kind of no-longer-seen ornament that could capture the imagination of children who stared into its enchanted depths.

There was only one item left.

With a careful touch, she picked up a small, rectangular box, its cellophane window yellowed and brittle with age. The brown, withered remains of a flower within bore no resemblance to the fragrant, snowy white gardenia it had been, what was it now, fifty plus years ago?

Her excitement crumbled and sorrow washed over her. For what might have been. And what was.

He called me Katie.

The meager bits and pieces of the past were Katie's, not Katherine's. Nobody called her Katie. Not anymore. But once, nobody had called her anything else . . .

" . . . Katie."

Snowflakes flurried against the glass, incandescent fireflies flitting through a blue-black night.

"Katie Bedford, would you please stop staring out the window and take this?" Mary Ann Hanson held up a hand-blown glass ball and glared with obvious irritation.

Katie reached down from her perch on the rickety ladder and plucked the ornament from her friend's hand. "I was looking at the snow. It's really coming down now."

Mary Ann's expression softened as if the beauty of Mother Nature's display washed away her annoyance. "It is pretty, isn't it? Just like a greeting card."

Katie wrinkled her nose. "I didn't mean that exactly. Oh, it's nice enough, I suppose, but I'm tired of snow. Winter's barely started and it feels like it's been snowing forever."

"Katie!" Mary Ann raised a chastising brow. "Don't be such a Scrooge. Why, snow for Christmas is practically perfect."

"I suppose," Katie murmured, her gaze wandering to the window once again. "But don't you ever wonder what Christmas would be like someplace warm? Someplace where you didn't have to fight icy sidewalks and slick roads all the time? Where the grass was green and flowers bloomed even at Christmas?"

"No," Mary Ann said staunchly. "Never. I love snow, especially at Christmas."

"Still . . ." Katie threw a last glance at the winter display outside the window and shrugged to herself. It was lovely, of course, but even inside the cozy community hall-turned-canteen, the cold beat against the glass and shivers skated along her arms.

Mary Ann released an impatient sigh. "Katie, are you going to hang that ball or sit up there on that ladder all night?"

"Sorry." Katie studied the tall, lush fir and quickly picked a spot for the ornament. "These are beautiful. Where on earth did they come from?"

Mary Ann shook her head. "Beats me. One of the chaperons said they must have been donated, anonymously I guess. There was a big box full of them at the door to the hall tonight when Mrs. Gillum and the others arrived to start setting up for the dance. It must have been somebody who took one look at this tree and thought it needed help."

"Mary Ann." Katie laughed. "I can't believe our very own spirit of Christmas present is saying such sacrilegious things."

Mary Ann stuck her tongue out. "It doesn't have anything to do with Christmas spirit, it's the truth. Our homemade decorations looked pretty darn pathetic." She tossed the tree a satisfied nod. "This is much better. Those balls give it just the right touch of—"

"Gaudy flamboyance?" Katie teased.

"I was going to say magic." Mary Ann glared. "Honestly, Katie, I don't know what's gotten into you this year. I really—"

"Enough, enough." Katie thrust her hands out in front of her in an effort to ward off any more of Mary Ann's comments. "I'm sorry. You're absolutely right. The ornaments do add a bit of magic."

"And there should be magic at Christmas," Mary Ann huffed.

Katie nodded and stifled a grin. "Absolutely. Now, give me a hand and I'll get off this thing."

Mary Ann cast her a mollified look and steadied her descent down the ladder. Katie brushed off the needles clinging to her skirt and glanced around the rapidly filling room. There would be a full crowd here tonight. She and Mary Ann had served as canteen hostesses every evening since their return home from school for the holidays. The place was always busy. But tonight was different. Tonight was Christmas Eve.

Mary Ann studied the room with a critical eye. "I wonder if he'll be here tonight."

Katie pulled her brows together in a puzzled frown. "Who?"

"Prince Charming, of course." Mary Ann's gaze never wavered from the growing assembly of young men.

"What on earth are you ta—" Abruptly the answer hit her. "Mary Ann Hanson, you're not on that husband hunt of yours again?"

"Um-hum," Mary Ann said, obviously more concerned with her search for Mr. Right than with Katie's words.

"I can't believe—"

"I can't believe you're not doing the same thing." Mary Ann turned eyes wide with exasperation toward her friend. "Look at us. We're not getting any younger. If we don't do something soon, all the good men will be gone. We'll be old maids."

Katie laughed. "I'm sure we have a couple of good years left. We're only twenty, not quite ancient yet. I don't think there's any need to worry."

"Sometimes I don't understand you at all." Mary Ann's eyes narrowed suspiciously. "Don't you want to get married?"

"Sure." Even to her own ears, her answer sounded a little strained. "Of course I do."

"Well, what better opportunity will you have to find a man than right here?" Mary Ann's wide gesture encompassed the room. "Just look at the selection: tall, short, dark, fair, soldiers, sailors, marines. You can practically pick and choose to suit your taste."

"A virtual smorgasbord of men," Katie said wryly. "Or maybe a better description would be 'potluck.'"

"Well, I don't care what you think. I think this is the perfect chance to meet someone special. To find that one man who's your destiny, your fate." Mary Ann tossed her head in a flurry of blond hair. "And I, for one, want that fate. I want to get married and have children and fall in love."

Katie raised a curious brow. "Not necessarily in that order, I hope."

"Don't be silly. Love comes first." Mary Ann's eyes widened as if she'd just been hit by a revelation. "What about love, Katie? Don't you want love either?"

"Of course I want love. And marriage," Katie said impatiently. This entire conversation, even with her closest friend, was getting far too near to a truth Katie didn't especially want to face. "But someday, not now. I'm in no hurry to go rushing down the aisle with anyone. And as for love . . ." Her gaze drifted across the room and lingered on a pretty woman barely ten years older than herself.

Pamela Gillum stood beside the refreshment table doling out cookies and punch and good spirits. She lived next door to Katie's family and, right now, lived there alone with her three children. Her husband was a captain in the Air Corps, stationed somewhere in England. Pamela held up well publicly, but Katie noted how the older woman looked when she thought no one watched. Then her composure crumbled. Scared was the best description. Maybe even terrified. Of every letter, every knock on the door, every newspaper headline. Fear etched tiny lines in her forehead and instilled a barely noticeable tremble in her hands and rimmed her eyes with red.

"I don't think this is the time for love," Katie said under her breath.

Mary Ann's gaze followed hers. "The war can't last forever."

Katie shook her head in disdain. "That's what we said last year. Remember? Right after Pearl Harbor? Everyone said this would be a short war. We'd wipe out the Japanese and march right into Germany and deal with Hitler and it would be over."

"But we can still—"

"Mary Ann, grow up," Katie said sharply. "Don't you read the papers at all? It's 1942. If you're hoping for a quick end to this war you can forget it right now and face the facts. This is going to be a long, hard haul. And all these guys you've got your eye on . . ."

She waved at the still swelling throng. "Look at them, Mary Ann. Half of them are younger than we are. They're just kids. We get to go home tonight when this party's over. They're going places they've never been, to do a job nobody should have to do. And a whole lot of them won't be coming home. Ever. Just like Harry."

"I know that," Mary Ann said quietly. "I just don't want to think about it. I'd much rather have a little fun and help them have a good time before they go. Is that so wrong?"

Guilt shot through Katie and immediately she regretted her harsh words. Mary Ann had a good heart, and there was no excuse for taking out her own frustrations about the war on her best friend.

"Of course not." Katie tossed her an apologetic smile. "I'm sorry."

"I'll tell you something else, Katie." The blonde squared her shoulders and met Katie's gaze straight on. "If I find my prince here, I don't care what happens next. If I have to spend however long this war lasts living like Mrs. Gillum, I can bear it. I could even take finding somebody and . . . losing him."

She shook her head. "I know you think it's stupid, and maybe it is, but I truly believe that when you find love you need to grab it right then and there. So what if life doesn't turn out the way you thought, if you don't get to live happily ever after, at least you'd have something. It might only be for a year or a week or just one night. Love is worth the risk." She glared with defiance. "It's got to be."

"I don't think it's stupid," Katie said softly. "I think it's very brave. I don't have that kind of courage."

"No?" Mary Ann stared at her for a moment as if considering her answer. Then an impish light twinkled in her eye. "But you do have long legs and Rita Hayworth hair and dark, mysterious eyes that make men weak. Let's face it, you're a dish. You don't need courage."

Katie laughed with relief at the return of her friend's good humor. "Maybe not, but I'll always need a friend.

"That you've got, pal." Mary Ann grinned, and the girls shook hands in an exaggerated gesture of friendship.

A moment later, an elderly woman bustled up to them with an authoritative manner that would have had even the most decorated generals at the War Department green with envy. With a few brisk, nononsense orders she directed the removal of the ladder by high-school-aged volunteers dressed like elves.

"Some of the local florists got together and donated these for the hostesses tonight." The energetic matron thrust two small, cream-colored boxes at them. "Gardenias, I believe. Isn't it wonderful how everyone wants to do their part for the war effort?"

The girls traded swift glances.

"Wonderful," Mary Ann echoed with a remarkably straight face.

Katie bit back a smile. "For the war effort, of course."

"Of course." The chaperon nodded firmly, oblivious to any possibility of amusement. "Now, you two have a lovely time this evening and be sure to follow the rules. They're there for your protection, you know." She cocked a stern brow as if daring them, right then and there, to break the myriad of rules and regulations designed for the express purpose of allowing healthy young men and women to have fun, but not too much fun. The girls stared back innocently. Apparently satisfied, the formidable guardian of virtue marched off to rally the rest of her troops.

Katie pulled the lid off her box and picked up the corsage. "Gardenias in winter. Very nice. Although they don't do well in the cold."

"Who cares?" Mary Ann plucked the fragrant flower from its carton. "I don't know about the war effort in general, but this certainly does do something for my own personal battle plans." She pinned the blossom on her sweater and cast an assessing gaze around the room. At once her eyes lit up.

"Spotted a potential target?" Katie said, smothering her amusement.

"You'd better believe it." Mary Ann tossed her friend a devilish grin. "See you later."

"Happy hunting." Katie grinned back, and her friend

sauntered off with a casual manner that belied the determination in her eye.

A burst of music from the far end of the hall caught Katie's attention. A group that could be called a band by only the loosest definition tuned up with all the subtlety of tortured animals. It was an odd mix of callow youth, who stared at the soldiers with naive envy, and older gentlemen, who cast wistful glances at the men in uniform as if remembering the victorious battles of their own wartime coming-of-age.

She scanned the now packed room, curious to see if anyone she knew was here. A silly idea, of course. All the local boys would be home with their families on Christmas Eve. It might very well be their last Christmas Eve together for a long time.

A wave seemed to undulate through the crowd and it parted for a moment, as if someone had drawn an invisible line down the middle of the hall. Her glance idly followed the open pathway, past one uniform after another, until stopped by a figure smack dab in her line of sight. Her gaze wandered up long, powerful legs, strong hands, and broad shoulders to a face fit for the hero of a movie. No, she amended the thought, make that the hero's best friend.

He was handsome in that kind of wonderful all-American-boy sort of way. Just the type of man she always seemed to fall for: tall with dark hair and darker eyes. He grinned a crooked sort of smile that said without words this was a man of confidence, a man who saw the humor in life, a man without fear.

His gaze caught hers, and a shock of recognition shot through her so strong it staggered her senses and knocked her breath away. At this distance she couldn't

tell if his eyes were blue or brown, only that they seemed to see into her very soul.

A startled expression crossed his face. Did he somehow share what she had just experienced? His grin widened and he nodded slightly as if in silent acknowledgment. She wanted to turn away from this odd intimacy with a total stranger but somehow couldn't summon the power to so much as move her head. Then abruptly the crowd shifted once again and he was lost to her sight.

Unexpected, unreasonable panic bubbled through her. Who was this man and why did he have such a dramatic effect on her? She'd never seen him before and would probably never see him again. Unlike Mary Ann, she had no intention of either hunting for a husband or snaring one, so this immediate connection with a stranger was shocking and scary and . . .

Fate?

The thought popped to mind with startling abruptness, and she fumbled with the flower in her hand. The delicate corsage tumbled to the floor, and she swooped down to retrieve it before it could be crushed in the crowd. She reached toward it, but just as her fingertips brushed the petals, a large, male hand gently plucked it off the floor. Her heart thudded faster, and she instinctively knew whose hand it was. Her gaze traveled up the length of his arm to finally settle on his face, the cocky grin she'd seen from across the room, the twin dimples in his cheeks, his dark eyes.

They were blue, dark as the night and just as endless.

"Do you believe in love at first sight?" His voice was mellow and rich and seemed to echo deep within her.

She stared, mesmerized, speechless. Every fiber of her being screamed *Yes!*

"No," she said coolly and pulled herself to her feet. "But that's a great line"—her gaze wandered to the bar on his shoulder—"Lieutenant. Almost as good as 'haven't we met somewhere before?' or 'you remind me of someone I know' or—"

"Didn't we go to school together?" he said, his voice solemn, his eyes twinkling. A challenge shone there, and she couldn't resist the urge to laugh out loud.

"That's better." He grinned. "I'd hate for the prettiest girl here to think I was some kind of a jerk."

She shrugged. "Well, with lines like that . . ."

"Funny," he said under his breath, "it didn't feel like a line."

His gaze met hers and they stared for a long, intense moment.

"Katie." She gasped, breaking the taut silence, and thrust her hand out to shake his. "I'm Katie Bedford."

"Michael Patrick O'Connor." He took her hand in his and she struggled not to pull back at the electric feel of her fingers in his. He nodded toward his shoulder. "Lieutenant O'Connor now, I guess."

"Where you from, soldier?" The routine words slipped out before she could stop them.

He cocked a dark brow. "Now, that's a line if ever I heard one."

"Sorry." The heat of embarrassment flushed up her face. "It's a standard-issue comment these days."

"Like everything else." He laughed again, and she marveled at the warmth that flushed through her at the sound. "I'm from Chicago originally. Fresh from college graduation."

"That's what I thought." She nodded.

"Oh?" The brow rose again. "Does it show?"

"No, of course not. I just meant . . ." She scrambled for the right words. What on earth was wrong with her tonight? She sighed. "Well, I'm not sure what I meant exactly. You just look . . . new at all this."

"I am new"—he gestured toward the room—"at this anyway. And by the way, it's not soldier."

"No?" A sinking sensation settled in the pit of her stomach. Obviously he wasn't a soldier. Even she could see that from the insignia on his uniform. He must think she was a total and complete idiot.

"Close, though. Army Air Corps."

"A pilot?" *Please, don't let him be a pilot.*

"You bet." Pride shimmered in his voice.

"How nice," she said weakly.

A frown creased his forehead. "I take it you don't like pilots?"

"They're okay." She shrugged. "My brother was a flyer. In the Navy." Even to her own ears, her voice sounded strained.

His question was casual, but a hint of concern touched his eyes. "Where?"

"Pearl Harbor."

"I see." He studied her for a moment, his gaze assessing and sympathetic. "Sorry."

"It's been a year. I . . ." She drew a deep breath and favored him with a shaky smile. "Life goes on."

"Sure." An awkward silence stretched between them. His gaze wandered to his hands and he looked surprised, as if he had just noticed the gardenia he still held. "Here." He thrust the flower toward her. "I almost forgot."

"Thanks." She accepted the corsage and started to pin it on her sweater. Her hands trembled slightly.

"Let me." With a few deft moves, he affixed the bloom to the wool cardigan. His dark head bent close and a subtle wave of scent washed over her. She breathed in the heady aroma of aftershave and spice and heat, and her knees weakened with an odd ache for something as yet unknown.

"There." He tossed her a satisfied nod and straightened up. Goodness, he was close. He was a good six inches taller than she and her eyes were on a level with his lips.

He was very close.

Firm, sensuous lips that seemed made for smiling or . . . kissing.

When did he get this close?

What would those lips be like against hers? Would they demand or coax? Would they be gentle or urgent? Insistent or tender—

"Miss Bedford?"

His voice jerked her attention upward to his eyes. Amusement glittered there as if he was well aware of her perusal. Once again, an annoying heat spread through her cheeks

"Katie," she sighed. "Call me Katie."

"Michael," he said.

His gaze meshed with hers, and she wasn't quite sure what to say next. She wanted to know everything about him. His hopes, dreams, and ambitions. She wanted him to know everything about her. Her secrets, her passions, her joys. Overwhelmed by her own reactions, she feared that every word she spoke would come out wrong. And it seemed terribly important to be clever and charming to this man.

The band burst into a rousing, if distinctly off-key, rendition of "Chattanooga Choo-choo." Michael winced, and she laughed at the chagrined look on his face.

"Sorry." He shrugged sheepishly. "I didn't mean to be rude. They caught me off guard."

"They're definitely not Glenn Miller but they're all we've got." She leaned forward in a confidential manner. "We'll be playing records when they need a break." She tossed him an impish grin. "Or when we need one."

He laughed, and the music abruptly seemed sweeter. "In the meantime"—he nodded at the dance floor—"would you like to dance?"

"Are you any good?" she teased.

"Am I any good?" He cast her a look of mock indignation. "I'll have you know I am one of the best. Why, women have been known to throw themselves at my feet for the opportunity to spin around a dance floor with me."

"Just like Fred Astaire, I bet," she said solemnly.

"Exactly," he said just as seriously.

"In that case"—she offered her hand and a resigned smile—"call me Ginger."

Michael took her hand in his, and his fingers fit around hers like a glove, natural and comforting and right. A grin still danced across his handsome face, but his eyes held a light that belied the casual tone of his words. "Call *me* lucky."

Lucky? He led her to the dance floor, and before the beat of the music swept away any possibility of coherent thinking, she firmly pushed back a nagging thought in the dim recesses of her mind.

These days, just how long would a pilot's luck last?

The evening and the music and the magic of the man beside her seemed to speed up the hours and the evening flew by. Every now and then she'd catch Mary Ann eying her with a knowing look and a smug smile, and Katie did her best to ignore her. It was easy. Michael occupied her attention completely. He was funny and smart and definitely not shy about his abilities.

"You are a good dancer," she said breathlessly as they spun to a stop at the edge of the floor.

"Told you." The twinkle in his eye belied the modesty of his tone. "I do a lot of things well."

"I'll bet." Friendly sarcasm dripped from her words.

"Surely you don't doubt the word of a man in uniform?" He clasped his hand over his heart and heaved an exaggerated sigh. "That's positively—"

"Un-American?" She grinned.

"Un-American, unpatriotic, un-just about everything you can think of." He leaned closer in mock menace. "I feel it's my duty to report this kind of gross violation of the war-effort act."

She stared, startled. "The what?"

"The war-effort act. Surely you've heard of it," he said in a solemn manner.

She pulled her brows together in confusion and shook her head. "No. Are you kidding?"

"Is this the face of a man who's joking?" His expression was stern but a teasing light lurked in his eyes.

"You are kidding," she said with relief. She didn't mind a good joke, but she didn't like the vaguest suggestion that she was doing anything even remotely disloyal.

"I still have to report this." He nodded at the bar on his shoulder. "I am an officer, after all."

"Well, Lieutenant." Her serious tone matched his own. "If you must, you must." She glanced around the crowded room and crossed her arms over her chest.

"But I don't know who you'll report me to. There doesn't seem to be a single, solitary general in sight."

"That is a problem." He frowned thoughtfully; then a slow grin spread across his face. "I've got it. Come with me, Miss Bedford."

He grabbed her hand and dragged her across the room. She struggled amidst her own laughter to keep up with his long strides.

"Where are you taking me?" she gasped.

"Right here." He pulled to an abrupt stop and she stumbled into him. "I believe this is the highest authority here tonight."

She lifted her gaze, and a giggle bubbled through her lips. Before her sat a most authentic-looking Santa. Who had been corralled into donning a Santa suit tonight? Judge Thomas maybe? Or Mr. Brisch? Regardless, he played the part to perfection.

"Santa, I have a serious infraction to report," Michael said in his best commanding-officer voice.

"Katie Bedford." Santa frowned in a chastising way she thought would have been reserved for misbehaving children. "What have you done to upset this fine young man?"

"Why, Santa," she said with innocence, "I haven't done anything. Nothing at all."

"That's not true, Santa." Michael shook his head sadly and leaned toward the oversized elf. "She doubted my sincerity."

"Katie!" Santa's tone was shocked but his eyes twinkled.

"Well," Katie said confidentially, "would you believe him?"

Michael clasped his hands behind his back, raised his eyes heavenward, and whistled a vacuous tune.

"You look like a choirboy," she accused.

"I was," he said virtuously.

"Now, now, children." Santa chuckled. "It's Christmas Eve. What can I do for you? What would you like for Christmas?"

"I can think of one thing." Michael cast her a wicked glance.

"Michael," she said, shaking her head, "you are incorrigible."

"Thank you," he said humbly

"When are you leaving, son?" Santa's tone was casual, but at once the mood of the conversation darkened.

"Tomorrow."

"Tomorrow?" A heavy weight sank in the pit of Katie's stomach. "But it's Christmas."

His somber gaze met hers. His voice was quiet. "It's a war, Katie."

"But—"

"Enough of that, now. There's still tonight to be enjoyed." Santa's voice rumbled through her, and she thought again what a perfect Santa this man made. "Come now, my boy, isn't there anything you'd like for a Christmas present?"

Michael smiled down at her. "I think I might already have everything I need."

The intensity of his gaze brought a flush of heat to her face.

"What about you, Katie?" Santa said softly.

She stared at Michael and wondered at the depth of feeling this virtual stranger triggered in her. "I don't think I need anything either."

"Katie." Santa's words were quiet but some vague underlying tone drew her attention to his face. She stared into his eyes and couldn't seem to pull away. She watched and they deepened to the color of a winter midnight. The color of the sky on Christmas Eve.

"The offer's good anytime. That's a promise."

At once his eyes lightened and the odd connection was broken. Santa shook his head as if to clear his mind. Then he grinned at the couple standing before him. "You two go and have a good time. And have a Merry Christmas."

"I think they're playing our song," Michael said.

Katie laughed. "We don't have a song."

"We do now." He pulled her into his arms and out onto the dance floor. The strains of "I'll Be Seeing You" floated through the air.

"I love this song," she said and snuggled closer.

"Me, too."

She gazed up at him and quirked a curious brow. "Really?"

He shrugged sheepishly. "Can I help it if I'm a born romantic?"

"A romantic?" Doubt colored her voice.

"Ah, Katie, once again you question my sincerity." He sighed.

She laughed. "Sorry. It's just not often you run into a man who admits to being a romantic."

"I not only admit it but I have a hard time believing this particular song fails to touch a sentimental chord in anyone. Even a man." He pulled her closer and spoke softly into her ear. Her blood pounded through her veins at the intimate contact. "Just listen to it, Katie."

She closed her eyes and lost herself in the spell of the music and the man.

"Listen to what it says." He hummed a bar or two,

then softly sang, "'I'll be seeing you in all the old familiar places, that this heart of mine embraces all day through.' Do you know what he's saying, Katie?"

"Hmm?" She didn't want to answer, didn't want her words or her thoughts to shatter the enchantment that shimmered around them.

"He's saying that everything they've shared will always remind him of her . . ." He paused for a moment and the music drifted by like a gentle wave or a warm breeze. "'. . . in every lovely summer's day, in everything that's bright and gay . . .' and more, Katie, everything he sees that's good and warm and joyous will always bring her to mind for him. He's talking about love."

"Love?" She echoed the word as if she'd never heard it before.

"Love, Katie," Michael said soberly. "The kind that lasts forever . . . 'I'll find you in the morning sun and when the night is through, I'll be looking at the moon but I'll be seeing you.'"

She pulled back and stared into the deep, endless blue of his eyes.

"It's a love song." His eyes enticed her down into their smoldering, hypnotic recesses and she couldn't turn away. "And a promise."

For a long moment, they stared and the world faded to a soft blur. She was afraid to move, afraid even to breathe, afraid to break whatever magic held them here, bound together in a fierce, intimate communion.

"Come on." He pulled her into the corridor where the light was much dimmer than in the main room. Some eager serviceman, or perhaps an equally enthusiastic young hostess, had tacked up a bit of greenery in the secluded area.

"Mistletoe?" She widened her eyes in surprise. "The chaperons would have a fit if they saw that."

"Then let's not let them see it." He pinned her with a direct gaze that melted her defenses. His eyes were dark with desire and intense with something she couldn't quite place. Something that took her breath away. "Kiss me, Katie."

He drew her into his arms and it was as if she'd finally come home. As if this was where she belonged, where she'd always belonged. His head dipped toward hers and she tilted her face to meet him. His lips brushed against hers, lightly at first, and the sparks she'd noted when he merely touched her hand flared into a blaze of need and wanting. Her arms snaked around his neck and he pulled her closer. The rough wool of his uniform pressed against her, crushing the gardenia that clung to her sweater.

Was it his heart that throbbed between them or her own?

His lips demanded more, and she met his insistence with eager abandon. Her fingers caressed the warm flesh at the back of his neck, and she marveled at the feel of hard muscle beneath velvet skin.

He pulled his lips to the line of her jaw and beyond to a point just below her ear. He nibbled and kissed and teased until she thought her knees would buckle and she would dissolve into a small, quivering puddle. Never had a simple kiss affected her like this. Never had she ached for the touch of knowledgeable hands on previously unknown places. Never had a man done this to her.

"Dear Michael," she murmured, "what will I do with you?"

"Marry me."

His words barely penetrated the thick haze of arousal enveloping her, and she uttered a mindless sigh in response.

Michael drew back from her and his gaze searched her face as if he sought answers to questions only he understood. His gaze locked with hers and it seemed as if time itself stopped just for them. As if they and they alone were the only two people in the world, in the universe, in all of creation.

"Marry me, Katie," he said softly.

"Marry you?" She gasped. "Is that what you said?"

"Twice now." A tiny twinkle of wry amusement danced in his eyes. "I love you, Katie."

The fog of desire that blunted her senses abruptly vanished and her mind sharpened with the meaning of his words. "Love? How can you love me? We just met. I don't even know you."

"I don't know you either, but I still want to marry you." The slight smile on his lips didn't touch the smoldering depths of his eyes. "And you're wrong, you know."

"Wrong?" She couldn't seem to catch her breath.

He nodded. "I do know you. I've known you forever."

"Forever? That's ridiculous." He was standing way too close. That's why she couldn't breathe. It had nothing to do with the passion in his eyes. Nothing to do with the fervent tone of his words. Nothing to do with how her body seemed to fit so perfectly with his own. She tried to pull away but he held her tight.

"I knew the moment I saw you across the room, we were meant for each other. It was the strongest sensation I've ever felt. Like being hit by a bolt of lightning. We're soul mates, Katie." His words rang with quiet conviction. "I know it as surely as I've ever known anything in my life; you're my destiny. My fate."

Fate?

She laughed weakly. "Fate? Now that's a good line. You *are* a romantic."

A frown furrowed his forehead and he shook her gently. "Don't laugh at me and don't take this lightly."

"You don't know what you're saying." Irrational, unexplained panic threatened within her.

"I know exactly what I'm saying."

"Michael." She struggled to find the right words. "You're caught up in the emotion of the moment. You're going off to fight for your country. You're just—"

"Don't treat me like I'm some green seventeen-year-old whose voice has just changed." Anger flashed in his eyes. "I'm an adult. Twenty-two years old. College educated. For crissakes, Katie, I'm a damned officer. I know what I want when I see it."

"You don't know anything." She jerked out of his grasp. "We're in the middle of a war. This is no time to make commitments or promises or anything else. Besides, you have no idea what happens to the women whose husbands are off who knows where facing who knows what."

She shook her head angrily. "I watch them, Michael, and I refuse to become one of them."

"Katie." Frustration simmered in his voice.

"No, Michael." She shook her head firmly, refusing to give in. It was too important, and too permanent, and too darn frightening. "I will not spend the next year or two years or ten years waiting for you to come home. Or for you to be killed. I will not cringe every time there's a knock on the door. I will not listen to the radio with my heart in my throat. And I will not bury someone I love again."

"It's because of your brother, isn't it?" he said gently.

"Harry?" Immediately the tall, sandy-haired big brother with the laughing eyes and teasing smile flashed through her mind. The thought hadn't occurred to her before, but Michael was right: Harry played a big role in her fears. "I guess so."

"Tell me." His tone was colored with compassion.

She shrugged impatiently. "There's not much to tell. Harry wanted to fly and see the world. He ended up in Hawaii. It seemed like the perfect assignment. Two days before he died we got a letter from him all about parties on the beach and learning to surf."

Michael eyed her intently. "It must have come as quite a shock."

A sharper, bitter laugh broke from her. "It came as a shock to the whole country. I was just a little more personally involved, that's all."

"I have no intention of dying in any damn war."

She shook her head. "Harry had no intention of dying either."

Their gazes locked for a long moment and silence fell between them. A myriad of expressions chased across his face: frustration, doubt, and finally determination.

He pulled her back into his arms. "You haven't said the one thing, the only thing, I'll accept as a legitimate excuse for being turned down."

"What?" she snapped.

He raised a brow at the sharp tone and lowered his head to hers. His voice was low and intense. "You haven't said you don't love me."

"Michael, I—"

His lips claimed hers, stifling any possible protest. A

rational, indignant voice, a voice of sanity, a voice of sheer terror screamed inside her head.

You don't love him! You can't love him! Not here! Not now!

But right here and right now, she was in his arms and her treacherous body betrayed her. For a split second she resisted, then her guard crumbled. Instinctively she leaned into his embrace as if to forge the separate into the whole, the two into the one. Her breath mixed and mingled with his as if the very air that provided life was incomplete unless shared. Heat pounded through her veins in a rhythm that ebbed and flowed with the throb of his lips crushed to hers.

He groaned and pulled his mouth away to feather kisses down to the hollow of her throat. "I knew it, Katie. You do love me."

"No, Michael." Her words were little more than a sigh.

Yes, Michael.

She couldn't answer, couldn't find the words, couldn't focus on anything beyond the glory of his lips on flesh heated with newfound passion.

"I saw a sign down the street." His voice rumbled against her neck. "A justice of the peace. Next door to a little inn."

"Judge Thomas." She struggled for sanity, struggled to remain coherent, struggled to ignore the intoxicating sensation of his hands splayed across her back, pressing her tighter until the clothing separating them seemed nonexistent and the flame of his passion arched between them.

"Marry me." His voice was rough with emotion, heavy with need, and the words shot through her with an icy force that jerked her back to reason.

"No." The word was a sob, wrung from deep inside her as if pulled by force or by necessity or by fear. "No."

A shudder of regret, a sigh of resignation shivered through him and he held her firmly, her cheek cradled on his chest. His broad shoulders sagged slightly as if he had finally accepted her rejection.

"Will you wait for me then, Katie?"

"Forever," she whispered.

He tilted her chin up and her gaze meshed with his. He brushed the flat of his thumb over her bottom lip and tossed her a sad smile that clutched at a place in her heart. "You know, if you'd marry me I'd have something to come back for."

"You'll have something to come back for," she said staunchly, steadfast in her belief that this was the right thing to do. "I promise."

"And I promise too, Katie." His eyes burned with conviction. "I will come back to you."

"I'll be right here." She mustered a smile that quivered in spite of her resolve to show nothing but confidence and conviction. "Waiting."

"Okay." He heaved a heavy sigh. "That'll have to do, I guess."

"I guess," she echoed.

They stared at each other for a second or an eternity. There was so much she wanted to say to him, so much she needed to say. But the words didn't come.

The overhead lights flashed on in the main hall, signaling the end of the evening.

"I have to go," he said simply.

"I know." He took her hand and they walked into the rapidly emptying main room, blinking in the bright light after the dim recesses of the corridor.

Her throat tightened and she bit her lip to hold back tears. "I'll walk you out."

"No." He shook his head. "That's okay. I'd rather . . ." He laughed awkwardly and ran his fingers through his hair. "I don't know what to say."

She pulled a deep breath. "Me neither."

He turned to leave, then swiveled back and yanked her into his arms. His dark eyes bored into hers with a fervor that crept into her soul. "You haven't said it, Katie. You haven't told me."

"Told you what?" Frantically she searched her mind. "I said I'll wait for you."

"No." He shook his head and stared. "You never said you loved me. Do you, Katie, do you love me?"

Love?

"I—" The word shivered through her, shadowed with indecision and doubt. Was this love? Could she admit the truth to him? Or more, to herself.

"Lieutenant?" an impatient masculine voice called.

"Coming." Michael threw the answer over his shoulder, then swiftly brushed his lips across her forehead. "Write to me."

She swallowed the lump in her throat and nodded.

His gaze lingered on her for a last second. Then abruptly he twisted and strode toward the door.

"Michael," she whispered.

Across the room, he hesitated beside the Christmas tree. His hand snapped out and plucked a glass ball from the fir. He swiveled to face her.

"Katie," he called, "you do need a present."

With an easy underhand pitch, he threw the ornament into the air. It swung high in a long, slow arch, catching and reflecting the light like a Christmas star.

She cupped her hands together and held them out before her. The ball landed with a gentle plop in the center of her outstretched palms as if guided by unerring instinct or pure emotion.

Michael tossed her a quick wave and the crooked grin that had already branded a spot on her heart.

"I'll be seeing you, Katie." Even from across the room she could see the smoldering pledge in his eyes, and she read his lips more than heard his words. It was enough. "I promise."

He joined the throng of uniforms swirling through the open door, and she lost sight of him. At once she wanted to run across the room, into the night and back into his arms. She wanted to hear his laughter and bask in the sparkle of his eyes. She wanted to feel the warmth of his body beside hers, as his wife, as his love.

But she couldn't seem to move. Her feet, her mind resisted the urgent cries of her heart. Her shoulders slumped with the realization: she was a coward, plain and simple. Too afraid of the possibility of loss and pain to recognize the greatest gift a man could offer a woman, at Christmas or any other time.

The door slammed shut and at once the noise in the room quieted to a gentle murmur. The only ones left were the hostesses and the chaperons and the odd assortment of males who made up the makeshift band. Only women and children and old men. It was the same in any war.

She was right not to marry him, not to commit her life, her heart to him. She'd write, of course, and she'd wait and she'd pray for his safe return.

Would a ring on her finger make it any harder?

She sucked her breath in sharply and clasped a hand

over her mouth. How could she have been so blind? What a complete idiot she was! Married or not, she was in the same boat as Pamela Gillum. But worse, much, much worse. Pamela at least had her husband's name and her memories.

Katie stared down at the delicate ornament in her hand as if it were a crystal ball that held the true meaning of life. But the revelation of some truths come too late. She'd sent Michael away with nothing beyond a simple promise to wait. She hadn't even told him she loved him, when everything inside her proclaimed the truth. Improbable and unrealistic and downright insane, it was still the truth.

She loved him.

And he was gone.

She fought a rising sense of panic. It will be okay. He'll come back. He has to come back.

He promised.

She wrote to him on Christmas morning. And the next day and the day after that. A flurry of letters winged their way across the ocean bearing a flood of emotion. She poured her heart and soul into every word, every line, every page. She wrote of her hopes and dreams for after the war, for the future, their future together. She wrote of love.

And she waited.

Katie returned to school with her mother's promise to forward all mail. She checked her box every day, sometimes twice. Nothing.

Weeks turned to months without word. Anticipation faded and doubt gnawed at the back of her mind like a voracious rodent. Were Michael's words just routine lines after all? Were they merely quick and easy lies designed to play on the wonder of a single night and the threat of mortality? Did he really mean everything he said? Did he mean anything he said?

I do know you. I've known you forever.

No. She refused to believe, even for a moment, that the tone of his words, the touch of his hand, the look in his eye was anything less than what she knew, deep inside some secret place in her soul, to be real. And right.

Faith kept her strong, hope kept her going, and love kept her alive. She would hear from him. He would come back to her.

He promised.

It was a frigid winter day when she found the bulky Manila envelope stuffed in her mailbox. She yanked it out with fingers numbed from the cold and icy tendrils gripping her heart. Her hands trembled as she struggled to tear the packet open. Her letters to Michael tumbled out, drifting to the ground. Amidst them fluttered a single, official-looking page.

Dear Miss Bedford,

I must apologize for the unforgivable delay in contacting you. Unfortunately, your correspondence with Lt. O'Connor was apparently held up and not discovered until recently. Your letters were not among his personal effects.

I regret to inform you Lt. O'Connor was killed in a training accident shortly after his arrival in England. I didn't know him well but he seemed like a fine young man. Please accept my condolences.

Sincerely,
Capt. Benjamin Gray

Pain speared through her with an intensity that ripped away her breath and stopped her heart and froze her soul. Her legs buckled beneath her and she sank to her knees. She could neither accept the straightforward words nor ignore them. For a long moment she huddled, numbed, as if by avoiding any movement herself she could somehow halt the world in its orbit, turn back the clock, deny what couldn't be denied. One line from the Captain's letter pounded in her head over and over in a refrain of accusation.

Your letters were not among his personal effects.

Michael never received her letters. He never knew how much she regretted her decision not to marry him. He never knew of her ardent, written vows to spend the rest of her life with him.

He never knew she loved him.

Like a dam swept aside by rampaging waters her defenses shattered. Great racking sobs shook through her and she wept for what was lost and what would never be. She cried for the love of a man gained in one night, destined to last a lifetime, now lasting no time at all. And her tears failed to wash away the one unrelenting truth of war and death and even life itself.

Promises can't always be kept. . . .

. . . promises.

Katherine stared at the aged box in her hand. Even now, fifty-four years later, the pain was as fresh and sharp as it had been on that cold, cold winter day. Somehow she'd always ignored it before. She rarely thought about Michael, relegating him to the dim reaches of her mind the same way she'd stored the hatbox and her memories in the back shadows of the closet. Occasionally a twinge of sorrow would tug at her heart. But only occasionally and always on Christmas Eve.

She had put him firmly in the past and gone on with her life. She finished school and fled to sunny California where the flowers bloomed even at Christmas and no one ever worried about icy roads. She got a good job and managed to hang on to it even when the war ended and the men came home. Every bit of passion within her went into her work, her career.

Every now and then she'd long for the magic she tasted so briefly on that one Christmas Eve. She married, twice, both marriages disastrous, both mercifully short. She never even glimpsed what she'd shared with Michael on a single evening in another lifetime.

Crazy old woman.

Disgust and anger surged through her. She ripped open the frail box and rolled what was left of the corsage onto her hand. Hard and dark and shriveled, it bore only the vaguest resemblance to what it had once been.

Just like me.

She gazed at the floral remains as if mesmerized. There was little of Katie left in Katherine. And no one to blame but herself. Her life would have been so very different had she, just that once, listened to her heart instead of her head.

You've lived your life. Made your choices. You can't go back.

Maybe she really had snapped. Maybe all the lonely years had finally sent her over the edge. It was insane to place all one's hopes and dreams and prayers on a promise muttered by a man in a red suit more than half a century ago. Or an odd quirk of lighting that changed the look in the eye of a department store Santa.

Her hand closed around the withered flower and she squeezed her fist tight. Better to crush this delusion, and all the bittersweet memories, right now and simply blow the dust away and face up to reality.

She opened her hand and her heart thudded in her chest. Blood roared in her ears and the room spun around her. She stared in stark disbelief.

In the center of her palm, the gardenia was as fresh and whole and sweet as the day Michael had pinned it on her sweater.

She couldn't seem to catch her breath. Her eyes blurred. The world around her faded. Only the stark white of the flower shimmered in her vision. It gleamed like a Christmas star or a wedding gown or a . . . snowflake.

" . . . Katie."

Snowflakes flurried against the glass, incandescent fireflies flitting through a blue-black night.

"Katie Bedford, would you please stop staring out the window and take this?" Mary Ann Hanson held up a hand-blown glass ball and glared with obvious irritation.

"Snow." Katherine gasped the word. "It's really snow!"

"Of course it's snow," Mary Ann said sharply. "Goodness, Katie, it's been snowing off and on for days."

Katherine couldn't pull her gaze away from the window. "It's beautiful."

Mary Ann's tone softened. "It is pretty, all right. Just like a Christmas card."

"A Christmas card," Katherine echoed. "I'd forgotten how perfect snow was for Christmas"—she sucked in her breath sharply—"Eve. It's Christmas Eve!"

Mary Ann threw her a look of exasperation. "Of course it's Christmas Eve."

Katherine widened her eyes with realization. "And it's 1942, isn't it?"

"Katie," Mary Ann shook her head, "I don't think—"

"Mary Ann Hanson." Katherine stared at the blonde from her lofty perch on the rickety ladder. "You're just as I remember you."

"Remember me? What's with you, Katie?" Mary Ann said with irritation.

"What's with me?" Sheer joy bubbled up inside her. Her excited gaze darted around the barely remembered community hall-turned-canteen, skimming past the growing crowd of young, uniformed men, skipping over Christmas decorations and sharp-eyed chaperons. Everything was exactly as it had been that night.

Katherine clapped her hand over her mouth. Surely it wasn't possible. This must all be a dream. Or maybe she'd died. Dropped dead right in her walk-in closet.

"Santa always keeps his promises."

"Katie?" Mary Ann's tone was cautious.

"You called me Katie." Katherine shook her head in wonder. "I can't believe it. And I don't care if I'm dead or asleep. I have a second chance."

"Maybe you'd better come down off that ladder," Mary Ann said carefully. "I think the height is starting to get to you."

"The height?" Katherine laughed with a surge of exuberance she hadn't known for years. "Mary Ann, the height is wonderful. It's incredible. From here I can see everything. Every inch of the room. Every person, every"—she caught her breath—"Michael."

"Who?"

"Oh, um, nothing." What could she say? What should she say? If this was real, and everything within her screamed that it was indeed true and tangible and solid, she didn't want to blow it. There was no way of knowing if her second chance lasted for just one night or the rest of her life. But it didn't matter. Tonight would be enough to treasure for a lifetime. One way or another, it had to be. "Never mind. Now"—her tone was brisk and no-nonsense—"hand me that ball and we'll get this tree finished."

Mary Ann eyed her suspiciously, then handed her an ornament. "For a moment you had me worried. What's the matter with you tonight?"

"Nothing, pal, not a thing." Katie placed the ball on the lush fir, nodded with satisfaction, and climbed down the ladder. She hopped to the ground and faced her friend with a grin. "Not one little thing. It's Christmas Eve, 1942, and everything is just about perfect."

"I don't know what's gotten into you." Mary Ann shook her head. "Five minutes ago you were complaining and crabby and not in any kind of Christmas spirit at all."

Katherine shrugged. "Go figure." She nodded at the tree. "It must be this magnificent Christmas tree that's completely changed my mood."

"It is lovely," Mary Ann said. "Those old-fashioned balls make all the difference. Somebody left a big box full of them at the door to the hall tonight. The chaperons found it when they arrived." She studied the tree. "I think they add just the right touch of—"

"Magic," Katherine said softly. "Christmas magic."

Mary Ann grinned in agreement. "You got it." She cast her gaze around the rapidly filling room. "I wonder if he'll be here tonight?"

Of course he'll be here. He had to be. Michael was the only reason for reliving this night. Still, already everything was a little different than she remembered it. What if he didn't come? What if—

"Katie, aren't you going to ask who?"

"What?" Katherine jerked her attention back to her friend.

Mary Ann sighed. "Honestly, Katie, I'd swear you were somewhere else tonight."

"Oh no, Mary Ann." Determination underlay her words. "I am definitely right here."

"Well, you don't act like it," Mary Ann huffed. "I was talking about the love of my life, you know, my Prince Charming."

"This is obviously a great place to find him." Katherine scanned the crowd looking for the one face she'd waited a lifetime to see.

"What?" Mary Ann snorted in derision. "No lectures on the evils of husband hunting? No comments on how we're only twenty and have plenty of time to find a man? No stern talks on the risks of falling in love during a war?"

"Absolutely not," Katherine said firmly. She pinned her friend with a steady gaze. "Mary Ann, if you never pay attention to anything else I ever say, pay attention to this. When you find Prince Charming or Mr. Right or whatever you want to call him, don't hesitate, not for a moment. Ignore sanity and reason and common sense and listen only to your heart. It doesn't matter if you don't end up living happily ever after. Love, whether it's for a lifetime or just one night, is worth anything."

Katherine's voice rang with conviction. "It sounds corny, but there is such a thing as fate. Such a thing as destiny. There really is one special man meant for you and you alone. And if you miss your chance to love him and be loved by him, you'll regret it for the rest of your life."

Katherine grabbed Mary Ann's shoulders and stared into her eyes. "You'll grow old alone and, at the end, your life won't have counted one little bit. And regardless of whatever success you may achieve, no matter what challenges you may overcome or mountains you might climb, nothing, positively nothing will ever compare to what you might have had with him." Her voice softened. "Knowing love, just for a moment, is worth anything. Even the pain of losing someone you love is insignificant compared to the agony of not loving at all."

Mary Ann stared wide-eyed. "Wow."

"Sorry." Katherine dropped her hands and laughed self-consciously. "I didn't mean to go overboard. I probably sounded a little nuts."

"No," Mary Ann said breathlessly. "What you said was wonderful. I never imagined you felt that way. Every time I talk about love and finding the right man you always seemed so—"

"Condescending? Conservative? Cautious?" Katherine wrinkled her nose at the accuracy of her words.

Mary Ann nodded sheepishly. "Yeah, I thought—"

"Girls." An older woman bore down on them in the manner of a veteran war horse and thrust two small, cream-colored boxes in their general direction. "Some of the local florists got together and donated these for the hostesses tonight."

"Gardenias," Katherine said, a wistful note in her voice. Her heart leapt. Events were unfolding much as they had before. It was only a matter of minutes before she'd see Michael again. And this time everything would be different.

"Indeed." The energetic matron nodded sharply and handed them the containers. "Isn't it wonderful how everyone wants to do their part for the war effort?"

"Wonderful," the girls echoed in unison.

"You two have a lovely time this evening and be sure to follow the rules. They're there for your protection, you know." The chaperon cast them a stern glance, then continued on her rounds, spewing orders like a general to the tiny troop of high-school-aged volunteers that trailed obediently at her heels like well-trained recruits or puppies.

Katherine pulled the lid off her box and picked up the corsage. Her hands trembled and anticipation threatened to overwhelm her.

"This might not do anything for the war effort in general but it certainly helps my own personal battle plans." Mary Ann pinned the blossom to her sweater and cast an assessing gaze around the room. At once her eyes lit up. "And I see a likely target right now."

"Good luck," Katherine said absently, barely noticing Mary Ann's comments in her own search of the room.

"Katie." Mary Ann hesitated as if she couldn't quite find the words. "I don't know what's going on with you tonight but"—she sighed—"well, good luck to you, too, I guess."

"Thanks." Katherine grinned and gave her friend a little push. "Now get out there and conquer new worlds."

"You bet." Mary Ann tossed her friend a devilish grin. "See you later."

"Happy hunting," Katherine said, relieved to get rid

of her. Oh, it was wonderful to see Mary Ann again but time was slipping away quickly and Katherine didn't know how much she'd have. So far, the evening progressed in much the same manner it had the first time. If that held true, next—

A burst of music from the far end of the hall caught Katherine's attention. It was the motley collection of volunteers they'd called a band. What happened now? Her heart raced and she searched her memories. Of course. She'd been idly looking around the hall. The crowd seemed to part, and there he was.

Her gaze skimmed over the room as she waited for a break in the milling mass of uniforms and enthusiastic young women. Nothing happened. Panic fluttered in her stomach. What if history wasn't going to repeat itself? What if nothing was the same at all? Maybe just being here again changed events. This could be some vindictive cosmic joke. What should she do now?

Perhaps if she went to find him? Again she scanned the room. He'd been standing somewhere in that area when she'd first seen him. She drew a steadying breath and took a determined step. The crowd jostled against her and the gardenia in her hand tumbled to the floor.

"Damn," she said under her breath. "I don't have time for this."

Quickly she swooped down to retrieve the flower before it could be crushed in the crowd. She reached toward it, but just as her fingertips brushed the petals, a large, male hand gently plucked it off the floor.

Michael!

Her heart seemed to stop. Her gaze traveled up the length of his long arm, past hard, broad shoulders to his beloved boy-next-door face. To the cocky grin she'd remembered over and over in fifty years of dreams. To his dark, endless eyes that glittered with promise and burned with a fire she'd never forgotten and never forsaken.

"Do you believe in love at first sight?" His voice was a caress, resonant with deep, unspoken meaning.

Katherine stared in stark disbelief and immeasurable joy. She yearned to reach out and place her hand on his cheek, to feel the warmth of his flesh beneath her fingers, to assure herself once and for all that he was real and she was here.

Her voice was barely a whisper. "Yes, I do. Do you?"

"I didn't." His smile didn't quite erase the perplexed look in his eye. "Until now."

She tilted her head to one side, cast him an appraising glance, and struggled to hide her true emotions. As much as she wanted to throw herself in his arms, she had to remember this was his first meeting with her. He hadn't lived this moment over and over again through more than half a century the way she had. She had to take it slow, with care and caution.

"Was that just a line then?" She flashed him a flirtatious smile.

"Not at all." He laughed, and she nearly wept at the well remembered sound. "Here, let me help you up."

He placed his hand under her elbow and they rose to their feet. Even this minimal contact sent shivers coursing down her spine.

"You flyboys are all alike," she teased.

He raised a brow. "How did you know I was a pilot?"

She nodded toward his insignia. "Your wings for one thing. Also, the only other time I was asked if I believed in love at first sight, the question came from a pilot."

"What did you tell him?" His query was offhand but there was an odd light in his eyes and her pulse raced.

"I said . . . no." Her voice was breathless and she fought to sound cool and blasé. "So, if it wasn't a line, then what was it?"

"I'm a romantic at heart, I guess." His gaze searched her face and his brows pulled together in a puzzled frown. "Have we met somewhere before?"

"That's a good line, too, but no, I don't think so," she said lightly.

Oh, yes. Once. In another lifetime.

"No, seriously, are you sure?" He narrowed his eyes thoughtfully. "Have you ever been to Chicago?"

"No, never." Her heart fluttered.

He can't possibly know. Can he?

"Funny." He shook his head as if to clear it. "I have such a strong feeling that we've met before. That I know you from somewhere."

"Déjà vu?" She laughed casually. "Or fate maybe?"

"Maybe." He grinned. "It's as good an answer as any."

"I feel as if I know you too," she said boldly. She obviously had his interest, now she had to hold it and pray that lightning would strike once again. Just like before. "I feel as if I know all kinds of things about you."

"Oh?" He quirked a dark brow. "And just what do you know?"

"Let me think." She considered him for a moment. "I know you're a lieutenant."

He nodded at the bar on his shoulder. "Too easy. What else?"

"I know you're from Chicago."

He shrugged. "Another easy one."

She cocked her head and eyed him reflectively. "You're headed to England tomorrow."

"Not bad," he said grudgingly. "Still, I bet most of the guys here are heading out tomorrow."

"Okay." She pulled a deep breath. "And your name is Michael. Michael Patrick O'Connor."

His eyes widened in surprise. "Very good. How on earth did you . . ." He grinned his crooked smile, and her heart melted at the sight of it. "Somebody told you, right? One of my friends set me up, didn't he?"

"Nope." She laughed with the sheer pleasure of his company.

"Then how—"

"Magic, Lieutenant." She leaned toward him confidentially. "Christmas magic."

"I see." A twinkle danced in his eye. "Does it only work for you or can anybody try it?"

She crossed her arms over her chest. "Just for me."

"I doubt that." He studied her for a moment. "I bet I know a lot about you, too."

She tossed him a challenging glance. "Really? And what do you know about me?"

"I know you've been decorating Christmas trees." He reached out and plucked a small sprig of fir from her hair. His scent of warm spice and male heat washed over her and her breath caught.

"Doesn't count." She shook her head as much to clear it as to deny his observation. "Too easy. What else?"

"You're an excellent dancer."

She laughed. "What makes you think so?"

"Great legs," he said in a matter-of-fact manner. Heat rushed up her face. Lord, she hadn't blushed in so many years the sensation was almost frightening.

"Good line," she shot back. "Anything else?"

He narrowed his midnight eyes in obvious appreciation. "I know you're the prettiest girl here. I know you

wear some kind of intriguing perfume that reminds me
of roses and cinnamon at the same time. I know your
eyes are dark and bewitching enough to make even a
man who can't swim want to dive right in. I know . . ."

"Yes?" She stared into eyes that went on forever and
seemed to search for answers to unasked questions.
"What else do you know?"

"I . . ." An absent note sounded in his voice, as if he
lost track of his train of thought, as if he too was
caught up in a moment of connection, a moment of
truth. He stared, his expression bemused.

He knows. He must know.

Abruptly he shook his head and the fragile bond between them shattered into reality. He smiled down at
her. "What I don't know is your name."

"Katherine Bedford," she said softly. "But everybody
calls me Katie."

"Katie." The name tripped off his tongue like an
embrace or a prayer. "It suits you."

"Does it?"

"Yeah." He considered her for a second. "You look
like a Katie."

"Well, Lieutenant—"

"Michael," he said firmly.

"Well, Michael," she smiled, "I'll tell you a little secret. Tonight I feel like a Katie."

He threw her a speculative glance. "I have no idea
what that means but I think I like the sound of it."

"So do I," she said under her breath. "More than you
know."

The band launched into an especially raucous version of "Boogie Woogie Bugle Boy." Michael winced,
and she laughed at the embarrassed expression on his
face.

"Sorry." He shrugged, chagrined. "I didn't mean to be rude. They caught me off guard."

"It's okay. They're not much but they're all we've got." She nodded toward the band. "At least they're enthusiastic."

"Would you like to dance?" The eager light in his eyes matched her own need to be, at long last, in his arms.

"I'd love to. But first"—she pointed to the corsage still cradled in his hand—"I'll take my flowers back."

"Sure."

She reached to accept the blossom from his outstretched palm, fighting to still the tremble in her fingers.

"Nervous?" He quirked an amused brow. "Not about dancing with me, I hope? Although, I must admit, I am a great dancer."

"Don't be silly. Of course I'm not nervous," she said sharply and snatched the flowers from his hand. She fumbled to pin the gardenia to her sweater. "It's just a little cold in here, that's all."

"Allow me." He pinned the blossom on her with a swift, efficient move. His head bent close and she ached to run her fingers through his dark, silken hair. "There."

He nodded with satisfaction and straightened up. How could she have forgotten how tall he was? He towered a good half foot over her and her eyes were at a level with his lips. Lips that had haunted her dreams forever. She could still remember the insistent demand of his mouth. The sensual pressure of his lips next to hers. The surge of passion from the merest puff of his breath against her own.

"Katie?"

"Michael." She stared up at him and his gaze searched hers with the same odd look he'd worn earlier as if he reached for something he couldn't quite grasp. She longed to tell him everything. That they'd been through all this once before. That they were destined to be together. That the love they found on this lone night was real and true and right. "Michael?"

"I just don't get it, Katie, there's something about you . . ." He shook his head. "I could swear I know you from somewhere."

She was tempted to tell him the truth. To spill it all and go on from there. No. Firmly she thrust the temptation away. What on earth would he think if she told him they were caught in a replay of history? There was no possibility he would even remotely believe her. Why, he'd think she was a lunatic or worse. Still, would there be anything wrong with using her knowledge of the future to give him a little push, to help him, just a bit faster, to fall in love? They had so little time.

"I guess I'd better confess, Michael." She cast him a confidential look. "It all has to do with fate."

"Fate?" His brows furrowed in confusion. "What do you mean?"

"Fate, Michael, destiny." She glanced to one side then the other as if checking to make sure no one was listening. "We're soul mates, you know."

"Soul mates?" He narrowed his eyes as if he wasn't quite sure how to take her comment. "Are you serious?"

"You bet." She grinned. Joking was probably the easiest and most subtle method of working her way back into his heart. "Relax, Lieutenant, it's all just part of that Christmas magic we've been talking about."

He laughed and grabbed her hand. "Then we might as well see if any of it will work on the dance floor." He pulled her toward the dancers, then stopped abruptly and stared at her for a moment. "You know, I kind of like the way that sounds."

"What?"

"Soul mates." He tossed her an easy smile and continued on his way to the dance floor.

"Lieutenant," she said, more to herself than to him, safe in the knowledge that the blaring music would cover her words, "that's the best news I've heard in half a century."

She wouldn't have believed it possible. This night was somehow better, brighter, and even more special than the first. Perhaps it was simply that she was relaxed and willing to give in to her emotions. Perhaps it was that she and she alone knew how very important the evening was. Or perhaps it was only the ever-present thought that the memories created in this one night must last a lifetime.

She didn't remember laughing quite this much on that first night, but then it had been a very long time since she'd laughed at all. He was funny and smart and every time he touched her hand or held her in his arms for a dance she had to make a conscious effort to keep her heart beating and her breath from catching in her throat. She'd tried not to think about the future all night, just as throughout her life she'd tried not to think about the past. Only here and now could she admit she had never completely closed away that Christmas Eve, and never gotten over him.

Now, he'd left her standing near the Christmas tree

to get them something to drink. Her gaze followed his every move. He walked across the room with a long-legged, athletic stride that spoke of confidence and courage. Confidence in ordinary day-to-day living and courage in the face of extraordinary danger. Something in his step clutched at her soul with a sharp reminder of how little life this man had left. And try as she might, there was probably nothing she could do to prevent his fate.

Pamela Gillum walked past with a determined smile on her face. Her expression didn't erase the tiny lines of worry that even makeup couldn't hide. Maybe she couldn't do anything to change Michael's destiny or anybody else's future, but she could do something to help this woman right now.

"Mrs. Gillum . . . Pamela," she said.

"Yes, dear?" The older woman turned toward her, a question in her eyes. "Can I help you?"

"I . . ." What on earth could she say now? How could she tell her that all her fears were for nothing? That her husband would indeed return home? Frustration flooded through her. Still . . . she drew a deep breath. "It'll be okay. Really, it will. He'll come home. I know it."

Hope glimmered in Pamela's eye, then softened to a look of sad resignation. "That's what we all hope for, dear."

"No, honestly." She reached out and grasped Pamela's arm. "You have to believe me. He'll be fine."

"Katie." Pamela cast her a chastising frown. "I know you're just trying to help but—"

"It's more than that." An urgent need to convince this woman filled her. She lowered her voice. "Please don't tell anyone, but there are some things that I just know. And I know your husband will survive this war." She shrugged helplessly. "I can't explain any more than that. You have to trust me."

Pamela stared, her gaze searching Katie's face as if desperately seeking something in her expression to convince her of the accuracy of her prediction.

"What deep, dark secrets are you two sharing?" Michael handed her a cup of punch and she dropped her hand from Pamela's arm.

"Nothing." Katie smiled weakly.

"I'm not sure why," Pamela said, shaking her head, "but for some strange reason, I think I do believe you. Lord knows I want to. It's absurd, of course, no one knows the future. Even so . . ." She drew a shaky breath. "Thank you, Katie." She smiled, nodded at Michael, and walked slowly away.

Katie heaved a sigh of relief. With any luck, she'd given Pamela something to hang on to and maybe relieved her anxiety just a bit.

"What was that all about?" Idle curiosity shone in Michael's eyes.

"Oh, every now and then I do a little fortune-telling." She took a sip of her punch. "Chalk it up to Christmas magic."

"I see. Something else to add to your many attributes."

She raised a questioning brow. "Are you making a list?"

He nodded solemnly. "And checking it twice. Let's see now." He ticked the items off on his fingers. "You're almost as good a dancer as I am."

"Thank you," she said dryly.

He pointedly ignored her interruption. "You're obviously intelligent, judging from the way you're quick with a sharp comeback."

"Thanks again."

"Beyond that, you're quite a dish." He tossed her a slightly lecherous glance and she laughed in response. "You believe in fate and destiny, and now I find out you tell fortunes as well." He narrowed his eyes in mock suspicion. "You're a witch, aren't you, Katie?"

She chuckled. "I've been called worse."

He snorted doubtfully. "I find that hard to believe." He stepped closer, cupped her chin with his hand, and gazed into her eyes. "Can you tell the future, Katie? My future?" He stared, and his voice deepened with unspoken meaning. "Our future?"

"Our future?" She could barely breathe with the nearness of his body to hers and the intensity of the look in his eye.

"It's awfully hot in here," he said softly. "Would you like to get some fresh air?"

"It's against the rules and I . . ." She paused. What did she care about the silly rules and moral barriers of a long-lost era? This was the only night she had and she wasn't going to miss out on one magical moment of it. Besides, her success, small though it was, with Pamela had her thinking. Maybe, just maybe, she could change things a little. And then maybe Michael wouldn't have to die so young and so soon. She nodded. "I'd love to. There's a terrace behind the building. I'll get my coat and meet you there."

"Don't take too long." His smile spoke of promises and passion, and anticipation shivered through her. He turned and strode away and she hurried to the cloakroom where she'd left her wrap.

Katie grabbed her coat and with a forced nonchalance

made her way toward the back door. Halfway there, a flash of red caught her eye and she froze in her tracks.

Her gaze meshed and locked with eyes deep and wise and kind. He sat in a huge carved wooden throne across the room surrounded by stacks of brightly wrapped packages. It was a scene straight from a children's book. Was this simply a local man playing a part for a Christmas party or was this a vision far beyond the limits of reality as she'd always known it? It no longer mattered. Whoever or whatever he was, she had to thank him for the chance to live this one night over.

She stepped toward him but he shook his head sternly, then nodded at the back door. He grinned and tossed her a casual salute. She smiled back and turned toward the door. Surely he already knew how grateful she was for this very special gift. Didn't he? The least she could do was tell him what this night meant to her. She swiveled back and scanned the area he'd sat in only a second before.

He was gone. There was no sign of a chair or packages or any evidence that anything was even slightly different from a moment ago. She chuckled to herself and continued to the door.

It was probably time for him to leave. After all, Santa had already delivered the best gift of all.

"Do you really want to be a pilot?" Katie asked as if the answer were of no importance.

"I've never wanted to be anything else." Michael leaned against the terrace wall. The snow drifted gracefully between them. "I've wanted to fly for most of my life. Funny as it sounds, this war is giving me the chance to live a dream." He cocked his head and studied her. "Why did you ask?"

She considered her words carefully. "It's dangerous, that's all. Especially now. I think you should reconsider flying."

His eyes twinkled and his words teased. "Are you worried about me, Katie Bedford?"

"Yes," she said simply.

"Good, I like that." His tone was abruptly serious. "I know we've just met but I feel somehow as if I've known you forever."

"Me, too."

He eyed her solemnly, his gaze considering. "And I think there's something you're not telling me. What is it, Katie?"

She stared down at the snow-covered ground. There was so much she wanted to say and so much she couldn't. She sighed and looked up. "My brother was a pilot."

"Was?"

She nodded. "He was in the Navy. Stationed at Pearl Harbor."

"I see." Sympathy shone in his eyes. "Were you very close?"

"Harry was my big brother." She smiled sadly. "He was a great guy and I really miss him."

"Katie . . ." Michael shrugged helplessly. "It's a war."

"I know that," she said, her voice sharper than she intended. She glared with all the emotion stored up in a lifetime of regret, and something inside her snapped. "I'm not an idiot. I know all about war. Men have been fighting and killing each other for centuries and for what? In the name of decency or patriotism or God? One war might end but there's always another one sooner or later. Now it's this World War and next is Korea and after that Vietnam—"

"Vietnam?" Confusion shadowed his face. "What are you talking about?"

"Never mind." She waved him off impatiently. There was no way she was about to explain the geopolitical conflicts of the last half of the twentieth century to a man planted firmly in 1942. "The bottom line is that when the smoke clears and the bodies are counted, what difference does any of it make after all? And it's not just men paying the price but the women and children left behind pretending to be brave but really living in constant fear. It's so damned unnecessary to have to sacrifice everything you care for, everyone you love—"

"Do you love me, Katie?"

Did she love him? She'd loved him for most of her life. She gazed into his eyes and prayed for the right words. The words that would draw him closer and not push him away.

"I just met you." Caution underlay her words.

"I think we already established that," he said softly. "Do you love me?"

"What do you want me to say, Michael?"

"It's crazy, Katie, but it's a crazy world we live in these days." He shook his head as if he couldn't believe his own words or his own feelings. "When I first saw you across the room, I thought you were the prettiest girl here."

"You thought I was a dish," she said accusingly.

"You are a dish." His voice was firm.

"And?" she prompted.

"And . . ." He combed his fingers through his hair as if struggling to understand his own words. "And I felt as if I'd been hit by a bolt from the blue. As if someone had reached out and smacked me across the face." He stared at her, confusion battling with wonder in his face. "Does that make any sense at all?"

Joy surged within her. "I think so."

His gaze locked with hers, intense and searching. "You talked about fate and destiny, and, God help me, Katie, I've always believed secretly, in the back of my mind, that there would be only one chance and only one special girl. I was always confident I'd know her when I met her. And I did."

He pulled her into his arms. "What was it you said? About you and me?"

"Soul mates?" she said breathlessly.

"Soul mates." He nodded. "That's it exactly. I feel as if, for the first time in my life, I'm whole and complete. As if there's a part of me that's always been missing until now." He shook his head in amazement. "It doesn't make any sense. It's insane and irrational and—"

"Magic?" She sighed the word. "Christmas magic?"

"No." He brushed his lips against her own and she struggled to keep from melting against him. "This magic isn't just for Christmas. This is forever, Katie."

"Forever." Her voice was barely a whisper and her heart nearly broke at the lie.

He gazed into her eyes for a long, silent moment. "Are you a witch, Katie? Can you tell the future? My future?"

"Yes." She gasped and stared with all the longing of a life lived without him. "I can tell, right now, you're going to kiss me."

The corners of his mouth quirked upward. "You are a witch."

"Then kiss me, Michael."

His lips claimed hers with an eager gentleness that

left her aching for more. Long-denied passion flared within her. She wound her arms around his neck and crushed her mouth to his. He hesitated for the barest moment as if surprised by her boldness, then pulled her closer, tighter, until even the clothing between them couldn't hide the aching need of one for the other.

Her mouth opened beneath the pressure of his and his tongue traced the inner edge of her lips in a sensuous path that left her weak with desire. Her hands grasped at the back of his neck, her fingers tunneling up through the thick satin of his hair. So long, she had waited so very long for the heat of his lips on hers.

"Katie." He pulled away and stared down at her. Snowflakes danced between them. "You still haven't answered my question."

She traced the line of his jaw with a trembling finger and marveled at the mix of rough texture and warm flesh. "I told you you were going to kiss me."

"Not that question. The other one." He gave her a tiny shake and her gaze jerked to his. Urgency, desire, and a touch of apprehension lingered in his eye. "Do you love me?"

She stared and a million thoughts flew through her head. Once before he'd asked the very same question. But confusion and fear and downright stupidity had held her tongue. She'd sent him off to war, off to die, without saying the one thing he wanted, no, needed, to hear. And she'd lived a lifetime of regret because of it. She would not make the same mistake again.

"I've loved you forever." She held her hand against his cheek. "And I will always love you. That's a promise."

For a second he simply stared, amazement coloring his face as if he could not believe his luck.

"Did you doubt it, Lieutenant?"

He grinned. "Never, Miss Bedford. Not for a moment."

He let out a whoop of elation, picked her up off the ground, and twirled her around until she laughed with sheer delight and they both tumbled to the snow-covered ground.

He leaned on one elbow, gazing down at her. Snowflakes swirled around them and she wondered vaguely why they didn't sizzle just a bit when they hit the heat generated between the two of them.

"I love you, too, Katie." His expression was once again serious, his eyes somber. "I almost wish I didn't."

"What?" She struggled to sit up. "Why?"

"You said it yourself a few minutes ago." He shrugged. "Men go off to war. Women stay behind and . . . wait and worry. They go through their own private brand of hell. I'd hate to do that to you."

"It's too late, Michael." She laughed softly. "No matter what happens from here on out, I love you. I will die a little every time there's a news report on the radio or a headline in the paper or a knock at the door. And that's okay."

She reached out and took his hand in hers. She studied his long fingers, his firm palm, and wished she knew which tiny crevasse was his life line. She pulled a steadying breath.

"Loving you, right here and right now, just for tonight is worth anything, any price, any sacrifice. I don't care. This is enough." She gazed straight into his eyes. "I wouldn't trade one single, solitary moment with you for an entire lifetime without you."

"We can have a lifetime." His tone was intense, his eyes deep and compelling. "Marry me, Katie."

"Marry you?" She could have wept with joy at the question. At long last she could do what she always should have done, to make up for her mistake, to have her second chance. "When?"

Astonishment swept his expression. "Is that a yes?"

She laughed. "You seem surprised, Lieutenant."

"Not surprised, baby, more like stunned." He turned her hand over and placed a kiss in the palm. "I can't believe I can be this lucky." He narrowed his eyes and searched her face. "To have found you here and now."

"Christmas magic, Michael?"

"Fate, Katie, destiny." He drew her closer against him and crushed her lips with his in a kiss hard and swift and breathtaking. Then he leapt to his feet and pulled her up beside him. "Didn't I see a justice of the peace sign about a half mile down this road?"

"Next door to an inn." Her heart hammered in her chest.

"Then let's go." He grinned and put his arm around her. They took a few steps and he stopped and studied her, his expression somber. "Katie, nothing in my life has ever seemed as right as this does. But if I'm rushing you into this, if you have any second thoughts, then—"

She gazed up at him with all the love stored within her. "I never wanted anything as much as I want this, Michael. I want to be your wife. I want you."

Concern creased his brow. "Are you sure, Katie? I didn't give you any time to think about it."

"Time?" She laughed softly. "I've had all the time in the world."

". . . till death do you part?"

"I do." The vow fell from Michael's lips with an intensity that echoed in her soul. Judge Thomas and his wife and everything around them faded to a dull haze. All she could see was the promise in eyes as dark as a winter night.

"Harrumph." Judge Thomas cleared his throat. "I said you may now kiss the bride." For a moment, Katie and Michael just stared. "Go on, son," the judge smiled knowingly, "it's the best part."

"Randolph," Mrs. Thomas clucked at her husband, then threw Katie a confidential glance. "He's right, you know."

Katie choked, Michael laughed, and the judge chuckled. Michael kissed her quickly, a brief brush of his lips that left her knees weak with what was to come. Mrs. Thomas produced mugs of hot cider from somewhere and the gathering toasted the newlyweds.

"I wish you the best of luck." Judge Thomas raised his cup in a salute. "You'll need it. I don't mind telling you, these wartime marriages are tough."

"But, Randolph, just look at them," Mrs Thomas said. "Why, anyone with half a brain can see they're obviously in love."

The judge snorted. "Everyone's in love these days. Hardly a night goes by anymore without love-struck kids knocking on the door, waking us up, and wanting to get married." He raised a bushy brow. "Even on Christmas Eve."

Katie and Michael traded swift glances.

"We need to be going," Michael said quickly, shaking the judge's hand.

"Thanks for everything," Katie added, slipping into her coat. "We really appreciate it."

"As well you should," the older man mumbled.

Mrs. Thomas walked them to the door and pulled

Katie aside. "Don't mind him, dear. He's a little cranky when he has to get out of bed unexpectedly. And don't worry about that business about wartime marriages."

She leaned toward Katie and lowered her voice. "I was a war bride, too. Randolph and I were married nearly twenty-four years ago." Mrs. Thomas let out a sigh of contentment. "And look at how well that turned out. We've had a long and happy life together."

Unexpected pain speared though Katie at the woman's words but she forced a smile to her face. This kindhearted soul had no idea that her helpful advice only served to remind Katie of what she and Michael would never share. They had this night and only this night.

"Ready?" Michael said.

"Sure. Thanks again, Mrs. Thomas." Katie threw her a grateful smile.

"You're welcome, dear. And have a wonderful life." Mrs. Thomas closed the door behind them.

Katie and Michael stood silently in the swirling snow. She wasn't quite sure what to say or do next and a surprising awkwardness settled over her. Finally she pulled a deep breath.

"The inn's right next door." The words blurted out and she groaned to herself at her lack of restraint. Lord, she sounded like a sex-starved tart.

Michael's brow rose in amusement. "I noticed."

"Well, do you . . . I mean I thought . . . maybe it would be . . ." This was ridiculous. She was a grown woman in her seventies, no longer young and innocent and virginal. How could she be so uncomfortable on the very brink of what she'd wanted for much of her life?

"Nervous?" His expression was serious but his eyes twinkled.

"No." *Yes.* "Of course not," she said loftily. "I am a married woman, you know."

He laughed, hooked his arm through hers, and steered her toward the inn. Aside from a larger building containing an office and the residence of the owners, the inn itself was more a series of tiny cottages than anything resembling an actual hotel. Michael led her to the cottage farthest from the office and grabbed the doorknob.

"Wait." Katie placed a hand on his arm. "Don't we have to check in or something?"

"Mrs. Thomas called and arranged everything when you weren't looking. It's all set." He pushed open the door.

"Well then." She breathed deeply and stepped forward.

"Hold on just a minute." Michael cast her a stern glare. "I believe you're forgetting something."

She pulled her brows together in a puzzled frown. "What?"

"I thought you said you were a married woman." He shook his head with mock disappointment.

She stared in confusion. "I am but—"

"But this." He swept her off her feet and up into his arms. She laughed and threw her arms around his neck. He stepped across the threshold and into the cottage.

"Welcome to the honeymoon suite, Mrs. O'Connor." He glanced around the room and his expression fell. "I wish it could be more."

"It's wonderful." She beamed up at him. He set her on her feet but she kept her arms wrapped around him. "Don't you know anything yet, Lieutenant? I don't care if it's a shack or a castle. Just as long as you're in it."

Relief shadowed his eyes. "I do have something to make it a little more like a castle." He pulled a bottle of champagne out of his coat pocket. "A little wedding celebration."

She arched a brow. "Mrs. Thomas again?"

"The woman's amazing." He paused and looked thoughtful. "Maybe I should have married her."

She tapped him on the chest sharply. "She's already taken."

He sighed with exaggerated resignation. "Then I guess I'm stuck with you." He laughed. "I'll see if there are any glasses in the bathroom."

He headed to the only other door in the room and she eyed their surroundings. It really was a pleasant little cottage with knotty-pine paneling and cheerful curtains at the window. A big old-fashioned wing chair filled a corner. The room was dominated by a double bed and matching dresser. She shrugged out of her coat and caught sight of herself in the mirror.

She caught her breath and stared, eyes wide with shock. She hadn't looked in a mirror all night. The face that gazed back at her was an image she'd nearly forgotten.

She'd always known that people had considered her pretty in her younger days, even beautiful, but it never really held much meaning for her. In her world, the world of business, a world of men, her looks were always more of a detriment than a benefit. An attractive face and shapely figure meant men typically thought she would be available for mergers that went far beyond the details of a business deal. She'd breathed a sigh of relief when she finally reached an age where she was no longer described as lovely, but "handsome."

Now she stared at dark, shiny hair that glowed with

health and vitality instead of the dull gray shimmer she was used to. At a face still untouched by the years with skin smooth and clear and not a line or wrinkle anywhere. And at a body firm and lithe and unaffected by the gravity and infirmity of age.

"You're beautiful, Mrs. O'Connor." Michael stood behind her, his gaze meeting hers in the reflection. He handed her a tumbler of champagne.

"We look pretty good together."

He nodded. "As if we were made for each other."

She took a sip of the wine and gazed at their images in the mirror: a pretty young woman, a handsome young officer. They looked like a photograph or a painting. A wedding painting. Two people in the prime of life with the world at their feet and their whole lives in front of them.

Except that for these two, the future was as much an illusion as the reflection in the glass. A shudder passed through her.

He wrapped his arms around her and she leaned her head against his chest. "Cold?"

She shook her head and her gaze meshed with his in the mirror. "I love you, Michael."

"I love you, too." He kissed the side of her neck and she watched him in the mirror. His lips traversed the sensitive flesh to meet the neckline of her sweater, and she sighed with the sweetness of his touch. His hands found the hem of her cardigan and slipped beneath the wool to caress heated skin, then moved upward to cup her breasts bound by her bra. She gasped and melted against him. His thumbs flicked the hardened tips through the cotton fabric, and need arched through her.

"Michael," she groaned.

She lifted her arms and he pulled the sweater over her head, swiftly unfastening her bra and letting it fall to the floor. For a moment, the two of them stared into the mirror, then all the passion pent-up through a long life alone demanded release.

She turned to him and fumbled with the buttons on his jacket. He struggled with her skirt. Within a few frenzied frantic seconds they stood together with nothing between them except the realization that their joining was as right as destiny and as inevitable as time itself.

They tumbled onto the bed and heated flesh pressed against searing skin. She could not get enough of his touch, of touching him, with hands and mouth and bodies entwined. Together, they searched and explored and discovered a passion she'd only known in the deep recesses of her mind where she'd kept him hidden and whole and alive forever.

At last his body joined with hers in a rhythm of man and nature. And she wondered dimly why she didn't shatter into a million pieces with the joy and wonder and glory of it all. Until finally the ever-tightening spring inside her exploded in a release of fire and flame and scorching desire. She cried out. He shuddered. Her fingers clutched his shoulders, pulling him closer and tighter as if to never let him go. Together they greeted an intensity of mind and body she'd never known and never suspected and would never forget.

And when at last they lay collapsed, side by side, in a dreamy glow of satisfied exhaustion, she leaned on one elbow to study him silently. His eyes were closed and he looked so much younger than she remembered. She tried to focus on every detail, every nuance, every expression on his face, committing them all to memory. To save and savor for the rest of her life.

And no matter what happened, memories of this night and this man would live in her heart always.

In a place reserved for Christmas magic and miracles and promises.

She woke at the first light of dawn, and he was gone. Fear sliced through her like a steel blade. She leapt from the bed, frantically searching for her discarded clothes and throwing them on in a blind panic. How could he have left without saying good-bye?

No! The answer reverberated in her head. Michael would never go without talking to her. He was not the kind of man to sneak out in the middle of the night. He wouldn't do that to anyone but especially not to her, his love, his wife.

She sank back down on the bed and caught her breath. Confidence and faith flooded through her, and her doubts vanished: he would be back. And when he returned . . . it would be to say good-bye. They had so little time left.

Quickly she finished dressing and then cast her gaze around the tiny cottage to make sure she left nothing behind. The minutes slipped past. Where was he? Impatiently she paced back and forth across the room. A radio sat on the table beside the bed and she flicked it on, hoping for distraction. Seasonal music floated through the air. Of course. How could she have forgotten? It was Christmas morning.

"Merry Christmas, baby." Michael's voice sounded behind her. His arms wrapped around her and pulled her close to his chest.

"Merry Christmas, Michael." She leaned back against him, content for a moment to merely bask in the glow of his warmth. "I didn't hear you come in."

"I didn't know if you'd be up yet and I hated to disturb you. I went to pay the bill." His voice was quiet. "I have to leave. Soon."

"I know." She drew a shaky breath. "Why, Michael? Why do you have to go?"

"Why?" Surprise sounded in his tone. "Katie, I'm in the Army. I'm an officer. I don't have much of a choice."

"Sure you do." She didn't want to look at him. Not yet. Her words were slow and measured. "Michael, you don't have to do this. There are places, in Central America and the Caribbean, where a man can disappear and no one can find him. With enough money—"

"Katie." He laughed and twirled her around to face him. "I don't know who you think you married but I'm just a regular joe. I'm not rich. I don't have that kind of money."

"But, Michael, I . . ." She stopped and widened her eyes with realization. She didn't have that kind of money either. Not in 1942. There were no stock portfolios, no investment dividends, no mansion in California. She wasn't Katherine Bedford with wealth and power at her fingertips but plain Katie Bedford. And all she had was love. She shrugged sadly. "I guess I don't either."

"Besides, Katie"—he lifted her chin with his finger and smiled into her eyes—"even if I had the money, I could never do that. I could never run out on my country. I'm heading off to do something that's not going to be pleasant and I don't mind admitting it's a little scary. But"—he shook his head—"when I signed on I gave my word. I won't back down on it now."

"An officer and a gentleman no less," she said with a feeble smile.

"Exactly." He nodded. "O'Connor men might not be wealthy in terms of money but we believe strongly in those things you can't buy, like patriotism and commitment and honor. I could no more abandon my country than I could abandon myself or . . . you."

"I know," she said with a deep sigh of resignation. "I knew before I brought it up. I just thought I had to try."

"You are worried about me, aren't you?" The concern in his eye belied the smug tone of his words. She nodded silently. He gazed at her for a long, thoughtful second. "Katie . . ." He paused as if unsure how to continue.

"Yes, Michael?"

"Do you . . ." Again he hesitated, indecision rampant on his face. Finally his words came in a rush. "Do you have any regrets? About last night? About getting married? Or anything else? Because if you do, we—"

She placed her finger across his lips. "Shut up, Lieutenant. I have a lot of regrets. More than you can possibly imagine. But not about last night and not about today." She bit her lip and fought to keep her voice steady. "I do regret that I didn't meet you a week ago or a month ago or a year ago. I regret that I have to let you leave without me, that I can't go with you like a camp follower from another century. And I regret, more than anything, that we've had so little time together."

"Hey." He kissed the tip of her finger. "We'll have time someday. We'll have the rest of our lives together."

Tears blurred her eyes but she smiled and nodded. He took her hands in his. "We'll have a wonderful life, Katie. And we'll have kids." He stopped and threw her a suspicious glare. "Do you like kids?"

"Kids?" She could barely choke out the word. The tears she'd held in check tumbled down her cheeks. She thought of the annoying little creatures standing in line with her to see Santa and the scorn she'd had for them—only now could she admit that it hadn't been as much disdain as it had been yet another regret. "I've always wanted kids."

"Good." A teasing light shone in his eye. "What do you think? Ten or twenty?"

"Children?" She gasped. "You're kidding, aren't you?"

"Yes, I am. But just about numbers." He stared at her sternly. "I insist only on a boy and a girl." He reached out and brushed an errant strand of hair away from her face, his voice gentle. "A little girl who looks like you."

"And a boy who takes after his dad." Hysteria tinged the edge of her laughter. *Hold on, Katie, don't lose it now.*

"We'll have it all, Katie. I promise." He gathered her into his arms and held her firmly against him.

She closed her eyes, wrapped her arms around him, and savored the solid feel of his body next to hers. Desperately she tried to deny the thoughts crashing around her. There was no time left. There would be no future together. No little girl who looked like her. No little boy who took after his dad. If only they could stay like this always. Capture this one moment and ignore the rest of the world, hide from the inevitable, cheat even time itself.

"Time now for a little change of pace." The tinny voice of the radio announcer broke into her thoughts. "Let's take a break from Christmas music for one of our favorite songs." The first notes of "I'll Be Seeing You" drifted into the room.

Michael released her, stepped back, and held out his arms. "Dance with me, Katie. One more dance and then . . . then I have to go."

She wiped the tears from her face with the back of her hand and nodded silently, unable to trust her voice. She melted into his arms and they swayed together to the bittersweet throb of the music.

"I love this song," he murmured.

She sniffed and snuggled closer. "That's because you're a romantic."

He held her a little tighter. "There are certain benefits to being a romantic, you know."

"Really?"

How can I let him go again?

He nodded. "You bet. For one thing, you acknowledge fate when it hits you across the face. And you recognize love when you find it."

"That's . . . swell."

How can I live my life once more without him?

"And you can appreciate a song like this one." He hummed a bar of music. "Listen to it, Katie. It's a love song and—"

"A promise," she whispered.

How can I say good-bye forever?

"A promise." He pulled back and his gaze locked with hers. "A promise that he'll never forget. That everything he sees, everything he does, everywhere he goes he'll be reminded of her."

"And?" She sobbed the word.

"And . . . it's a promise that he'll come back." Conviction shone on Michael's face. "I will come back to you, Katie. I promise."

"I know." The lie slipped out easily. What else could she say?

"Write to me?" The corners of his mouth quirked upward. "Mrs. O'Connor."

"You can count on it, Lieutenant."

A car horn sounded outside.

"That must be my cab," he said quietly. "I thought he could drop me off, then take you home."

"No." She shook her head sharply and smiled. "I'd rather just say good-bye here. I'll get home on my own."

"Okay." An awkward silence settled between them. There was so much she wanted to say but mere words weren't enough. He brushed his lips against hers, turned, and stepped to the door. Her throat ached with the tears she struggled to hold in check.

He pulled the door open and cast one final glance back. He grinned the crooked smile that had lived a lifetime in her memory and tossed her a cocky salute.

"I'll be seeing you, Katie." Her heart shattered with his words and the fervent vow in his eyes. "I promise." He stepped through the threshold and pulled the door closed behind him.

And once more she was alone.

Unrestrained tears coursed down her face and she stared at the door, at the last place he'd stood. And she waited.

She had no idea if she'd return to 1996. No idea if, instead, she was now destined to live her life over. To survive again all the empty years of pain and yearning, all the years without him. She pulled a deep breath. As daunting as the prospect was, it was not too high a price to pay for one special night, for the opportunity to really know love, for a second chance.

She stood and stared at the door for a minute or an hour or forever until there were no more tears left to fall. Finally she gathered her things to return to the home she'd hadn't seen for years and the life she would have to build again. To wait for the inescapable end: the news of his death.

Katie stepped outside into the silent winter. The pale early-morning winter light matched the somberness of her mood. Snow covered the ground, fresh and new and untouched like a canvas waiting for color. Like the rest of her life. She trudged toward the street, calling on vaguely remembered memories to help her navigate her way home.

A sad smile pulled at the edges of her mouth, and an odd sense of joy mixed with the pain inside her. It was all worth it: every ache, every tear, every wrenching emotion.

Michael had gone to his death and they would never be together again. But this time, he left with the sure and certain knowledge that he took with him her love, her heart, her soul. And no matter what twists and turns her future might now hold, she would never again deny what she'd refused to admit the first time they met.

She would love him forever.

She promised.

She wrote to him later that day and the day after that and the day after that. It was a futile effort, of course, a total waste of time and energy. There was every possibility he would never receive her letters. Still, there was always hope. And who knew just how long her second chance would last?

She didn't tell her family about her marriage. Somehow, given all that she knew, it seemed pointless. She returned to school with her mother's promise to forward any mail. And she waited with a sense of impending tragedy that grew with every passing day.

Weeks stretched endlessly without word. She existed in a strange kind of limbo, checking her mailbox every day, sometimes twice, at once resigned to the arrival of a bulky Manila envelope and terrified by the prospect.

Each day that passed was hopefully another day that Michael lived. She wondered if, because she'd married him, this time there would be no oversized envelope, but instead the yellow sheet of a telegram or a personal visit by an impersonal military representative. But their wedding had been so hasty, it was possible the Army had no official record of their marriage.

And so she waited.

She didn't know what to expect when word came. More and more she was convinced that with official notification of Michael's death, she would learn of her own fate. Would she go back to Christmas Eve 1996, with her life behind her and nothing ahead but a deteriorating body and an empty existence? Or would she be forced to relive a long and solitary life? She didn't especially relish either prospect. But it surprised her to realize that she could calmly face whichever future faced her now. There was a strange sense of peace, of acceptance and serenity within her she'd never known. She'd had her one special night with the one and only man she was destined to love.

And it would indeed last her a lifetime.

It was a frigid winter day when she checked her box for the second or maybe even third time in a span of a few hours. Damn. The mail still hadn't come. It seemed that erratic mail delivery was the one constant from generation to generation. At least when she knew the mailman had come and gone she could breathe a little easier. Each day without word was at once a frustration and a relief.

She turned away from the boxes with disgust and froze. The world around her spun to a stop. The air grew thick and her breath caught in her throat. Shock widened her eyes and focused her gaze. Disbelief clutched at her heart and she stared in stunned silence.

At a crooked sort of smile.

At blue eyes, dark as the night and just as endless.

At the hero's best friend.

"Do you want to dance, Mrs. O'Connor?"

"Michael?"

He grinned. "The one and only."

In a heartbeat she was in his arms, laughter mingling with tears in a joyous mix of amazement and revelation. She pulled back and stared. "Oh, Michael. I can't believe . . . how can you . . . I thought you were dead."

He cocked a dark brow. "Baby, I'm a lousy letter writer but that doesn't mean I'm not among the living. Actually, I got shipped around a little bit after this." He gestured to the crutches propped under his arms. They'd escaped her notice until now. "Nobody seemed quite sure what to do with me until they came up with the brilliant idea of sending me home to recover."

Her heart thudded in her chest. Was he merely injured this time instead of killed? And if Michael's fate had changed . . . "What happened?"

"It's kind of silly." He shrugged in a self-conscious manner. "A couple of nights after I got to England, well, I was pretty low. It seems I missed my wife." His eyes simmered with a promise of passion and her insides fluttered in response. "I had a few too many one night, and on the way back to the base ran into a flock of sheep."

"Sheep?" She struggled to suppress the exhilaration rising within her.

He shook his head. "Actually, they ran into me. Anyway, I managed to overturn the jeep. They tell me I was in pretty bad shape for a while. I don't remember much."

"Sheep?" Laughter bubbled through her lips. "I have sheep to thank for you being here?"

"Sheep and . . . you."

"Me?"

He pulled her close with one free arm. "If I hadn't been trying to drown my sorrows about not being with you, I wouldn't have had the accident."

She sucked in her breath sharply. "Oh, my."

"Funny thing, too, Katie." His brows drew together in a puzzled frown. "Until the accident, I kept feeling like I was doing things I had done before. As if I was repeating motions over or reliving a life already lived." He shook his head. "It sounds crazy. Do you know what I mean?"

"I have a pretty good idea," she said softly.

"That strange feeling disappeared after the accident. And that's another weird thing. The plane I was supposed to be flying on for a training exercise, the day after the accident, crashed." A shadow crossed his eyes. "Everybody died."

"Good Lord." The revelation struck her with an almost physical force and she resisted the need to collapse against him. At once, everything made sense. This time, Michael survived. This time a little too much to drink, stray sheep, and above all else, the knowledge that she carried his name and would wait for him forever had made a difference. This time, he kept his promise.

He pulled her tighter against him. "I'm not home for good, you know. I'll be going back as soon as I get the okay. But for now—"

"For now"—she beamed up at him—"you're here and we're together and everything has changed."

Confusion washed across his face. "What do you mean?"

"Never mind. It doesn't matter." She laughed with unrestrained delight. "Nothing matters now except that you're alive and we're both here and—" She caught her breath and stared.

"What is it, Katie?"

"And"—she struggled to swallow the lump in her throat and fight the tears that stung the back of her eyes—"and we'll have children and grow old and spend the rest of our lives together."

He grinned. "That's the whole idea."

"It really is a second chance," she said under her breath and vaguely wondered why her heart didn't break with the miracle of it all.

"Katie." Michael brushed his lips along her forehead. "I don't know what you mean by a second chance and I don't really care. All I know is that the girl I love is in my arms and I'm going to spend the rest of my life making her happy. And that's a promise."

The tears she'd restrained coursed down her cheeks and his face blurred, but the strength of his body next to hers was solid and real and lasting. And she knew without question there would never be a Katherine

Bedford who made millions from nothing and had her face on the cover of *Time* magazine. But there would be a Katie O'Connor who'd know all the joy and laughter and love that life could offer.

His lips met hers and she greeted him with the eagerness of a lifetime spent waiting for this one moment. And before passion swept away all possibility of rational thinking she realized the truth of what she'd never even suspected before.

Love is a promise to keep.

EPILOGUE

December 24, 1996

"I can't stand the thought that she won't be around anymore." The tall, dark-haired young woman wiped a tear from her eye.

The slightly older blonde seated beside her nodded silently.

Their gazes fixed on the front of the church. Winter morning light filtered softly through stained-glass windows and caressed the holiday decorations scattered with joyous abundance throughout the sanctuary. The casket before the altar was at once a sorrowful counterpoint to the festive setting and yet, somehow, appropriate.

"I just never really thought of her as dying," the brunette said. "She wasn't all that old."

"Oh, she was old, Diane." The other girl's voice was solemn. "She was seventy-four."

"I know but—"

"And everybody in the family kept saying after Grandpa died, Grandma wouldn't last long."

Diane stared at the casket. "Can you imagine loving somebody so much you can't live without them?"

"Sure." The blonde paused and shook her head. "Maybe. I don't know. Do you remember the story about how they met?"

Diane laughed softly. "Who could forget? It was as much a part of Christmas at Grandma's as the tree and stockings." She recited by heart. "Christmas Eve at a community canteen. Right before he shipped out to World War II. It was love at first sight." A wistful note crept into her voice. "It was so romantic."

The blonde chewed on her lower lip for a long moment as if getting her words and her thoughts in order. "I know this sounds kind of stupid but does all this seem . . . well . . . sort of right? Like fate or something?"

"Sandi O'Connor!" Diane's eyes widened with shock. "How can you even think such a thing?"

Sandi wrinkled her nose. "Calm down. I didn't mean it like that." A frown creased her forehead and she struggled to find the right words. "It's just that Christmas was always so important to her. Because of Grandpa, of course, but . . . do you remember what she used to say about Christmas?"

Diane nodded. "She said it was all a matter of believing. Believing in the promises of the season. Believing in the magic . . ."

"And?"

"And"—a smile quirked the corner's of Diane's mouth—"believing in Santa Claus."

"She really did believe in Santa, you know," Sandi said quietly.

"I know. I always thought it was funny." Diane shook her head in disbelief. "A grown-up believing in Santa like that."

"But don't you see?" Sandi leaned toward her cousin. "The way she felt about Christmas, the way she believed in miracles and promises and Santa"— Sandi shrugged—"it's almost like, at this time of year, with the spirit and excitement and magic of the season, this is when she would have wanted her life to end. What better time to say good-bye?"

"Maybe," Diane said slowly. "I understand what you're trying to say but still"—she released a heartfelt sight—"I'm really going to miss her."

Sandi put her arm around her cousin and gave her a squeeze. "So am I. But she did have a great life."

"She had a wonderful life," Diane said stoutly.

"Look." Sandi tilted her head toward the front of the church. Two young girls armed with violins took their places off to one side of the altar. "Your mom asked Carol and Deb to play today."

"The same song they played at Grandpa's funeral?"

Sandi nodded.

Diane sniffed back a fresh tear. "She would have loved this."

The first tremulous strains of "I'll Be Seeing You" echoed through the church. In the last pew, a portly, elderly gentleman slowly rose to his feet and headed toward the door. A slight smile played on rosy lips nearly hidden by a thick white beard.

He paused for a moment and cast a satisfied glance around the church filled with children and grandchildren, family and friends. The end result of a life filled with love and laughter and joy. Bottom-line assets that could be totaled on the only balance sheet that really mattered.

"Merry Christmas, Katie," he said in a murmur so soft no living creature could possibly hear it.

"Santa always keeps his promises."

☐ **YES!**

Sign me up for the Love Spell Book Club and send my
FREE BOOKS! If I choose to stay in the club, I will pay only
$8.50* each month, a savings of $6.48!

NAME: _____

ADDRESS: _____

TELEPHONE: _____

EMAIL: _____

☐ I want to pay by credit card.

☐ **VISA**   ☐ **MasterCard**   ☐ **DISCOVER**

ACCOUNT #: _____

EXPIRATION DATE: _____

SIGNATURE: _____

Mail this page along with $2.00 shipping and handling to:
Love Spell Book Club
PO Box 6640
Wayne, PA 19087
Or fax (must include credit card information) to:
610-995-9274
You can also sign up online at **www.dorchesterpub.com**.
*Plus $2.00 for shipping. Offer open to residents of the U.S. and Canada only. Canadian
residents please call 1-800-481-9191 for pricing information.
If under 18, a parent or guardian must sign. Terms, prices and conditions subject to
change. Subscription subject to acceptance. Dorchester Publishing reserves the right to
reject any order or cancel any subscription.